Kelley turned and Claire came into his arms, as though they'd known each other for years. . . . They made love on a big brass bed, no fumblings, no questions, just a sweet straight urgency. And then they were kissing again, lying on their sides, smiling with everything, eyes, mouths, limbs . . .

"Come with me to Dallas," he said.

"I have work to do, Kelley."

"On the weekend?"

"Mmm hmm. If you want to get your radio commercials on the air. Did you look at them?"

"No. Do you like them?"

"Uh huh."

"Okay, so do I."

She laughed. "I think it pays to be sleeping with the boss."

"Hey," he said sharply, "don't do that, okay? That's not what this is." He watched her. "Or is it?"

Harold Robbins Presents:

Blue Sky

A novel by Sam Stewart

PUBLISHED BY POCKET BOOKS NEW YORK

Distributed in Canada by PaperJacks Ltd., a Licensee
of the trademarks of Simon & Schuster, Inc.

"I Get a Kick Out of You" © 1934 (renewed) Warner Bros. Inc. All rights reserved. Used by permission.

"Who's Driving Your Plane" © 1966 by ABKCO Music, Inc. All rights reserved. Reprinted by permission.

Another *Orignial* publication of POCKET BOOKS

POCKET BOOKS, a division of Simon & Schuster, Inc.
1230 Avenue of the Americas, New York, N.Y. 10020
In Canada distributed by PaperJacks Ltd.,
330 Steelcase Road, Markham, Ontario

ISBN: 0-671-52678-2

First Pocket Books printing November, 1985

10 9 8 7 6 5 4 3 2 1

POCKET and colophon are registered trademarks of Simon & Schuster, Inc.

HAROLD ROBBINS PRESENTS is a trademark of Harold Robbins.

Printed in Canada

Harold Robbins Presents:
Blue Sky

1

ON HIS LAST night in Paris, the woman he'd observed a few times in the hallway, the woman who was much too impeccably dressed, and had jangling bracelets and a Cartier watch and a flashy wedding ring, said to him, "Well?" She was idling in front of her door at the Crillon, a room-key resting in a manicured hand. Kelley had just gotten in from his dinner. Kelley had looked at her, slowly, appraisingly, figured, Why bother? decided, Why not? and then left his own room-key in the nest of his pocket.

It was brief, pragmatic, insensitive, fine. Kelley slept soundly for forty-five minutes and woke from a nightmare.

The woman said: "So."

He landed on an icy runway in Newark at a quarter of eleven. Being eager to look at what his rivals were doing, he'd ascended into nationally advertised sky and discovered, as expected, they were doing quite well. The flight had been uneventful, efficient. The ticket, a one-way coach-fare from Paris, purchased at the counter of the Crillon Hotel, had set him back four-hundred forty-nine dollars. Blue Sky could handle it for three hundred less. Beginning in April. Maybe. With luck.

Kelley was a die-hard believer in luck. He was not superstitious. He was not into guardian angels or stars, he was simply observant. His faith had been tested in crapshoots and cockpits. You did what you had to do, luck did the rest—or didn't. It was no more exotic than that.

Luck, for example, had been with him at Customs. He could have hit an agent like the one in Chicago—a real professional hassler, a pasty little guy who just looked at Kelley's tan and the stamp from Geneva and the hatred exploded. "You been skiing." Like he knew all there was about skiers and especially the skiers with the Rolex watches and the Mark Cross bags: fornicating wastrels, oligarchic bums, and the money came from trafficking in quality smack. The guy went through everything including the ribbon of Colgate toothpaste. But this time, in Newark, the agent had recognized his name from the passport and the pigskin duffle bag had gone unexplored. And this time the contents had a probable value of a hard three-to-five. Kelley'd once visited a juvenile facility in upstate New York where he'd talked to the warden. On his desk was a sign that said THE LUCK STOPS HERE.

He shouldered the duffle bag and plunged through the crowd. Crossing the terminal, he caught the impression he was slogging through a knee-deep barrel of mud—the inevitable impact of jet lag and Scotch and something, he admitted, more dangerous and subtle: he'd been running on empty for a very long time. On the escalator leading to the first mezzanine, he ran into Heidigger—the new kid, the one who understood the computer. Heidigger would say to it, "Don't give me crap," like that; very serious; "don't give me crap," and the twenty-seven terminals would fall into line.

Heidigger breathed at him, "'Lo, sir. You're back."

Kelley said nothing, though he tried to look friendly. The kid looked embarrassed, maybe shy, Kelley thought. He wanted to tell the kid, "Relax. Life is short."

"Gonna snow," the kid blurted.

"Guess so," Kelley said.

"McDermott wants to see you."

"I'd've guessed that too."

"He went down to the gate because he wanted to see you but I guess he didn't see you."

"Relax," Kelley said.

McDermott was the company's financial director. The money-thing was rapidly getting out of hand, although Kelley tried to keep it in its proper perspective: Monopoly paper. Trivial Pursuit.

Once again, he was conscious of the Whiz Kid behind him, who appeared to be going through a great paroxysm of awkwardness—a lot of whistling and thrumming; a major distraction with a newsmagazine. He'd rolled it up tightly and was currently enjoying its use as a swagger stick; bouncing it around along the escalator rail.

Kelley said, "Is something the matter this morning? Or let me put it this way—is something unexpected the matter this morning?"

As they moved to the landing and headed together for the decorated door, the Wunderkind appeared to give it serious thought. He loped beside Kelley, who patiently waited for the birth of information and was suddenly rewarded with the newsmagazine and, "The only thing I know about is page sixty-three."

Kelley just nodded. Heidigger, ahead of him, was opening the door, and Kelley stepped through it to the general offices of Blue Sky Airlines. The sky hadn't fallen. The office was the usual confusion of noises—click of computers and the flash of the phones. "To Syracuse? Yessir. Twenty-six dollars. No, I'm not kidding, sir. No, that's the price." The girl on the telephone, grinning at Kelley. "No, I'm not kidding, sir," she said to the phone.

He glanced over quickly at the warren of cubbyholes

and desk-top computers. Three hundred operators answering the questions, hacking the schedules, confirming the flights. This was his entire reservations operation. No counters in the terminals or offices in town.

Which was why he could offer you a no-kidding price.

He moved down the corridor, passing the posters of his long-ago ads: "FLY-BY-NIGHT AIRLINES," "FARE-WEATHER FRIENDS." And the best of them: "ALL GOD'S CHILLUN GOT WINGS." Rosetti's advertising knack at its best.

The doorway to George McDermott's office was open but he noticed gratefully that George wasn't there. Good. He could do without George for the moment. What he desperately needed was a ten-minute nap. Or a two-week vacation. Or a few million bucks.

In his own private office, he shucked off his overcoat and stripped off his tie. Frannie, his secretary, came through the door—a slim black woman with exotic cheekbones and cool watchful eyes that seemed capable of voodoo. Kelley'd once called her an ironic hand in a velvet glove. She glanced at the magazine he'd tossed on the desk.

"Have you read it?" she asked him.

"Do I want to?" he said.

She gave it a second of deadpan thought. "Well . . ." she decided, "you could look at the pictures . . ."

He laughed. "That bad, huh?"

"Well . . . I don't know," she said soberly. "I honestly don't. If you want my opinion, it *isn't* that bad. But then I'm an old-time sucker for the underdog. You want the opinion of your marketing director, Ashe said, quote, 'If you look like a loser, you're lost.'"

"That's not an opinion," Kelley yawned, "that's a fact. People get afraid you'll go bust and they'll be stranded. The agents don't book you, they're afraid they'll be sued. So from things being a little off, you go into a real nosedive."

"Oh," she said grimly.

He suddenly laughed. "Ladies and gentlemen, this is your captain, we are now traveling in a vicious circle."

Frannie just stood there and nodded, unamused. "How was Paris," she said, "or was that funny too?"

"No," he said, "that was what they used to call in the old movies 'a tough fight, ma.'" He eased to the sofa and lit a cigarette. "To begin with, they told me we could fly into Paris, no trouble at all, but the closest we could *land* would be the Deauville airport. You know where that is? That's ninety miles north. The last time anyone landed there was D-Day. And you know what the French say? They have a phrase. They say *Je suis desolé.* 'I am desolated.' They say that very nicely while they're sticking in the knife. Anyway, I did about four days of talk and we now land at Orly. I've only got it three times a week, but I got it."

"You're something," she said.

"Yeah. Very tired."

"Something like a cross between Henry Kissinger and Indiana Jones is what was going through my mind—you want coffee?"

"Not yet."

"Want McDermott?"

"Not ever, but give me twenty minutes.—And while we're on it, what's the cause of his uproar?"

"My guess," Frannie said, "would be the auditor's report. They delivered it yesterday."

"You know any numbers?"

She looked at him slowly. "Who, me? I'se the maid. Although judging by the pharmacological ambience, I'd say you got, easy, ten-milligram trouble."

"Funny." He yawned, and stretched a few knotted muscles in his back. "Anything else you'd like to brighten my day with?"

5

Frannie shook her head.

"A roster of phone calls? A list of appointments?"

"They're all on your desk. The bright spot *might* come at six with Rosetti, who wondered if you'd meet him at the Westbury Bar." Frowning, she studied him. "You want to put it off?"

"No, today's Friday. Is today Friday?"

"It's Thursday and I think you're getting punchy," she said. "I think you need your milk and Fig Newtons and your nap." Leaving, she closed the door quietly behind her.

After she'd gone, he stayed punchy for a while, staring at the wide-angled window to the field, and watching as one of his 737's taxied to the runway. He waited, watching till it got off the ground. Then he lit a Gauloise and opened the magazine to page sixty-three.

The headline that greeted him was "BLACK-AND-BLUE SKY."

He put down the magazine, crossed to the cabinet, and poured himself a good stiff Cutty-on-the-rocks.

"BLACK-AND-BLUE SKY."

The picture was from 1971. Where President Nixon (Jesus—Nixon) was shaking his hand about the DFC. He looked at his own rather nasty young face as though trying to determine who the kid there was: kid with the scowl and the gunfighter mustache, still with the rakish-looking patch on the eye. Kelley: the semi-piratical Ace. Karen had been with him. "Thrilled and delighted," she'd confided to Tricky. Though nothing much "thrilled and delighted" her now.

He lifted the magazine and faced it in earnest.

BLACK-AND-BLUE SKY

Blue Sky Airlines, the first-born darling of deregulation and a pioneer in cut-rate unrestricted fares, is taking what appears to be the beating of its life. Record losses reported for the first three quarters of the year are only the beginning of the carrier's troubles, according to an analyst at Rockwell & Carz, who adds: "We'll have to look at how the fourth quarter goes. For the moment, I'd have to call it down but not out. On the other hand, the count," he concluded, "is eight." The once-revolutionary Newark-based carrier is reeling from the one-two combination punch of an overoptimistic program of expansion, directed by its founder and chief executive, Burke M. Kelley, and a predatory price-war on virtually all of its domestic routes. "The majors are really going out for his blood," said a Wall Street analyst, referring to Kelley. "They really want to get him. It's get-even time." But getting Burke Kelley hasn't ever been easy. From the very beginning he's defied all the odds, and a lot of insiders think he'll do it again.

THE DARING YOUNG MAN
ON THE FLYING TRAPEZE

"The Viet Cong couldn't shoot him out of the sky," said Blue Sky's Chief Operating Officer, Charles Stryker, "so I don't believe a couple of desk jockeys can." Kelley, whose Vietnam combat experience earned him two medals and a near-fatal wound, had established Blue Sky as an upstart, highly competitive airline operating solely in the state of New York. From its launch-date in 1972 with a couple of re-conditioned DC-3's and a youthfully exuberant media blitz, the airline and its dashing 26-year-old founder were immediate targets of competitors' wrath. With an offering of "Midnight Rambler Specials" to the upstate college-towns of Syracuse and Utica for anywhere from $13–17 and a "Midnight Gambler" to Saratoga Springs, he threw down the gauntlet to the regional airlines whose rates were up to 312% more. "Air Power to the People" went his first set of ads, and the regionals answered him with all-out war, costing him a total of $5 million in posted losses for the first two years. But

Kelley kept at it with a barnstormer's brio. He referred to his company as "Flying Duck Airlines" ("at least we've been flying, not sitting," he said) and joked at the losses. ("I come from a coal-mining town in Kentucky," he once said to *Newsweek*, "where losing five dollars is a major calamity. But losing five *million?* Oh man—that's a joke.") The joke, as it happened, was on everybody else. Blue Sky Airlines survived it and prospered. Seven years after its shaky beginning, with the coming of the Airline Deregulation Act, Kelley expanded into interstate routes, again with his defiant fare-slashing rates. Again there was warfare. Again, with a mixture of brilliant maneuvers and brash gambles and sheer force of will, Kelley and his upstart carrier won. In a time when the airline business in general was suffering reverses, Blue Sky soared, and its handsome young chief began living the highlife.

"FASTEN YOUR SEATBELTS"

The daring young man (who's about to turn 40) is about to take the bumpiest ride of his life. The airline, still with its non-union pilots and its no-frills travel and its second-hand planes, is getting into visions of transatlantic travel. "And serious trouble," a competitor said. "He's over-extended. He's mortgaged to the hilt. He isn't, let me put it, in fighting condition but he's practically begging us for Air War III. Fasten your seatbelts. I think he's about to get a nuclear war."

"You finished it?"

Kelley squinted up at the doorway. McDermott had his coffee in a silver-plated mug—one of those presents for the man who has everything except self-restraint. Kelley had once had to swallow McDermott as part of what he'd known was a devilish bargain. George McDermott was the bitter pill. Fortyish, blondish, sharper than a cleaver, he belonged to that species of the Rational Man for whom Kelley had nothing but the deepest mistrust, having known them by the fruits of their work in Saigon. The pols and the generals, the spooks and the brass—the Minds that so exquisitely prevailed over Matter.

Kelley said, "Come in, George, as long as you're in," and added rather churlishly, "Suppose I'd been fucking. You ever hear the rule about knocking on a door?"

McDermott raised his pale and provocative eyebrows. "You're upset," he conceded. "I can understand that. And then on the other hand, I did knock, twice, though I guess you didn't hear me. However, I'm sorry."

"However." Kelley grinned and then shook his head slowly, though whether at his own childishness or the other man's beautifully shit-eating poise, he wasn't quite certain. "Relax. Have a seat." He fumbled another cigarette from his pocket and watched George McDermott settle down in a chair. "And in answer to the question on everybody's lips: No. I'm not finished."

"No of course you're not." George said it rapidly and firmly. He reminded Kelley of the V.A. doctor who'd assured him, No of course you won't lose your left eye, we're going to remove it. "But of course you'll have to make a few changes," George said.

Kelley just nodded, as he had to the doctor, but apparently McDermott was a better interpreter of Kelley's particular mode of disagreement. He leaned forward earnestly. "Listen to me, Kelley. I don't believe you're grasping the extent of your trouble. On March thirty-first you've got a short-term payback of twenty-two million, you default and you're dead. The long-term lenders wouldn't touch you with a pole, and your fourth-quarter loss has been *thirty*-two million The war's over, Kelley. You're bleeding from a vein. You've got total liabilities of two-hundred twenty-seven—"

"Stop," Kelley told him. "I have grasped the extent."

"No. No, I don't believe you've grasped it at all. At ten o'clock this morning Standard and Poor's downgraded your debt issue. They've rated it 'primarily speculative' now. And once they get ahold of the fourth-quarter figures—"

"Then sit on 'em."

"Who?"

"The figures," Kelley said. "How long can you hold them?"

"Legally?"

"To start with."

"The SEC gives us ninety days to file."

"March thirty-first."

"On the other hand—"

"No," Kelley said. "That's the best hand we've got. Go on. You want to add something?"

Sighing, McDermott leaned back in his wing chair and took a sip of coffee. He'd come from a line of investment bankers; he'd been suckled on numbers. "Yes. I want to add that it won't help you, Kelley. Ninety days of voodoo . . . ?" He shook his head quickly. "Whatever's on your mind—be careful. You could get yourself indicted for fraud."

"And tune in tomorrow for Chapter Eleven.—Is that what you're saying?"

"You've grasped the extent."

"Take it easy, George, Rome wasn't burned in a day."

"Nor constructed in ninety," McDermott said flatly. "If you want to save the airline, you know what to do. Sell planes. Cut routes. Forget about Paris, and forget about your gimmicky wind-shear detector—"

"Which can only save lives."

"Not proven."

"Not yet," Kelley snapped. "Give it time."

"You haven't *got* time," McDermott exploded.

"That's what I've been telling you. You've run out of time. You're gambling with disaster. Every minute you—" He stopped himself and took a deep breath, then started more evenly. "You pay me to advise you, I'm advising you, Kelley. Start raising your fares. Now. Tomorrow. If God had really wanted all his kids to have wings—"

"He'd have gone out of business?"

McDermott looked startled. "Exactly," he recovered. "That's exactly the point."

Again Kelley nodded. "See, and I think you just missed the point, George. I mean what you're saying is, 'peace at any price.' 'If they're licking you, join 'em.' Which doesn't—I mean if we're talking war strategy—it doesn't really have a whole lot to recommend it. But the *point*, or let me put it the *exact* point is, that I never started out to be just another airline. I wanted to be an alternative airline. You follow what I'm saying? Third way to go. See, what we've got in the air-business, George, we've got First Class and Coach. And you know why it's 'Coach'? Because nobody wants to be called Second Class. And there isn't any Third Class. In America, Third Class is go take a hike. So I figured I want to start a Third Class airline. No competition. Nobody else is in the business at all. Hey listen—you want to buy a seat to L.A., spend eight hundred dollars, get a meal and a blow-job at twenty thousand feet? Do it, man. Have it. You want to spend *four* hundred dollars, do that too. But if you *don't* want to spend four hundred dollars, if you don't *have* four hundred dollars, then that's why I'm here, and if I go down the tubes, then a whole lotta people gonna have to stay home. So don't tell me I don't know what I'm gambling with, George, because no one knows better. But that's the way it is. And I've cut all the routes I can possibly cut, and I've sold all the planes I can possibly sell, and you're wrong about wind-shear and wrong about Paris, but I honestly and truthfully appreciate your efforts and I'll certainly think about everything you said."

McDermott rose stiffly: "I think you know I'll have to report this to the Colonel."

"I think I know you already have," Kelley said.

The phone was on its sixth or its seventh ring. Kelley counted ten and then picked it up slowly. When he heard Karen's voice, he thought, Well—surprise! she really wants to know about the meeting in Paris.

"I wanted to remind you of the dinner," she said.

"What dinner?"

"Christ. Tonight. Eight o'clock." She was apparently calling from a telephone booth. In the background, someone said, "Never again." "Black tie," she continued. "At Zeedee's."

"Shit." He was not in the mood for Zachary David or anybody else with adorable nicknames. What he wanted was a Chinese dinner in bed. "Do we have to?" he said.

She sighed at him. *"You* don't have to, my love. As far as I'm concerned, you can sit in your corner and pull out your plum. But I thought you'd want to be there and scotch a few rumors. For instance, the one about your recent death."

"It'll take a lot of Scotch."

"Your suit's at the apartment and I have to ring off."

"'Ring off,'" he said. "Jesus. We're British, no less." But she'd already missed it.

He swiveled in his desk chair and squinted at the picture in the round silver frame. Karen of Yore. Girl in a jumpsuit with "Blue Sky Airlines" written on the chest. Well . . . her chest had been his personal sky and he'd certainly dived right into it. Crash! he'd rapidly hit upon the stone of her heart. No; in fairness, it hadn't been rapid. He'd floated for a while. . . .

His thoughts were interrupted by a series of phone calls.

The airport in Washington was socked in with snow and more was predicted.

The caterer's contract was up for renewal.

The head of the Maintenance Department on the line, telling him a few more wind-shear detectors had arrived from the factory. Installing them without pulling planes out of service "means overtime," he said. "Do you want me to do it?"

"Go on," Kelley told him. "The way it goes now, we're in for a penny so we're in for a pound."

The "penny," he reflected as he hung up the phone, had been something like two and a half million dollars. To work out the kinks. To apply for the patent. To get it approved by the FAA, and then finally to locate a factory to make it. From Idea to Object had taken six years and been worth every day, though as George had pointed out, "If you want to have a hobby, go out and buy a yacht. At least you could sell it." As to whether he could sell the wind-shear detector, the question, he conceded, was up in the air.

He looked at the stack of messages Frannie had left on his desk. A dozen people wanted to see him "ASAP"—one of those unfortunate office phrases; it made him feel he'd be a sap to see them. The only one he really felt up to was Duke—Johnny Dukovic, the head of the Operations Department.

He got him on the phone and a few minutes later, Duke came rapidly wheeling through the door, a notebook on his lap and a truly ear-grinding squeak in his wheels. He'd once, Kelley knew, been an airborne marine, a flying cowboy in a khaki Stetson, roaring through the skies. He was still part cowboy—booted and jeaned, with a gunfighter mustache and shaggy brown hair. He now played center for a violent wheel-chair basketball team called the Wheeler Dealers.

He continued to squeak his way into the room.

"Squeaky," Kelley said. "The eighth dwarf."

Duke tossed his notebook on the side of the desk. "Nice," he said, "nice. And Frannie starts singing 'Squeak Low, Sweet Chariot.' Personally I'd like to see a little less irony around here and a little more upfront slobbering pity."

Kelley said, "I take it you lost last night."

"These guys're called Heavy Metal," Duke said. "To give you an idea." He lit a cigarette and thumbed at the copy of the newsmagazine. "You read what our good friend Chambers had to say?"

"Speaking of heavy metal," Kelley said.

"Man wants to hit us with a nuclear war."

Kelley just shrugged. "His airline's been hitting us for almost a year. He doesn't need nukes, it's the snipers that're getting us."

Duke hooked his arms around the posts of his chair. "You think he'd be going in for psy-war too?"

"Meaning?"

"Doing little raindrops on our head."

"Go on."

"Okay, try this one for size. This morning a girl in Reservations comes in. Pam. You know Pam? She's shacked with a pilot. The guy does the six-o'clock flight to Chicago. Computer tells her the flight was booked full. The *pilot* tells her there was room for the entire population of Toledo, a symphony orchestra and half the Rockettes."

Kelley said nothing. He was letting the thought run loose in his head. And forget it, he told himself. That kind of thought, you want to keep it on a leash. Muzzled. "And you're making it a Federal case?"

"I don't know," Duke said. "I don't know what I'm

making. Except that we were turning customers away on a flight that was empty. We had twenty-one people taking off on that flight. It was booked for the whole damn hundred and thirty."

"Uh huh." Kelley nodded and swiveled in his chair. "Well, what I think you do," he said slowly, "is you set up a head-count. Whenever the computer says a flight is booked full, you count actual heads.—We've never done that, have we?"

"No airline does it. There wouldn't be a reason."

"Well . . . we might have one," Kelley said flatly, and let it go at that.

Alone, he swiveled his chair to the window and squinted at the gray unpromising sky. He could picture the sky as the OK Corral. He could picture Chambers, the long-time president of Federal Airlines, who looked just a little like Lyndon Johnson, straddling a 747 like a horse: "Sky isn't big enough for both of us, pardner." Pschew!

Or would Chambers shoot him in the back?

No, he thought quickly, that was cop-out theory. Chambers didn't *need* to shoot him in the back. Kelley had put himself out on a limb so far that a little bit of bird-shot would do it; fair and open and right between the eyes.

Frannie came in with the auditor's report. It was bound in a shiny red vinyl cover, bearing the name of the accounting firm. He wondered vaguely if a solvent business got a *black* vinyl cover. Frannie said, "Judging by McDermott's expression, it ought to have a skull and crossbones on the top."

Kelley said, "Keep out of reach of children. —Seriously, Frannie. If you and Duke want to look at this, fine. But nobody else." He looked at her. "Any other news of the day?"

"Warner's got a couple of ad proofs to show."

"It can wait till tomorrow." He eyed the report,

flipping through the pages as Frannie walked out. A half-hour later, he tossed it on the blotter and went to the cabinet and poured himself a drink. It was lousy reading. A desperate play with no second act. And the only way out was an act of desperation. McDermott's solution: cut back the service and hike up the fares; destroy the airline in order to save it. And that was the one thing Kelley wouldn't do.

He looked at the picture of Stryker on his wall. His Chief of Operations, *Newsweek* had said. What it hadn't known to say was that Stryker was the one man Kelley really trusted. If Stryker were here he could have said to him, "Listen, am I crazy or what?" And Stryker would have told him either "crazy" or "what." And Kelley would have listened.

Instead he went over and poured another drink.

2

THERE WAS A sharp wind coming in off the field and Kelley felt it cut through his camel's hair coat. His head was pounding. It was twenty after nine by the unadjusted clock that was ticking in his head; twenty after five by the timepiece of Newark, and he'd booked himself to drink with Rosetti at six.

The company chopper was waiting on the field. Burnett, the usual pilot, was off and Kelley had a sudden ineluctable impulse to take it by himself.

He said to the pilot, "Take a break. Go home," and got into the cockpit.

The guy, still standing on the ground, looked baleful. "I live in New York."

"Take a bus," Kelley told him as he opened the throttle and squeezed the collective. The rotor blades whined. "And zero six niner is ready for take-off," he said to the radio, adjusting his belt, and then, *hiss!* the energy was charging the turbine, the needles plummeting from red into green and the radio instructing him to "up and away." He opened more throttle as he pulled the collective, and *up,* he was flying.

The ground below him receded into criss-crossing patterns of light.

His head stopped ticking. He could practically feel himself begin to unwind, his own motor slowing as the other one raced across the dark winter sky. Becoming

17

ungrounded, he looked at the pale impression of the moon, as round as a target. It was either, he decided, a lover's moon or a bombardier's moon, depending on your general location in time. He thought of Mick Jagger's "Who's Driving Your Plane?" It must have been—what? maybe '70—summer—flying chewed-up pistons from the base at Can Tho, only half the time, making it back, you were stoned, and the black guy, McClure, with the fading cassette playing over and over, "Who's driving your plane? Are *you* in control or is it driving you insane?"

The lights of Manhattan made a pattern below him. He headed for the heliport on East Thirty-fourth Street, gaping at the tangle of the traffic below. People on the move with the ultimate illusion they were people on the move. "And who's driving your plane, and who's driving your plane?"

"Fuckin' kamikaze!" the co-pilot screeched. They were taking almost every kind of ground fire now, the sky turning brilliant with the tongues of the tracers. Mortar rounds whumped in from somewhere below, and the rock'n'shock rattle of the automatic fire. "You're getting us *massacred*, you goddam bastard. Go back!"

Kelley nodded. He kept going down, the two-engine Caribou rolling through a sky full of phosphorescent murder. If the ammo on the deck got a hit they were done; cooked; exploded. You never had a gunner when you flew re-supply, you just winged it and prayed. So he kept going down, Roginsky beside him and the crew chief in back going totally apeshit while Kelley went cool, his mind just switching onto automatic pilot. Like a roller coaster rider, it was out of his control; he was going with the action and he kept going down because some guys needed ammo.

"Rocket!" He swerved and the fly-by exploded—ka-

BLAM—like a Walt fucking Disney cartoon. He was Road Runner, Sky Runner, genuine committable third-zone crazy in a Technicolor sky. "Turn *back!*" He was lucky, he was riding on his luck, and he saw them, below him, advancing like a wave with their rifles pointed upward, a hundred, maybe two, maybe three hundred men. They were heading for the outpost where the guys needed ammo, and he kept going lower till he looked at the shine of their unbelieving faces as he whammed right into them, bodies going everywhere banged against the plane, and Roginsky still hollering, "Fuckin' kamikaze!" and Kelley only thinking how he must've got twenty, maybe thirty.

He landed on a napalmed clearing. The ramp had descended in a record-breaking rush and the chief was off-loading; hands reaching upward, hands throwing crates. Kelley just sat there, stoned on his fortune, the all-time-favorite enticer of luck. Vaguely he was conscious of the ramp going up, the crew chief yelling at him, "Go, baby, go," and then Kelley heard a sound, a short, hard definitive *smack*—like the door closing after the luck that ran out. He was looking at blood. The bullet had angled in under his helmet. He could only see blood, and Roginsky was hollering, "Fuckin' kamikaze," and the crew chief was hollering, "Go, baby, go," and Kelley, with a bullet-hole bleeding on his face, flew them back to the base camp.

Now as he headed for the lights of Manhattan, he really had to ask himself, empirically speaking, Now is that or isn't that a cautionary tale? He decided, as he landed at the East Side Heliport, it probably wasn't. It was just something else. Or otherwise . . . he figured as he stepped from the chopper, Or otherwise, the captain and master of my soul is a fuckin' kamikaze.

It started to snow. He watched it from a taxi on the East Side Drive—the fat white snowflakes arriving on

19

the edges of the dirty river like pearls before swine. It occurred to him idly that he liked this city exactly because it contradicted itself. He'd once seen a cockroach crawling on a diamond in a Tiffany window; he'd shown it to Karen and she'd only said "ick," but to Kelley it was everything, the cosmic nutshell: life going on because the Yin fucked the Yang.

In spite of the traffic he arrived at the Westbury promptly at six and went into the barroom—The Polo Lounge; pictures of polo players dotted the walls around a dark wooden bar. He found a banquette against a non-athletic wall and ordered a Cutty from a lean black waiter, enjoying the particular aim of the room. The mingled odors of Scotch and leather and burning tobacco. The patrons, relaxed, unwinding, nobody selling any bridges.

He wondered what Rosetti would be selling today.

Also why he wanted to sell it in a bar.

Correction: a lounge.

He'd first met Rosetti in '72 when Rosetti was an ordinary super-bright kid in a flashy little hot-shop on Madison Avenue. Rosetti was bearded, had a windowless office with a poster of a weeping American Indian, a few sharpened pencils and a tinful of grass, and played Rolling Stones records while he scribbled on a pad.

The agency itself had been new and uncertain. They were looking for a wide-open chance to show off and along came Kelley. He'd interviewed half-a-dozen soberer shops, met lime-scented men with Connecticut accents, and finally landed in the ink-stained hands of the four kids from Brooklyn: Davanian, Rosetti, Rosco, and Schwartz. Or as *Ad Age* put it, "the agency was launched by Blue Sky Airlines, which the agency launched." It was true. They had each put the other on the map.

Rosetti came in now, late, looking harried. "Cold-

er'n a witch's tit," he said sullenly. "Jesus. This town."
He slid into the booth. "Can't get a taxi, can't get a
car—double-pneumonia you can easily get. How's
stuff?" he said, lifting up a manicured hand and wag-
gling for a waiter. "How's Paris? How's life?" He was
looking for the waiter.

Kelley told him, fine. Rosetti said, "Good. That's
good, really good." He was looking for the waiter.
"God*damn*it," he said.

Kelley looked him over, sipped slowly at his Cutty
and decided that Rosetti was a creature of fashion.
Rosetti had been hip when it was hip to be hip; only
now he'd gotten sharp—Essence of the 80's—all bright
and aggressive; clothes by Armani, body by incredible
effort at the gym. Rosetti passed a hand along his
clean-shaven jaw. "Think you could get a little service?" he said. "Just try it. Everybody's buckin' for
boss." The waiter came over and Rosetti made a big
deal about ordering a white wine spritzer. He didn't
want the house wine. He wanted a half bottle of Clos
Blanc de Vougeot, and a very, *very* little spritz of the
soda. Ever since he'd stopped smoking, he confided to
Kelley when the waiter went away, his palate had really
gotten hip to what's what.

"Like strawberries," he said. "You ever taste a
strawberry? I mean *really* taste it."

Kelley lit a cigarette and said nothing.

"Pussy." Rosetti started warming to his subject.
"Has a taste—aw Jesus—like I couldn't believe it."

Right; and how about bullshit, Kelley thought. Still
he said nothing. He waited till the waiter came back
with the bottle, opened it, poured, let Rosetti take a
sip, and then added the soda. Rosetti nodded. The guy
went away and then Kelley said, "What?"

"What what?"

"The what about what're we doing here, for instance. I take it you didn't bring the ads to the bar."

"Yeah," Rosetti said. "No, but they're terrific. We've got a new concept. The other one really wasn't doing very well, so how's this: 'That's class.' "

"What's 'that'?" Kelley squinted.

"Blue Sky. We want to tell 'em it's a classy way to go. You like it?"

Kelley nodded.

The waiter came back with another bowl of peanuts.

"Sucks," Kelley said.

"Well," Rosetti told him, "it's a question of image."

"It's a question of bullshit. Come on," Kelley said. "I'm being murdered in the aisles.—How about Paris? Have you done any thinking?"

Rosetti took a long slow pull of his drink. "Thing is," he said slowly, "what I've got here's a problem. Not just about Paris, it's the whole—it's everything."

Kelley said nothing.

Rosetti dug a manicured fist into peanuts. "Okay. We've been friends for too long to deal crap. What I've got is a conflict. Federal Airlines approached me last Monday. It's eleven million bucks' worth of annual billing and I couldn't turn it down, Kelly. Not—" He considered that sentence and dropped it.

"You mean now that it looks like I'm folding," Kelley said. He dragged on his smoke. "What the hell. I don't blame you."

"It's not like it's—"

"Quit while you're ahead," Kelley said.

Rosetti leaned forward. "So what about you? I mean I figure you're personally worth about, what? Twenty, maybe twenty-five, thirty million bucks."

Kelley shook his head. "No cigar."

"Meaning close. But most of it, I bet, you got socked into stock. So why don't you dump it? Sell out. I heard Lester Quaid wants to buy you."

"He did about a year ago."

"Well . . . he still does."

Kelley looked up. "Okay, so I take it he's been after your stock."

Rosetti looked down. "No."

"Meaning close. Okay. What the hell. If you tossed it in now you could still make a profit. Considering you bought in at fifty cents a share."

"I wouldn't do that."

"Right. Okay," Kelley said. "Have it your way." Rising, he slapped a few bills on the table. "Hey listen—I've got to go struggle into Karen's black tie." He started to move and then turned and looked back. "Nice knowin' ya, kiddo."

"No hard feelings?"

"No feelings," Kelley said.

He walked to the apartment—the place where he stayed when he was staying "in town." As opposed to "in country," as he'd lately come to think of the house in Oyster Bay—the house turning into a minor battle-field, zaps and strafings in the marital war. The Fifth Avenue apartment had been furnished at a time when the decorators' fashion-word had been "Santa Fe," and he liked it—the wood-beamed ceilings and adobe walls, the handwoven rugs, the fireplace, a lot of windows on the park.

In the master bedroom he tossed down his duffle bag, stripped quickly and showered. It was only after he was naked and clean, a brown nubby towel wrapped around his waist, that he started unloading the contents of the bag. In with the clothes was a tinsel-wrapped two-pound gift-box of chocolates. On the bottom layer was half a kilo, more familiarly known as just over sixteen ounces, of weed. Grass. Pot. When they busted you, they called it marijuana. He stared at the box, sixteen ounces roughly translated into five full years. Chancing it across the international borders had qualified as all-time-major stupidity, a really genuine record-book dumb, but in Paris the stuff had been offered to him easy, no waiting, no hassles, no greedy little jerks with their "haveta talk to Birdy," or seven trips to Harlem, so it came to a question of a trade-off in hassles. And besides, he needed it, quality and quantity. And possibly—also—he'd needed to play a little game with his luck.

He put the box on the bed and looked around, half-disgusted, at the clutter on the floor. A few thousand dollars' worth of Karen's wardrobe, like silken stepping stones, formed a kind of path between the closet and the bed. Even aeons from now, an archeologist, he guessed, could elucidate the social content of the week by the pattern of the artifacts. Karen: going from a lunch to a party to a theater to a dinner.

Turning, he discovered the note she'd left him, wedged between the ashtray and the night-table lamp. *At Candy's. Come, call, or meet u ZD's.*

Sprawling on the bed, he picked up the telephone and dialed, but not Candy. He listened to it ring about four or five times, with the quaint country ring of an old rural phone, and then Margaret answered.

"Hi," he said.

"Burke?"

"Yeah. How's it goin'?"

Her voice lowered quickly. "Well . . . you could say it was an upchuck morning followed by a terribly depressed afternoon. On the other hand it's snowing and I brought him a big dish of snow and he ate it."

Kelley laughed softly. "What's that? White magic?"

"Now that you mention it, possibly," she said. "How was Paris?"

"I thought I'd tell both of you tomorrow. Could Charlie use a visitor?"

"Only if it's you. But I don't think you'll make it.

The roads could get lousy and the airport goes out if you *breathe* on it hard. We're expecting a foot."

"And expect me too."

She paused. "Hey, I know you can walk on water, but *snow?*"

He laughed. "Let me ask you a question. That magazine quote—about the Cong and the jockies? When did he give it?"

"Oh," she said. "That. Years ago. They must've pulled it from the files. I think it's from the same vintage as you laughing merrily at five million dollars."

"Yeah. Well, my sense of humor's improving."

"I've noticed. Look—I got clamoring kids and a sputtering roast. I love you dearly but I'll see you tomorrow. I mean, if you make it, but I think you're insane."

"Join the club," Kelley said.

He looked at his watch, dialed a local number, got a Haitian maid and asked for Mr. Wagner.

Ab came on the line sounding fairly out of breath. "Kelley? It's good to hear from you and I've got about five minutes to get out to a squash game. Can I call you back later?"

"Can I have about three of those five minutes now? You were out this afternoon—"

"It's a business call, then."

"I'm afraid so, Ab."

"I read about your trouble."

"Then we just saved a minute. Suppose I tell you that the fourth-quarter figures were such a disaster that I have to keep them quiet while I try to raise money. What would you tell me?"

"As a lawyer?"

"Right."

"Be careful of fraud."

"Somebody else told me that this morning."

"Well . . . he was right." Wagner paused. "Okay. Now you tell *me* something, Burke. In what we used to call your heart of hearts do you think you'll stay afloat—and don't answer me yet. Because legally a crime begins with intention. If you think you'll go bust and you keep spending money, then legally you're stealing from existing creditors. They're Peter and you're robbing them to pay off Paul. You wear a white collar so they don't call it robbing, it's 'diversion of assets' but it's basically the same thing. Are you with me so far? Fraud comes in if you try *raising* money. Be careful as hell. You go up to a guy, you say, Hi there, sucker, you want to buy a lemon? then you're perfectly clear because you've told him the truth. But as soon as you try to make it sound any different, tell him for instance it's a yellow rock or a blue sky, as soon as you misrepresent—that's fraud."

"So you're telling me it's worse than I thought," Kelley said. "You're saying if I *spend* money I'm a thief and if I raise it I'm a crook."

"That's about it, Burke."

"Thanks," Kelley said. "And, Ab?"

"Yeah?"

"Give 'em hell on the courts."

3

THE STREET IN front of Zeedee's brownstone was packed. Kelley turned the corner and it looked like a meeting of the chauffeurs' legation. Guys eating sandwiches in silver Mercedes and Rolls-Royce Phaetons, keeping the heat on, enjoying the radio; Make-Believe Ballroom like you wouldn't believe.

The sounds coming out of the townhouse were different. Kelley heard the calm incantations of Bach as he fiddled with the big brass knocker on the door. Above it was a sign that said PROPERTY PROTECTED BY HOLMES ELECTRONICS.

The butler showed him into a living room big enough to land a Citation, and crowded with impressionist paintings and flowers in elaborate bowls. Zeedee had landed maybe two dozen people—a consummate selection of the Brave and the Fair. The model and the maverick auto designer, the French ambassador, the banker with the wife who'd had a facelift in Spain. ("Imagine—*Spain!*" Karen had hooted.) Karen wasn't there.

Zeedee craned his neck around the back of a sofa, looking trim and golden in his formal jacket, his tie just askew enough to show he had class.

Zeedee said: "Ah! Our triumphant pugilist returns from the ring. Let's look at you. No, no, it really isn't bad. Just the smallest *smallest* bit of black around the eye." Zeedee on a jag. "And of course you know all of these wonderful people and you know where the bar is."

Kelley proceeded directly to the bar. He had a slight buzz on. Finally. He had himself nicely on the slide. A few more Scotches and he'd reach the plateau. He ordered a double, then stood for a moment with his drink in his hand and listened to the voices and the measured music. Looking up, he saw a woman in the corner of the room. He'd never seen her before, not in person or in print, but she looked like a girl who was aware that she counted. She was standing with a couple of tall, distinguished-looking movers and shakers and drinking black coffee from a small china cup. He could picture the sequence. He imagined her saying to the bartender, "Coffee?" and the bartender, very nonplussed about the thing, informing the butler, who instructed the maid, who inveigled the cook to make a small pot of coffee. Okay, he thought idly. There goes a girl who knows exactly what she wants. She was dressed very simply; everything in gray, except not looking dull. Long full skirt, cashmere turtleneck, low-hanging silver-and-turquoise belt; earrings of the same stuff dangled from her ears. He liked the way the thick dark hair was cut short, but then longer on the top, falling in her eyes, giving her the look of a serious urchin. She threw back her head now and laughed. She had a nice full musical laugh. Kelley looked over at the guy who'd been talking, who appeared to have as much sense of humor as an egg, and decided she was definitely working the room; and then wondered, For what? She turned, as though suddenly aware he'd been watching, or possibly, he figured, aware all along. Her eyes held his for a second: Do I know you? Would I like to? Kelley said absolutely nothing with his eyes. She was holding a burning cigarette in her hand and walked away to put it out.

Kelley got cornered by Maria Van Kamp. How's Paris? she asked him and Kelley told her fine, and then asked, How's jeans?

"Jeans?" she said. "Is anybody still wearing jeans? Good God! I haven't seen anyone in jeans—"

"I thought you designed them."

"I *did* design them, darling, which is not to say I designed them. I mean, who designs jeans? they're *jeans,* for Christ's sake, but at any rate, *that* golden goose has been cooked. I was into Jap Wrap for a while, only that's dying too. I mean, face it, who wants to go around swaddled like a mummy, and then, on the other hand, who has the time? Takes forty-five minutes getting *in*to that stuff, so I'm just getting out of it. I think I'm into sheets and towels for a while. They're soothing, don't you think?"

Kelley said he'd often been soothed by sheets and occasionally, towels.

He politely excused himself, saying he had to make a telephone call and then going to the bar and getting a refill, redoubling his efforts, as it were, to get smashed. The banker was talking to a Broadway composer. The composer was mentioning a "two-comma deal" and bitching at his taxes. "How about *brain* depreciation?" he was saying. "You got oil wells depleting. How about your brain?" The banker turned to Kelley and smiled at him, friendly. "Sounds interesting," he said, "what do you think?" and Kelley said, "I'm too depleted to think," and walked away from the banker.

He was still heading for the phone, call Karen, he figured, tell her he was leaving because he wasn't doing himself any good here being nasty to bankers. Not that there was anything to gain from a bank. The banks would be the first ones to shutter their windows and double-lock the doors.

He pulled at his drink. He was almost to the hall and then the girl was in front of him. The girl with the cup, saying, "You're Burke Kelley," in a neat husky voice. She had bright green eyes. He'd never in his life met a girl with green eyes. Maybe it was somehow the turquoise reflected. No; they were green. She was giving him a slightly tentative smile. "Hey look," she said quickly, "I've been trying to meet you for practically a month."

Kelley shook his head. "I'm not that hard to meet. —What's your name?"

"Claire McCarren."

"Done," he said. "See?"

She smiled. "Have you really been traveling all month? Or is that just a monologue your secretary does?"

"Frannie never lies. San Diego, Milwaukee, Atlanta, Geneva, Chicago, Hawaii, Paris . . ." He squinted. "I think that was it."

"Sounds hectic."

"Oh yeah. Especially Milwaukee." This time she grinned; the girl was a dazzler. He remembered how she'd dazzled the soft-boiled egg. "Okay then, so what can I do for you?" he said.

She took a deep breath. "Well, if you put it that way—" She paused. "I want to handle your advertising work."

"Why?" he said bluntly.

She shrugged. "Okay. You want Harvard Business School reasons?"

"No. Did you go to Harvard Business School?"

"No."

He laughed. "So what else've you got?"

"Talent. I'm good. And I'm not girlie, I'm tough. And I've thought about your problems."

"Why?"

She looked up—half-amused, not thrown. "Because you've got them," she said. "Because I think you could use me and God knows, Kelley, I could sure use you.

Because I just started my own agency. Because then I heard Rosetti made a big pitch to Federal—so I figured you were shopping. Is that enough reasons?"

It hit him. Not that it mattered very much, but Rosetti pitched Federal, not, as he'd implied it, the other way around.

She misread his silence, was talking pretty fast. "Look—I don't usually hit people up at dinner parties. Could we make an appointment? Or have you hired someone else?"

"Tell me something," Kelley said. "Just one thing. That guy before. What did he say that was funny?"

She frowned at him. "What guy?"

"Tall, thin, white-haired. You laughed."

"Oh. Him." She paused. "He made a pass."

"And you laughed at him?"

"Well . . . a guy talks to you for four minutes and invites you on his yacht, I think it's pretty funny. Besides, what else would you do? Scream, faint, get testy?"

Kelley laughed. "You got a card or something?"

"Mmm." She had a small silver change-purse hanging from her belt. "It just so happens." Extracting the card from it, she looked at him warily. "I did know you'd be here, you know."

"Okay," he said. "What am I supposed to do? Scream, faint, get testy? How long've you known Zeedee?"

"I don't know him at all," Claire McCarren said quickly. "I got brought. But I am kind of curious about him."

"Are you?" He gestured with his eyes up at Zeedee, who leaned against the mantel and whispered to the lady with the Spanish jaw. "Well—take a look. What you see is what you get."

He watched her as she followed his glance up to Zeedee. "Meaning?"

"What do you see?"

He liked her reaction—pushing her lips out, giving it a moment. She shrugged and looked back. "Tall handsome blond being terribly charming."

"Okay, that's it," Kelley said. "That's all. There ain't no more. The newspapers once used to call him a sportsman, because they couldn't think of anything else to call him. Or at least nothing printable. He raced cars in the sixties, married twice in the seventies, inherited his money and never worked at anything except being social."

She cocked her head at him, amused again. "So—how do *you* know Zeedee?"

"Through my wife," Kelley said.

A guy said, "Claire?" Kelley watched him advancing. He was also a blond and he moved with the sureness of a rightful owner. Kelley knew the face, vaguely, from somewhere; he pictured it saying something terribly plucky from a television screen.

"Burke Kelley—Tom Cubbitt," Claire McCarren said smoothly.

"You made a try for the America's Cup," Kelley remembered.

"Yeah. Fuckin' Aussies." Cubbitt shook his head. Kelley also remembered that he owned a few Southwestern television stations. "What I came to ask you," he was saying to Claire, "is if you're ready for a seriously alcoholic drink." He put an arm around her waist.

"Actually, I'm ready to eat a horse," she said.

"Good luck," Kelley told her. "At ten you'll get a very polite piece of lamb." He saluted her with his glass. "Tomorrow would be fine," he said, and headed for the phone.

The second-floor study was loaded with books and, as Kelley remembered it, autographed pictures. Zeedee's father with Roosevelt, Truman, Stevenson, Wagner. Zeedee's father, Daniel David, like his father before him, Isaac David, had made his money in titanium ore, and spent at least a fairly sizable portion on the Democratic Party. Deedee David had once been a backbone of the liberal establishment and, as somebody put it, "a credit to his race." Deedee had then made his famous comment that as soon as you start to think of Jews as a race, the next thing, you're trying to run them off the planet. Deedee had hoped that his first son, Warren, who'd died in a ski accident, would become the first Jewish president, though Zeedee claimed none of his family were Jews, and especially Warren, "who ate more pig than any man alive." And in fact, Warren's reputation with the ladies had been getting out of hand when the Fates tossed him out of the running at Aspen.

Or at any rate, that was how Zeedee told it. One thing you really had to hand to him was that at times, at least, he was mordantly funny.

When Kelley opened the wood-paneled door, Zeedee looked up as though a shot had been fired.

"Oh," he said. "You."

"Sorry," Kelley said.

"No. It's okay. I thought it might be Daddy coming back from the grave." He did *Twilight Zone* music. "Never can tell." He was sitting at the desk with a microscope in front of him. "Checking the purchase," he said off-handedly. "Never can tell what these devils'll do."

The powder on the microscope slide-bar was coke. Kelley saw a quarter-key bag on the desk—about twenty thousand bucks' worth of hard-rock candy. "Good good good," Zeedee mumbled. "C'mere." He made a beckoning motion with his finger. "Take a peek, man."

"Well, I don't know," Kelley said. "Last time a guy told me that I had to look at a naked lady."

"This is better," Zeedee said.

"Could be. Naked lady turned out to be a painting."

"Blew a dime there, did you."

"Quarter," Kelley said and bent to the eyepiece. Under magnification, the powder turned to fragments of striated crystal that sparkled in the light. He'd once met a guy who'd invested in diamonds and went around with a little portable eyepiece, wanting you to look at the close-up of facets, like some people want to show pictures of the kids. Except how do you tell a man his children are boring.

"Pretty poison," Kelley said.

"Yeah. Want a toot?"

"Hell no. I don't want to dance all night, I want to sleep." Kelley walked into the open bathroom and splashed a little tepid water on his face.

"Not a big drug man, eh?"

Kelley rubbed his face with a small white towel. "What are we—having a contest?" he said. "I can take more shit than you can?"

"Just asking," Zeedee said. "You don't have to get hinky, man."

"Hinky, man"—Zeedee being hip, relaxed, with-it; talking opera with the French ambassador ten minutes ago, now doing Street. Kelley thought: he ought to put a sign on his door—"Street Language Spoken Here." Next to the one about the Holmes Electronics.

"Thing is, pal, you really don't know what you're missing, that's all. Think you've flown before? Shit."

Kelley folded the towel, yawned. He was bored with the whole attitude, the whole junkie-adventurer myth, guys who saw themselves as mental frontiersmen, trailblazers of the further realms, like all those people dropping acid in the sixties and going weird places.

Kelley, instead, had gone to Vietnam. Not that he'd remained any chemical virgin; he just knew the line between need and romance.

"Now you talk about *this* stuff," Zeedee kept talking, *"this* naked lady here is high, and I do mean *high*-percent pure. Chook's good. Get a bastard, he can cut it with anything—procaine, lidocaine, borax, speed, *sugar,* for Christ's sake. Anything. Milk!"

"Guy's feeling mean, he could cut it with arsenic."

"Oh Jesus. Shit. Has that ever happened?"

"Everything's probably happened," Kelley said. "You can think of it, it's happened."

"You ought to know Chook, though," Zeedee went on. "Character. Got a lot of friends higher up."

"On what?" Kelley said, coming out of the bathroom. "Have you heard from my beautiful wife, by the way? Did she call?"

"Did who call?" Zeedee was lining up the coke, dividing the powder into little white lines.

"Forget it," Kelley said, and picked up the phone. "You mind if I dial information? Blow another dime?"

"Easy come." Zeedee stuck a little straw in his nose.

Kelley said, "Number for Marcus Imry. Operator? Not the photography studio, the Imry apartment. Residence. Right."

Zeedee said, "You palling with Marcus these days?"

"Hardly. But Karen likes to pal with his wife. She left me a note she'd be at Candy's tonight."

"He ever make a pass at you?"

"Not that I know."

"Well . . . it's like Ogden Nash used to say. Candy's dandy but Marcus is quicker." Zeedee blew in. "Oh man, oh Christ, oh Jesus, you gotta *try* some of this."

Kelley hung up. No answer at Candy's. He looked up at Zeedee, who was telling him, "Really," leaning back in his chair. Zeedee, getting rushes, little bursts of encouragement from his bloodstream. Sitting up straight now, he suddenly waggled his nose-straw at Kelley. "I got it! I absolutely no-shit got it."

"Good," Kelley said.

"No, not just *good,* man. Wonderful. Great. The answer to everything."

"Nice. A little nasal mysticism, eh?"

"Oh yeah, make fun, make fun," Zeedee said, "but what do you think all those other guys were doing. I mean up in the mountains when they saw burning bushes."

"Not coke," Kelley said. "That'd have to be the Andes."

"Technical. You're being technical and picky. They were *on* something. Mesc. Grass. Hash. But I tell you—listen—guy carries ten big tablets down a mountain, guy's doing coke. That's heavy shit, man." Zeedee cackled. "Where was I?"

"The answer to everything."

"Oh. Yeah. Listen. *Chook!*" He looked up at Kelley, expecting him to grasp this superb profundity. Kelley said nothing. *"Chook!"* Zeedee said. *"Your* problems, see?"

Kelley said nothing; then: "Listen—I have to go home and go to sleep."

"No-no. You have to go to Chook's and get rich. Or solvent. Don't you get it?"

"No," Kelley said.

"Oh Christ. And a little child must lead them. Look—*you* need investors, Chook needs investors. You follow me? Pay-off's at twenty-to-one."

"Hey, pal," Kelley said, "you go to your party, I'll go to mine."

"So . . ." Zeedee sighed and wagged his head sadly. "History repeats. Here I am the first actual Jewish Christ—the other one converted too early to count—

36

and here I am offering the key to salvation and you're kicking my ass in with 'go to your party.'"

"Go to your party," Kelley said.

"Someday, someday—" Zeedee moved from the desk and started wrapping up his treasure, "someday you too will come to know and to fully appreciate the role of the Christ."

"I already know what it is," Kelley said.

"You do?"

Kelley nodded. "Yeah. To get nailed."

4

THE PARK AVENUE doorman was not a happy man.
There had already been about a dozen complaints. The
police were being called, and it would land on his head.

"Anything at all that goes down in this building lands
on my head, brother. That's how it is." He had a voice
like Rochester, deep scratchy black voice. He gave up
buzzing at the Imry apartment. "They don't know," he
said. "They don't know they got the music louder'n a
pimp-suit on Saturday night. So you want to go up
there, you got my permission. You feel like you want to
rob, rape and pillage, well you just go ahead. Apartment twelve H." He called after Kelley, "Tell 'em
Groucho sent you."

You could hear it from the elevator, the stereo
equipment blasting out a hard-ass Aussie vision. Kelley
rang the bell, then wondered if he might have to kick
down the door. He tried the handle; the door was open.

The apartment was packed. It was New Year's Eve
either fifty weeks early or still going on. They were
jammed like sardines in the twenty-foot foyer. Kelley
started thinking of the human wave, what he'd give for
a good-sized two-engine plane—vaROOM! He dived
into thundering chaos, elbowed through heavy metal
and leather, elbowed through a clot of sequins and hair,
and came out in a living room almost as crowded.
There seemed to be a large contingent of sibilant

homosexuals, there was a lot of androgyny around; there were guys who looked like they posed for muscle magazines and women who'd been carefully reconstructed to look like girls. He was wondering, Who the hell *are* these people? Do I know these people? Why would I know them? Somebody poked him in the back with a thumb.

He turned, didn't know her.

"Hi there," she hollered over fifty thousand decibels of screaming Eurythmics. "You got here all right." She was one of those cookies from a *Cosmo* cover, all neckline and eyes. The eyes had been manufactured with the sexy-look already in them. Less work for the owner. "Anita," she told him. "Anita Ramone. Remember me?"

Kelley said, yeah, sure, how've you been? Except the trouble with that was, she told him. At length. She'd been to California. They'd given her a test.

"Wasserman?"

She tilted her pretty little head. "Who's he?"

"Nothing," Kelley said. "No one. Joke. Hey listen— nice seeing you, Ramona."

"Anita."

"Anita," he assured her, and tried to get away as a middle-aged rocker who'd been taking it in said, "Syphilis, darling. Wasserman's the test they used to give you for—"

A lot of people with rainbow-colored hair. A guy with a nose-ring. A guy in drag, or a fatefully unattractive woman. Marcus Imry, the putative host, elegant, lithe, and unnecessary-looking, as *Vogue*-ish as always, relaxing in a circle of elusive young men. Marcus's marriage to Candy was a joke—Zeedee had pegged it as "the consummation devoutly to be wished"—but apparently it offered them a mutual reward. Candy had connected to the envious position of the permanently chic, and Marcus had bought himself passage on the ark. Marcus was burbling in somebody's ear. Kelley was opening the door to the pool room. A naked redhead with her legs spread apart had arranged herself neatly on the corner of the table and was offering another kind of corner pocket. The players were a gaggle of baby tycoons. *"Ouch!"* the girl said as the six-ball hit. "No kidding, that *hurts."*

He got to the bedroom. Karen was sitting on the bed with Candy and a mountain of coats—two little Blondies on a bed full of everything that once roamed the forest.

Kelley said simply, "Police! Freeze!" and for a moment they paled, turned, and stared at him with sickened expressions.

Then Karen said, "Funny."

Kelley said, "Not so funny. They've been called."

Candy said, "Really?" and Kelley wondered briefly if Candy had a clue to what reality was. She looked like an anorexic on a diet.

"You might want to lower your noise," Kelley said.

Candy jumped up but decided, thinking on her feet, "Well fuckum."

Kelley said to Karen, "You want to be here or what?"

Karen said to Candy, "His master's voice."

Kelley said, "Nice of you to show up at Zeedee's."

Karen said, "Yes, and so nice of you to call."

Kelley said, "You couldn't hear World War Three in this fucking apartment, what you'd hear is the phone."

Karen said, "Screw."

Kelley said, "It's stupid to ask you if you're coming so I'm telling you I'm going."

Karen said, "Good-bye."

Candy said, "Hey I forgot. Welcome home."

The cops arrived while he was crossing the lobby—a couple of reedy-looking Puerto Ricans. Groucho said,

"You're gonna need riot gear, friends," but the cops just sneered.

"They'll learn," Kelley said.

The doorman nodded. "You want to try for a taxi, I could put on the light, and then we could sit down and have a nice long discussion on the state of the republic and after a while I could order in breakfast."

Kelley shook his head. "You won't believe this," he said, "but that's possibly the finest offer of the day."

"Well," Groucho said, "blond lady comin' might change your direction."

Karen, mink-wrapped, heading for the door. Kelley said nothing as she moved up beside him. Karen said nothing as she took him by the arm.

Groucho said, "'Night, folks. Have a nice time."

Karen got her feet wet walking the two long blocks to the apartment, a walk conducted in the silence of a possibly haunted tomb. He wanted to say, What the hell's going on? Where are you? Who are you? "Nice friends you got," he said. "What *was* that?"

"A party."

"Why was I able to deduce that myself? I mean a party for what?"

"For some of Candy's friends."

"Oh," Kelley said. "I thought maybe it was a welcome wagon for some newly arrived Martians."

"That's your trouble," she said.

They walked further in silence.

"Dead Heat was there."

Kelley wasn't certain what to make of that statement so he left it alone. They turned into their lobby, their own rather stuffy Anglo-Saxon doorman tipping his hat to them.

Silence in the elevator.

"Is that a rock group?" he said.

She looked at him. "Welcome to the twentieth century."

He decided that meant it was a rock group; maybe.

In the apartment, she dropped her coat in the hallway and looked at her ruined red satin shoes.

In the bedroom, she hurriedly kicked the things off and then kicked them again out of sheer anger. She stood there barefoot in her red silk evening dress, blond hair tumbling, looking like one of those sci-fi women getting ready to unleash a little planetary wrath.

Kelley spread his hands. "Hey—you didn't have to leave."

"It was getting boring."

"Oh."

"And this is boring too."

"Yes it is," Kelley said.

"I think I feel sick."

"Then get into bed."

She shook her head quickly. "Not that kind of sick."

"I don't know what you mean," Kelley said, and started taking off his clothes. "I want to fix a sandwich. You want something?"

She looked at him. "You really don't know what I mean, do you?"

Holding on her eyes, he caught a glimpse of their panic.

"Edge of the world," he said softly.

She nodded. "Hold me."

He moved to her, feeling the silk with his own bare body, already getting hard, holding her, finding her lips against his own very open, very soft.

"I don't mean this," she whispered.

He pulled slightly back, confounded, once again.

"Just hold me," she said.

"Any further instructions?"

"Oh don't be a bastard," she said. "Please."

"Just a daddy."

"Just hold me," she said and then later: "Oh Jesus, Burke, make me be nice."

He took her to the bed, tossing the long silk garment to the floor. She was getting even thinner. Her breasts had been big round gorgeous handfuls, now they appeared to be dying on the vine. He cupped one in his palm and then licked at the nipple, then took it in his mouth, feeling her impatient hand on him, pulling, not playing, just telling him urgently to get down to business. She was clinging to him. "Fuck my brains out," she whispered, and it seemed to him less like a prelude to passion than an outcry of desperate and literal prayer. And for Kelley, as she seemed to be attaining her goal, it became nothing better than an act of anger—some fugitive desire to ram some kind of sense into her.

Afterwards, she pulled away from him quickly and stared at the ceiling, silent. He understood that. There was nothing to say. There'd been a swift flight and a crash landing. So maybe your bones felt a little bit shook, but the impact was brief and already receding. So what could you say except possibly, "Taxi."

"Have you got any pills?" she said. "I'm jizzed and I'm out, and I'd really like to sleep."

He reached for a cigarette. "You shouldn't mix too many downers with booze."

"I haven't been 'boozing' as you so quaintly put it."

He let it go.

She didn't. " 'Booze,' " she said. "Christ. You sound like a redneck."

"Blackneck," he said. "You get a red neck from working in the sun, you get a black neck from working in the mines."

"Are we onto your sad childhood?"

"It wasn't sad, it was grungy—there's a difference and I was merely correcting your terminology.—You want to wind up like Karen Ann Quinlan?"

"Did she misuse 'redneck'?"

"She misused downers and mixed them with booze, or whatever you'd call it."

"Quits," she said wearily, "if you'll get me some pills."

He filled a small bathroom glass with water and brought her a couple of yellow Valium.

"Kidstuff," she said, but swallowed them, dribbling the water on her chin. She turned off the light and flipped on the Sony: a weatherman, glibly updating the blizzard. Chicago, Washington, Boston, upstate New York. Pictures coming in of a blitzed Buffalo; middle-aged guys getting heart attacks, shoveling. Kelley lingered in the doorway for a moment, tying on a bathrobe. "Twenty-three inches and still coming down," the weatherman burbled. "Airports throughout the Adirondacks are closing and—"

Kelley walked out. Like a farmer watching his crop being ruined, he'd come to look at weather as a personal insult. How many planes would be idling on the ground? At how much an hour? For how many days? And Margaret had been right. Chances were he couldn't make it up to Glen Falls, couldn't drive to the farm, couldn't get to see Stryker.

He stood for a moment in the darkened living room looking through the window. A couple of inches had fallen on the city and were now getting frozen. The park was covered. The trees stood frozen like Lot's wife.

He crossed to the desk and opened the tinsel-wrapped chocolates from Paris, found a package of papers, rolled himself a joint and went back to the window.

Any minute now he was going to have to sit down

and have a long serious talk with himself about money, lay waste a few powers, think about the getting. One: he would of course have to telephone the Colonel. He'd have to play it very careful with the Colonel; pick a tone that would appeal to him, and still wouldn't sound as though a tone were being picked or an appeal being made. And if that didn't work? He'd have to go hunting. If his stock was "primarily speculative" now— then fine—there were plenty of speculators left, guys as eager to take fat tax losses as to make killings. There was big money in this country that would any day rather whore than turn honest; put it in a goldmine, put it in a canister, put it anyplace except in the mouths of black babies; so he wouldn't be taking it from anybody's mouth, he'd be taking it merely from some kind of Panamanian shell-game or possible investment in *Star Wars VIII*.

He had very mixed feelings on the subject of money. Like the rifle clubs telling you, guns don't kill, people do, he knew it wasn't money that created corruption, it was simply one of many available tools. He admitted to having enjoyed his own money. He'd enjoyed making it. When it started coming in he'd made some clever investments; bought gold at four hundred, sold it when it peaked at its almost phenomenal eight-fifty-six. He'd had the same kind of amateur's luck with the market, knowing very little, but sensing progressions, timings, stirrings in the wind. He'd enjoyed spending it too; up to a point. He'd bought himself a lovingly reconstructed Beagle, a seven-seat twin that reminded him not so much of a beagle as of Disney's Pluto. Great dumb-looking plane. He'd bought a maroon Ferrari and the Fifth Avenue apartment, an attractive villa on the southern coast of France and then he'd been sated, bored with it. And then of course Rosetti had been right: most of it he'd squirreled into company stock. Meaning, simply, that his bet wasn't hedged and what happened to the company would happen to him. He could, if he wanted to, think about that. About the fact that if money wasn't guaranteed joy, its absence was pure unadulterated shit, so from a personal standpoint he wanted to stay at least a yard above the creek. And barring that—hold onto the paddle.

But losing the airline . . . ? What would he do? Even stoned, as he was rapidly getting at the moment, he could not see himself as one of those incredible Born-Again types. Like cops becoming actors, actors becoming presidents. No; he was dealing from a one-card hand. The only thing he knew about was airlines—maybe. He was basically a pilot with a long string of luck. And for months he'd had a feeling—not a premonition, nothing that sexy—just simply a feeling that his rocky love affair with luck was at an end.

Well, it had still been a pretty good run.

He took another long deep hit of the grass and the tune went through his head, he forgot the connection, wasn't sure why it did, but there it was, humming,

> *He floats through the air*
> *With the greatest of ease,*
> *The daring young man*
> *On the flying trapeze.*
> *His actions are graceful,*
> *All girls he does please*
> *And*—something, something, something. . . .

5

GETTING OUT OF the V.A. hospital, Kelley hadn't figured he was any kind of hero; the way he could see it he
was nothing but a twice-lucky sonofabitch, having, one,
saved his ass and, two, saved his eye. The eye had been
close. The wound was infected and the doctor pronounced that since the eye would be eventually useless
anyway, they might as well remove it. Kelley had
pronounced that since the doctor's dick would be
eventually useless, it too should be removed, and a
one-eyed Kelley would be well inclined to do it. He'd
joined the army solely to learn how to fly. The recruiting poster hadn't mentioned Vietnam, it had said
"Earn Your Wings" and he'd earned them in spades.
He'd learned to fly choppers and, rarity of rarities,
fixed-wing too, and he'd paid for the privilege with two
tours in Nam. He was not now about to be permanently
grounded; he put up a fight. His case was referred to a
Dr. Quintero, a general conservator of human parts,
who brought off the trick, and by the time Kelley got
himself released from the service and also from the
ward, all he had to do was wear a patch for a year.

He walked out of the hospital into the fog-bound San
Francisco day, stood on the steps with his bag on his
shoulder, looked at the fog and took a deep free breath.
Then he just stood there, knowing he didn't know
where the hell to go. There was no destination, no

particular plan. His parents had died; his father of black lung disease, his mother, at forty-six, of old age. He was twenty-five years old, had fifty thousand hard-fought dollars in his pocket and no place to put it.

He walked around the city. San Francisco in the summer of '71 was still hippiedom's heaven. There were girls in long gauzy dresses, barechested boys with headbands and beads. Peace, people said, Love, people said, and then looked up at Kelley and hollered out, "Killer!" It was neither the first nor the last time he'd hear it and at least he had it relatively straight in his head. You could, if you wanted to, be against the war, but The War had absolutely nothing to do with the luckless bastards who were over there dying, who had as much to do with foreign policy as the taxpayer has to do with taxes. The grunts were just payers. If they needed Medevacs and hot ammunition, then someone had to bring them. Period. Argue philosophy later; or sooner.

He found himself a good dark neighborhood tavern, tossed his bag onto sawdust and ordered a Cutty. There was a group of hippies drinking beer at a table, a nice-looking redhead and a couple of guys, no hasslers at the moment. He sipped quietly at his Scotch and decided that the time had come to have a plan. He had more money than he'd ever dreamed of, but not enough to purchase his particular dream. He wanted his own airline. His own personal chunk of the sky. A plan had been hatched on the dregs of a three-day pass in Saigon. They'd discussed it stoned and discussed it sober. Blake, Turner, Kelley and Scott. It would be, they decided, a short-haul taxi. Buy yourself a couple of slick little Beeches and tool around strictly in the hub of a city. Flying New York had been Turner's contribution, a competitive statewide airline was Kelley's, only everyone had raspberried Kelley's idea. Not that it mattered. No one, as it happened, was buying any planes.

Blake went down in a blaze at Quang Tri.

Scotty bought the farm on a strip at Dong Ha.

Turner was missing and presumed to be dead.

And Kelley took a bullet through the bone above his eye.

Lighting a cigarette, he glanced in the mirror. Even in the gloom with his depth-perception shot, it occurred to him he looked like a hardcase villain, like someone he personally would not want to mess with. He was slightly surprised then, a few minutes later, when the redhead came over and sat at his left. He could see her watching him in the mirror. Finally he turned and said, "What do you think?" She had level brown eyes. She said, "I don't know yet." Kelley said, "Fine. Let me know when you decide."

"Would you give me an interview?"

"Interview?"

Her name, she told him, was Barbara Lewinter, though Kelley came to call her The Berkeley Barb. She was, as she admitted, "heavy into peace," had continued to be an active demonstrator, had written for the *Barb* and was now doing "free-lance stuff for magazines." She was doing an "In-Depth Study on the Mind of the Returning Veteran." She asked him where he was staying so she could call him sometime and arrange an appointment. He told her he didn't know where he was staying. She suggested Sausalito ("It's always sunny there, even when San Francisco's in a fog") and offered to drive him.

The sun was, indeed, out in Sausalito. There was a room for rent a couple of blocks from where she lived, in an old clapboard building, upstairs from a restaurant, a block from the water. Table, bed, chair and a hotplate. Kelley's first home. She walked him to a store where he bought a few dishes and basic groceries and asked her what she thought of his Returning Mind. She said: "You're laid back." He told her he hadn't been laid back in quite a while, having come from the hospital.

In bed she was very soft, very sweet; very natural and loving. She said, "You'd make a really good hippie, you know?" He said, "I just did."

He tried it for a while; kept the room and the girl, grew a bandit mustache, grew stronger in the sun, tried surfing, but he didn't have the temperament to drift. In the age of the drifter, he was someone out of sync. To the surfers and the part-time players on the beach, to the girls who misinterpreted the slow quiet surface, the voice with its lingering Kentucky drawl ("You talk," the Barb said, "like Kristofferson sings."), he appeared to be a model of Aquarian cool. To the men he'd flown with he seemed to be almost fanatically reckless, a compulsive, someone put it, who's in love with the edge. To the women he'd slept with he seemed to be in love with nothing but the moment. Only Turner, his friend in the army, understood him, understood that he was motivated only by a push for absolute freedom. "You have to keep proving you're free to do anything," Turner had told him, "even free to die. And sometimes you act as though you already had it."

"Had what?" Kelley asked.

"The freedom of the dead."

He rented a car and drove to San Francisco, checking the libraries, checking out the books on airline management, airline economics, airline operations. He began reading papers like *Aviation Daily;* he read corporate histories, going for a fix on the minds and the moves that had turned raw dreams into solid success. If not exactly educated, Kelley had a quick and agile intelligence. Smart enough to know when he didn't know enough, he kept probing and seeking. He checked out the air-traffic charts of the country and the number of airlines that were slotted for each. The point was you wanted to stay within a state so the feds couldn't regulate your rates or your routes. And Turner had been right. New York would be the right kind of place to begin. Geographically large enough to offer economical intrastate routes with enough population to provide the traffic. The more he read the more certain he became that overhead costs could be kept down far enough to pass on a lot of significant savings and still make a profit. He decided, ideally, he'd like to have a couple of beat-up Dakotas. With piston engines and thirty-six seats, a Dakota could carry a full load of passengers two hundred miles—New York City to Syracuse, for instance—for seat-mile expenses of five bucks a head. "And for that kind of money," he explained to the Barb, "you could beat your competition six ways to Sunday, and on *Sunday*," Kelley said, "you could charge half fare."

The Barb rolled over and asked him, "How much?" She was dressed in her usual beach costume—jeans and a long voluminous T-shirt. This one was pink. "To start an airline, I mean."

"About five hundred thousand dollars," Kelley said.

She made an O with her mouth, nodded only once and went back to her reading.

Kelley traced the number with a stick in the sand, circled it and looked at it.

"Oh oh oh oh oh," he said.

The Barb looked up from the depths of *The Bell Jar*.

"I was just counting the o's."

"Mmm. You've got plenty of o's," she said flatly, "it's the five part I think you have to worry about."

"If you worry," Kelley said, "you get a wart on your nose. Didn't your mother ever tell you that?"

"No.—Don't you ever worry?"

He shrugged at her broadly. "You see any warts?"

He flew to New York, bought himself a brand-new hundred-dollar suit, a sincere blue tie, and accosted the banks. Nobody argued with his figures or his plans; the word "airline," he learned, could stop any banker faster than a shot. As though everyone in town were under mass hypnosis: at the word "airline" you will shake your head rapidly and hold up your hand.

Airlines, he was told, had a roller-coaster cycle. They folded more frequently than canvas deck-chairs and attracted "neither lender nor investor confidence." Further, there remained the intractable problem of Kelley himself. With no experience and no education, he quickly concluded, the only way he'd ever get money from a bank was to get himself a mask and an M16.

The Barb insisted he work the *I Ching*. He rolled the coins and got fortune 35: *Chin—Progress*, with a 6 at the beginning:

> *Progress, but turned back.*
> *Perseverance brings good fortune.*
> *If one meets with no confidence one should*
> *   remain calm.*
> *No mistake.*

According to the Santa Barbara directory, William Jefferson was still a resident of 127 Olympic Boulevard. Kelley drove down on a Sunday afternoon, having no idea what the Jeffersons were like or how they'd react. If they'd call him a bastard. If they'd call the police. Because Jim Jefferson, age twenty-four, Vietnam victim, improbable Ace, had a quarter of a million in private insurance, payable as soon as the body hit ground. Kelley himself had had two hundred thousand. The companies were selling it to everybody, war-clause suspended like a shot, because the actual odds of being murdered in a war hadn't ever been as certain as the companies' greed.

Jefferson had just been a terrible bet.

His parents lived in a four-room apartment in a stucco building with a red tile roof. Outside the window was a sick-looking palm. The father, Kelley learned, was a postal employee and the mother was a mother. Hysterical tears and "would you like some more cake?"

Kelley was mournful, kind, and attentive. He told them that Jimmy had fought the good fight, not mentioning the fact that the fighting had been vicious, repulsive and dumb, or that Jimmy caught a savaging dose of the clap or had learned to talk words you couldn't send through the mails. That was the wind-up. He started the pitch by painting them a picture of something like a cross between a company outing and a scout jamboree—kids camping out around a crackling fire in a picturesque wood swapping boyhood dilemmas and improbable dreams. "So you see," Kelley said, "our dream was this airline. The four of us together. Just Jimmy and Billy and Scotty and me. Only Jimmy was the one really put it into words. The way Jimmy put it, he said, 'This is more than an airline, you know.' He said, 'This is real public service.'"

"Did he say that?"

"Yes ma'am, that's what he said. And I figure, you know, if I brought the thing off, it would be . . . well, let's call it a fitting memorial to wasted young lives." He looked at the mother. "And Jimmy's last wish." He looked at the father. "And of course I'd pay you back within the next seven years and let's say I'd pay you at six percent interest. Now I happen to have a few papers drawn up . . ."

He left Santa Barbara with a certified bank-check for seventy thousand.

They were lying on the beach. The Barb rolled over and told him, "That's fraud."

Kelley said, "You better get out of the sun. You're turning the color of your T-shirt, kiddo."

This one was orange.

"Good," the Barb said. "You can squeeze me for breakfast. Now answer the question."

Lighting a cigarette, he squinted through smoke. "There didn't seem to be any question about it. You said, that's fraud."

"Well isn't it?"

"No. I'm paying them better interest than a bank and meanwhile the bank's paying interest to me. So what's fraud about that?"

"Jefferson," she said. "I've heard about a Turner, a Scott and a Blake. I never heard about a Jefferson."

"So?" Kelley said. "Maybe I forgot to mention him."

"Oh." She rolled over and looked at the ocean. Then she said, "You better get out of the sun."

"Me?" he said. "Why?"

She looked at him hard. "You're turning the color of a bad penny."

Kelley said nothing. For a while he looked at her looking at the ocean. Then he said, "Listen—you know what's on the penny?"

"Lincoln."

"The words, 'In God We Trust.'"

"So what are you saying?"

"Trust me," he said, and then laughed.

She didn't. Instead she got up and took a walk down the beach.

The Blakes, he discovered, lived in El Paso.
He left El Paso with a certified check.

He now had a hundred and fifty thousand dollars and the Barb took a more or less permanent walk.

He was sprawled on the beach with another big stack of the flying magazines and the *121 Aviation Manual,* reading the rules about safety requirements. Engrossed. He figured he was totally engrossed because he didn't even notice there was anything arising on a shell from the ocean or popping from a bottle. The girl was just there. Looking like an ad for anything, name it—Colgate, Jantzen, Coppertone, round-trip fare to California.

"You a flier?" she said.

"Uh huh. Want to fly with me?" Just to be funny.

She nodded. She kept on nodding her head. She either had a nice little deadpan sense of humor or none whatsoever.

He still wasn't sure. "You want to try landing, or you just want to stand around tossing your hair?"

"What would happen if I sat?"

"Well listen, the usual stuff. I could offer you a cigarette, ask you your name . . ."

She sighed. "Oh wow. Could we skip all the dumb part? My name's Tina, I work for Western Airlines, and I live around Waldo." She cocked her beautiful Golden Girl head. "You want to see where?"

Kelley said there weren't many things on the planet he would rather see more.

She had a small house with a large bed. Neither of them had a lot of clothes to get out of. They were on the bed and she was all over him. She said, "My God, I saw you on the beach and I thought, I gotta have that."

"Sex object," he said.

She had his sex object in her hand. This was definitely some kind of movie he was in. This wasn't real life: sitting on a beach, reading, Miss California comes up, "I gotta have that."

"Oh . . . Jesus . . . *Christ!*" he exploded. "Where'd you learn that?"

"From Popsicles," she said.

"Unreal."

The door opened. The guy standing there, Kelley hoped, was also unreal. He was built like a truck. A big wild Irishman with flaming red hair. For a time there was a nasty frozen tableau. The girl rolled over. Kelley checked the area for usable weapons. The guy said nonchalantly, "At it again, eh?" and walked over to the bureau and pulled out a shirt. "She can wear out a pile-driver, that one." He started changing his shirt.

Tina said sweetly, "Sit on it and twirl."

Kelley said, "You're not her husband, I suppose."

"Fuckin' A."

Kelley nodded, pulled the blanket up over his shriveled joint, cleared his throat softly and said: "Nice shirt."

The linebacker laughed. "I'd tell you who I am but I'd rather have you go to your grave wondering."

Kelley said that was indeed likely. Lighting a cigarette, he turned to Tina, offering the pack, but apparently his first impression had been right: no sense of humor. She sat there naked and upright on the bed, wearing an expression of rage so glaring that it went through his mind: put it in a box, *Barbie Goes to Bellevue,* and throw in a doll-size straitjacket.

"Faggots," she screaked at him. "Two fuckin' faggots."

The guy laughed again. "I'll be out in a couple of seconds, by the way."

"So will I," Kelley said. "This is too deep for me." Rising slowly, he pulled on his trunks while Tina started cursing, mostly at the guy who was apparently "Stryker." Stryker very calmly picked up his keys. Kelley took his manual and reached for his shirt. Tina started furiously cursing at Kelley and not just cursing now but *really* cursing, in old Hungarian Gypsy tradition, a list of the seriously Gothic fates that awaited his scrotum. She threw in a couple of other things too—a hairbrush, a book; a coffee cup crashed against the door as they left.

They walked in silence down the flagstone path. All things considered it seemed to be an almost companionable silence. Stryker had a couple of inches on Kelley, maybe six-foot-three, about as solid as rock, about thirty. They were almost at the end of the path. A yellow Mustang was parked at the curb behind Tina's little Volvo.

They looked at each other.

Stryker said, "Well."

Kelley said, "Exactly." Wanting to laugh now but still not certain if there'd have to be a fight. Stryker was staring at the patch on his eye, looking down at the manual and back at the patch.

"Nam?"

"Uh huh."

"And you're a flier, I take it. Not by any chance in the Hundred and First?"

Kelley squinted. "In fact."

"Well no shit. Me too," Stryker said. "I got out of there in must've been late sixty-seven."

"Missed the good part."

"Yeah. So I heard." Stryker grinned. "So what can I tell you, man. The girl goes for anything that rises in the air."

"Flighty."

"That's the word that's been evading me. Right. Hey listen—need a ride?"

"Sausalito'd be good.—You can just kind of drop me on the road," Kelley said as they settled in the car, Stryker pulling out with a screech of Pirellis, Kelley easing back, getting comfortable, flipping down the visor in the front. The sun was still ripe; he figured he might as well go back to the beach.

"Weird," Stryker said.

Kelley said nothing.

"Ex-husband," Stryker said. "That hit you as weird?"

"Neither."

"Huh?"

"Neither husband nor ex."

"Yeah. Okay. I get it."

They drove in silence for a time. Stryker was staring through the windshield ahead. "Bought the house, you know. I figured, wow, I lucked out. Oh man, I can tell you that is one crazy bitch. She goes to the supermarket, she'll do it with the butcher, she'll do it on the shelves. I'm only exaggerating slightly," Stryker said, looking up in the mirror. "Makes you feel better though, she really only does it with good-lookin' guys."

"What would make me feel *better*," Kelley said slowly, "is you tell me she had her distemper shots."

"Yeah." Stryker laughed. "Christ, she gives language lessons on the docks. Got a mouth on her, right?"

They sat with that sentence between them in the air. Then Stryker started laughing.

"Must've been fun while it lasted," Kelley said.

"No. Pure hell, pure hell," Stryker told him. "I used to fly for Western, gave it up, left town, had to get a little distance. I got hired by this guy—big Texas bread. I'm his private pilot. His 'air chauffeur.'" He shrugged. "What the hell, he pays me like I'm Captain Friendly at the majors. Goes to Vegas a lot. I get time off there. Gets up to San Francisco maybe three times a month which is why I keep the house. Well . . . one of the reasons. I got it cheap four years ago and I'd rather, you know, own a house than own money."

"Tina still live there?"

"Tina? No. She just uses it to fool around in. She's married again."

"Oh," Kelley said.

They were silent for a moment. Stryker put a little more speed on the motor, zipping along around the oceanside cliff. He looked down briefly at the *121* that was resting on the seat. "Got an actual setup, or is that just dreaming?"

"Well, let's call it just thinking," Kelley said.

"You got enough bread?"

"That's one of the things I'm not thinking about. Saw an ad for some planes. Cox, Nevada. You know where Cox, Nevada, is?"

Stryker said, "Yeah. 'Bout sixty out of Vegas." Then he said, "You want to go look at 'em or something, I'm flying back empty. Leave around noon."

"Tomorrow?"

"Right. You're just dreaming."

"Noon from where?"

"Oakland." They were coming to the Sausalito turn-off. Stryker pulled over. "Lane Twelve," Stryker said. "Show up, you can ask for Colonel Hollis's plane. By the way," he held his hand out, "I'm Charlie Stryker."

"Kelley," Kelley said.

It occurred to him later that God did work in mysterious ways.

3 Dakotas, 1 certified fly-away,
2 need work. All logs, manuals
available. Rite price down. See
Ed. Mobile Air.

STRYKER HANDED BACK the ad. "Even used, beat-up,"
he said, "you're still talking two hundred thousand
worth of plane. And then two need work."

"I can read," Kelley said. They were sitting in the
deli at the Sands in Vegas. "And be careful. You're
getting mustard on my dreams."

"Seriously," Stryker said. "You have enough
money?"

"Nope. I come up about fifty thousand shy." Kelley
pulled at his beer. "And then two need work."

"So what do you do if you like 'em?"

"I punt," Kelley said. He reached for the check. "I
don't know what I'll do. I don't *ever* know what I'll do.
I surprise the hell out of myself sometimes. So you want
to come with me, you can see what I do."

Mobile Air turned out to be a small used-plane lot
for small used planes—mostly two-to-six-seaters, a lot
of single-engines and crop-dusters. The advertised Dakotas were, as advertised, a trio of veteran DC-3's—fat

clunky things, but still they had a passenger load of thirty-six and a maximum cruising range of fifteen hundred miles. The plane had been the workhorse of commercial aviation and military transport from the thirties to the fifties, when Douglas stopped making them for lack of public interest.

"Talk about don't make 'em like they used to," Ed Spinnaker said, "this baby here's the one yer talkin' about."

The baby appeared to be at least seventeen. Kelley walked around it. "This the fly-away?"

"Yep."

The skin was flaky; the tires were okay. He peered through the nacelles and looked at the engines. The two Pratt and Whitneys had been cleaned to a shine.

"Just like I told ya," Ed Spinnaker said. He had the face of an old skyhawk.

"You flown it?"

"Flew her grandmother in the Philippines, kid. Flew this one last week. When I tell you fly-away I mean fly-away."

Her older sisters weren't doing so well. The engines were congealed oil and rust; drooping flaps. "Hydraulic system's shot on this one," Kelley said.

Spinnaker lifted the baseball cap on his grizzled head and put it back in its place. "*Said* they need work. You'll want to see the logs."

He went off to get them as Kelley climbed into the second plane. Its army designation would be C-47, a cargo transport, a zero-seater. The deck was like a furnace. The cockpit was worse. There was a lizard on the pilot's seat. Kelley picked it up and held it very gently in the palm of his hand as he sat, quietly, and thought of Saigon. Thought about Turner, dead or at best living in a cage. Thought about Blake and Scotty in the ground. He looked at the instrument panel of the

Dak; it appeared to be a maze of dusty dials. Like looking at a strange new woman in bed and wondering, Where are the right buttons?

Charlie poked his head through the cockpit window of the neighboring plane. "Duck soup," he said flatly. "So easy a child can fly it."

"Meaning you can't."

"True," Charlie said. "I don't know where anything is in here, but there isn't too much. This isn't exactly amazing avionics."

Spinnaker came back with the logs—all nine of them, the one for each craft and one for each of the six engines. Kelley gave half of the logs to Charlie and they sat in the small shed that served as an office, drinking warm Cokes and poring through the pages, then swapping the ledgers. Spinnaker had bought the planes from the army. They hadn't been flown since the mid-sixties. The army had completely overhauled the fly-away just before they'd junked her.

"Well, it's always good to know your taxes went for something constructive," Charlie said. "Gives you a nice warm feeling, doesn't it?" He looked up at Kelley. "So what do you think?"

"Two new engines, complete overhauls, exterior paint, interior everything."

"Figure a hundred and a half just to fix 'em."

Kelley said nothing. Then he whistled into the top of the empty bottle. Then he said, "The cargo plane." Then he said nothing. Then he said, "What if you had a plane that flew passengers in daytime and cargo at night?"

"You'd either have very uncomfortable passengers or comfortable cargo. What'll you do—put the boxes on the seats?"

"Take the seats out. Have snap-out seats."

"Could you do that?" Charlie said. "Shit. You could do that, couldn't you."

"You *could* do that," Kelley said. "Couldn't you."

"You could do that," Charlie said. "You'd make back your revenue—"

"Right." Kelley put down the vinyl logbooks and headed for the field where Spinnaker was working on a Cessna 150.

"What're you asking?"

Ed Spinnaker studied him, squinting in the sun. "What do you want 'em for?"

"Planters," Kelley said. "What do you mean, what do I want 'em for?"

"Pardon my saying, boy, but you don't look none too airworthy yourself, so I just got to wonderin'. Cargo or passenger?"

"Passenger."

Spinnaker sniffed, nodded, rubbed slowly at his lip. "Tried it myself, ya know. Nineteen-fifty. Went broker'n an egg."

Kelley said nothing.

"Hundred for the fly-away. Other two together be a hundred and a quarter. And don't try to bargain with me, boy, 'cause I just bargained with myself. I want forty-five down."

"Or sixty down, one-eighty for the lot. The sixty in cash."

Spinnaker looked at him. "What do you mean by cash?"

"Little green presidents," Kelley said. "From under my mattress to under yours."

Spinnaker squinted, then nodded slightly, as though he were afraid there were bugs in the desert. "Now how you gonna test her? This fella here?" He thumbed at Stryker.

"I can do it," Kelley said.

"Oh no no. Not in *my* plane, you can't. You got a license at all, it's a third class only. One-eyed Jack goes to hell in my plane, I go broke in a jail cell."

"Right," Charlie said. "Give me the handbook."

In the car he said, "Swell. I got a date, I'm supposed to stay home, read your handbook."

"Don't worry about it."

"Why not? I'm not flying what I don't understand."

"I said don't worry about it, you're not flying."

"Good. Who is?"

Kelley turned a full one-eighty to look at him.

Charlie said, "No, not with me as your co."

"Relax."

"When you're giving me a wonderful choice. Either I kill me or you kill me."

"Relax. Don't worry about it," Kelley said.

He got back to his room at the Sands around seven. He showered, shaved, and then stared at his bandit reflection in the mirror. The Barb had been right. He was definitely the color of a bad penny. It surprised him to discover that he missed her a little. They'd been friends and then she hadn't felt friendly anymore. He acknowledged her reasons, though without feeling guilt. He'd done what he had to. For all he could figure, Jefferson and Blake had been roundly amused; if they weren't, they could come back and haunt him for a while. That too would be fair.

He dressed quickly in an old pair of jeans and a clean blue shirt, poured himself a drink, and then paced to the window and leaned against the sill. It was a tiny room with delusions of grandeur—white French furniture and wine-colored drapes—and an unobstructed view of the parking lot below.

He watched a Lamborghini disgorging its load—a hefty-looking guy in a dove-gray Stetson with a big-chested redhead clinging to his arm. He heard her laugh softly and say, "Aw shoot," and then found himself wondering who the guy'd shot at to get the Lamborghini.

He'd been thinking like that. There were very few legitimate ways to get bread. The system wouldn't give you enough to let you beat it; you could get enough to live on but not enough to fly. And the upshot was this:

He did not have enough. With every single penny he'd earned, saved, conned and cajoled, he could possibly fix up two of the planes and then he'd have a couple of planes on the ground. The certificate to fly them would cost him another fifty thousand bucks and he'd *still* have a couple of planes on the ground. No crews, no gates, no office, no staff, no insurance, no ads.

It was time for a move.

He took the cashier's check out of his wallet and looked at it carefully.

"Exactly Forty-Eight Thousand and 00/100 dollars."

The amount of money in the bank that was his. Combat/hazard pay. Less per hour than a corporate lawyer makes for killing a clause.

In his hand. Right now.

He took it over to the bed, sprawled out, lit a cigarette, and looked at it some more.

He thought of his mother saving up for a year to buy cheap lace curtains.

He thought of the suit his father was married in and got buried in twenty years later.

He thought of himself, chopping wood, seven hours in the sun, to take a girl to a movie; couldn't think what girl.

He stubbed his cigarette and went down to the casino.

"A-ten a-ten a-ten a-ten a-ten's the point," the stickman chanted. "Come with it easy, come with it hard, the point is ten."

The shooter was a grim little man with a large stack of chips arranged neatly at the rail. Luck made him sweaty. The room was cold enough to freeze lava and here he was with big fat beads on his face.

Kelley had a hundred riding *Don't Pass;* now he pitched five hundred more at the Seven, like pennies at a curb, and waited, his brown hands braced on the rail, his jeans jacket open, and one booted foot tapping rhythms on the floor.

The wet man rolled.

"Seven, line away," the stickman called it.

Kelley collected, adding the chips to the pile in front of him, a few thousand dollars ahead of where he'd been. He ordered another Cutty on the rocks from a girl with a beehive of platinum hair as the stickman was calling out, "Next shooter up."

The next-up shooter was a liver-spotted man with yellow-white hair and a dusty black suit. The crowd just didn't like the looks of this guy; money went down on a fast crap-out. Kelley held back.

"Shooter rolls eight. Eight is the point."

Kelley said, "Hard way," and put down a hundred on the hard double four.

The old man looked at him with watered blue eyes, then nodded and rolled.

"Nine. The point is eight, the shooter rolls nine."

Kelley's bet rode. Nobody covered it, not even the old man himself, who appeared to be betting only two-dollar chips. He kept rolling. No sevens, but no eights either. Other bettors got lucky on beside-the-point rolls. Ten, nine, six the hard way, three, deuce, four, six again. The dice didn't want to leave the old man's hand. Kelley doubled his bet, then doubled twice more, played Eight, Big Eight, let the hard bet ride, and had twenty-one hundred dollars on the table as the old man headed for his fourteenth roll.

"Seven, line away."

The chips went to the house and the dice went to

Kelley, who was back where he started, the dice having given, then taken away.

He chose two dice from the five that were offered by the stickman's stick, then held them for a moment and asked himself whether he was lucky or not. He got no feeling about it either way. He didn't even feel like a man who was about to gamble on his life, he just felt like a guy standing at a table with some cubes in his hand. He bet *Pass*, bet Seven, hesitated, bet Eleven, and without making any big rattling ritual, shook the dice once, and tossed.

"Eleven."

The pay-off was fifteen to one. He'd just won a total of eight thousand dollars. He shoved it on the pass-line and rolled: a six. He bet six hard and easy, covering each with a thousand-dollar buy; rolled eight, rolled eleven, rolled five, rolled four, and then rolled the two threes. He was now another nineteen thousand ahead. The table limit was sixteen. He bet sixteen on *Pass*. There was a stirring at the table, everybody catching the fever of a streak. The old man at his right said, "Keep it up, son. I'm ahead twenty dollars." Kelley rolled seven. Then he rolled a four, a nine, a ten, a six, and a four. He'd more than doubled his money. There was a thick crowd around him. There were calls of encouragement. He looked quickly at the girl who was still watching him from across the table. If she was a movie star he'd been out of touch too long to have gone to her movies but she would have played the Ultimate Heartbreaker role. The girl put a hundred-dollar chip on the *Pass*. Kelley felt the dice go cold in his hand. He'd never believed in that particular metaphor, but then, there it was—a dead-certain instinct that zapped from the tips of his fingers to his brain, not the other way around, and that told him, it's over. He lit a cigarette with about two hundred eyes on him and squinted at the girl. The problem that came to his mind was in the nature of a paradox. If his luck had run out he'd get craps on the first roll or seven on the second. If he bet *against* himself he'd actually win with those rolls, but if luck were against him . . . shit, he'd produce a natural and lose. Appointment in Samara. So be it. Okay. He moved sixteen thousand to the *Any Craps* line. The girl raised her tawny eyebrows. By the rules of the game, she couldn't change her bet. Kelley shrugged and then rolled.

Deuce.

Craps.

He'd won a hundred and twelve thousand dollars.

He now had a little over two hundred thou.

And he knew, he *knew,* he'd pushed luck to her limit. He bet a thousand on *Pass*, rolled four, rolled seven, and went to the bar.

The bar was black. Black vinyl tables and black booths and a black piano with a black piano player noodling Gershwin. It was almost empty. Kelley took a booth near the noisy piano so as not to be able to hear himself think, and ordered a Cutty. There was nothing to think about anyway. Except that he needed to double what he'd won. He could have this drink and go back to the tables but the feeling persisted: the lady said "no," don't push it, not tonight.

After a while the girl came in with the guy she'd been standing next to at the table. He was rangy and hyper; salt-and-pepper hair, cashmere sweater over bare skin, white ducks, no socks. Catherine Deneuve. That's who she looked like. Or possibly was.

The dusty old man, the one who'd won twenty dollars on Kelley's landslide, wandered in too. He squinted through the gloom and walked directly to Kelley's table. Kelley wasn't sure that he wanted this now, but the old man seemed very purposeful when he said, "Mind if I set?" and Kelley gestured at the seat.

"I don't mean to bother ya too long, son, I just had a question."

Kelley offered him a drink. When the waiter came over, he ordered a bourbon and asked if he could trouble Kelley for a smoke. "What I'se wonderin'," he said as he accepted Kelley's light, "is just how come you quit."

"Sevened out," Kelley said.

"No no. Now, you quit, son, be*fore* you sevened out. 'Sides, even so, most gamblers I ever met, they'da stuck to that table like they's tethered to the rail. So I want to know what happened. You get cold feet?"

"Cold dice."

"Heard a little ivory voice kinda whisper you're done."

"Something like that."

"You a quitter? I mean as a general proposition?"

"That's three," Kelley said.

"Beg pardon?"

"You said you had a question. That's three."

"Gettin' a mite squiffy there, are ya? Well, can't say's I blame you, old codger comes up, cadges drinks, bums cigarettes, asks a lotta dang fool questions. Still and all, son, you do inspire curiosity. I'd've pegged you for a real hardnose, myself. Man who'd go lose an eye—how'd you lose it, by the way?"

"Same cat that got your tongue."

The old man guffawed. The waiter came back with a neat bourbon and the old man downed it in one neat gulp, then stood. "Well now, I'll leave ya to yer own sweet dreams. Much 'bliged fer yer time, son. 'Bliged fer the laugh. And don't let the cat get yer money now, hear?" He walked away, still smoking the cigarette, holding it between a thumb and three fingers, the way winos do; keeping a good grip on it.

Kelley sipped his Cutty and thought about messages from ivory voices. The idea, he admitted, sounded pretty dumb. He called for the waiter, ordered another double on the rocks and asked if he could have some sugar. In cubes, he said. The waiter, who must have heard everything by now, said flatly, "In the Scotch, sir?"

"No, on a plate and let me borrow your pen."

When he got the cubes, he dotted them like dice and tossed them on the table: snake eyes. He tossed again: four, three, seven. Then twelve—another craps. Then six, then seven. The girl and her rich boyfriend appeared to be watching him with snide amusement. He thought, Fuck you. When he finished his drink, he wrapped the dice in a napkin with a hundred-dollar chip and wrote on the napkin: "With deep sympathy for your loss."

When he left, he told the waiter to bring it to the girl.

When he got to his room he regretted the gesture as cheap and adolescent.

When his phone started ringing, he thought it was the girl to say, Fuck you too.

It was Charlie Stryker. "I heard you broke the bank."

"Hardly. It was more like a small crack."

"You call that small, we're from different planets."

"I need double," Kelley said.

"Well, don't worry," Stryker yawned at the phone. "Luck loves a winner."

"Hey—I'm not *worry*ing," Kelley protested. "I'm just—actually, I'm worrying. Yes."

"See how much happier you were when you were poor?"

"Don't push it," Kelley said.

"Okay, but I thought you'd be comforted to know that I'm taking your goddam manual to bed."

"And I don't want to hear about your sexual perversions."

"Okay," Stryker laughed.

Kelley said, "You're not a bad person there, Charlie."

"I know. That's my trouble."

"Well," Kelley said, "stick with me, kiddo, and you'll learn how to change."

7

STRYKER CALLED IN very early in the morning. The test flight was off because he had to fly the Colonel up to Frisco for the day, "but we can do it tomorrow."

Kelley lost a thousand dollars at the tables and drove himself out to see "the fabulous wonders of Hoover Dam."

("It was," as he explained to Stryker, "a dam.")

He returned to find a message was waiting at the desk; a small envelope that said "Mr. Kelly," spelled wrong. A hundred-dollar chip fell out when he opened it. The note said, *"I never take money from strangers. I do like champagne."* There was no signature. Kelley asked the clerk if he happened to know who'd left it at the desk and was told (oh yes indeed) a Miss Houghton. The number of her room was a state secret. "If you want to send a bottle," the clerk said flatly, "what I can do is, I can notify the bar-service people, I can have them keep calling till they find her in the room, or otherwise you'd find her yourself in the casino."

Kelley, for the hell of it, tossed him the chip.

She was easy to find. They had tall spotlights set around a table. People looked on behind a red velvet rope while the lady rolled dice and the rich-looking sharpie in the cashmere sweater kept dancing around her going click with his camera and "wonderful beautiful terrific" with his mouth. She was wearing a long straight cream-colored dress, hair piled up, little wisps and tendrils of it brushing at her cheek. Around her was a group of what appeared to be models—a gaggle of well-heeled guys in tuxedos, a sight seen in Vegas only slightly less often than a total eclipse. The girl turned around, distracted by something, and Kelley saw the clothespins gripping the gown. Amused now, he stood behind the rope for a moment.

"Hold it. Hold it," the photographer shouted. "I want to try something else."

The girl rolled her eyes and moved away from the table. One of the men in tuxedos started rubbing her back while the bouncy photographer squinted into space, undoubtedly beckoning the evanescent muses of *Harper's Bazaar.* His eye caught Kelley and remained with a narrowed speculative look. He was either thinking or chewing up his lip because he hadn't eaten lunch. Now he walked over and conferred with the girl, who looked up at Kelley and called him with a sweet little mischievous expression and a curl of the finger; same gesture she used to launch ships, Kelley thought; little curl of the finger and WHAM! full speed out of Adriatic ports.

Kelley shook his head. She mugged disappointment, pushing out her lip. He laughed, but he was thinking what he'd do to that lip, and this time he went to her, just another schooner pulled in by the tide.

"Mr. Kelley," she said. Close up, she was actually overwhelming. "This is Marcus Imry, the very famous photographer who earns about eighty thousand dollars a day and who wants to take your picture and put it in a magazine and pay you a dollar." She giggled at Imry. "Did I handle that well?"

Kelley said nothing. He was trying to maintain an objective attitude, not to take her beauty as a personal assault. He signed the release and collected his dollar. A woman came over with a tray full of makeup, eyed

73

him, said, *you* don't need any help, and then he was standing with the girl at the table, his jeans jacket open, his faded T-shirt exposed to the spotlight of haute couture.

"Okay," Marcus said. "Okay, you're a rich Texas rancher, okay? I hate it. Forget it. You're a poor grifter. Terrific. She *thinks* you're a poor grifter, and she doesn't want to fall in love but she does, turns *out* you're a rich Texas rancher. Okay. Now I want you to look at her, sexy as a grifter, but a grifter who *knows* he's a rich Texas rancher. Now you got it?"

Kelley squinted. "Marcus? What I got so far is a buck."

"Right. Okay. Just look at her sexy."

He looked at her, standing beside him at the table, slim and tall in the cream silk dress, hair the color of pale champagne, of caught candlelight, alchemists' dreams.

"You're a good actor," she told him at dinner.

"Don't," he said.

"What?"

"Ask for compliments."

"Was I?"

"Uh huh."

She'd changed to a simple blue shift and had taken her hair down. And every head swiveled when they'd entered the room. "You are, though," she said.

She said it "y'ar," and he asked her what part of the South she was from.

The girl made a face. "We could definitely call it the bad part," she said. "One of those nasty little backwater towns. You know. Kind of town where a boy even tries to look sexy at a girl, she's a hot tool of Satan."

"Right. What's the boy?"

She laughed now. "A boy."

She had a nice little laugh, clear and unaffected, almost like a child's. It occurred to him she might be

74

younger than he'd thought. Not easy to tell behind the clothes and the words. She said, "backwater town." She said, "hot tool of Satan," but there seemed to be something very fragile about her, and something . . . no; he wasn't quick enough to guess. He'd just have to wait.

"So how'd you get away from it?"

"Texas?" she said. She put down her wineglass and fiddled with the stem. "Well," she said soberly, "one Sunday morning they all got in the truck and they crashed with one of those big gas tankers. Whole family but me. I forgot to mention they were on their way to church. Anyway, my mother had a sister in Chicago, and that's the way—" She lifted her head up quickly and looked at him, her eyes on his. "Now why did I tell you that? My usual answer is 'ran away from home.'"

Kelley said nothing for a time. Then he said, "I guess it's my priestly face."

"Well hardly," she said, and studied him. "Possibly a witch doctor though. Are you?"

He laughed. "Sure. Why not. Somewhere in the lineup a Mohawk chief raped a trapper's daughter."

"Really?" she said. "I can't tell if you're joking."

"No, I'm not joking. I fell from a tree full of warriors and trappers. It's a hell of a story. The fabulous story of America, right? The warriors lost and the trappers got trapped." It occurred to him she didn't understand what he was saying; it also occurred to him he didn't much care. He just wanted to keep on talking to that face, to those eyes that watched him so intently as he spoke.

"But you didn't get trapped at all," she said quickly.

"Hell no. I joined the army," he laughed. "I saw the world. Though recently I've only seen the left side of it."

She frowned at him solemnly. "Is that . . . permanent?"

75

"No," he said. "The patch comes off, I'll see the right side too."

"And you really think there is one."

"You mean a right side? I don't know how you mean that."

"Things turning out right."

He grinned at her. "Well . . . we'll see, won't we."

She studied him slowly with her head tilted. "You know what's so wonderfully attractive about you? You look like you believe things'll turn out right. No—like you'll *make* things turn out right."

"Either that, or I'll die trying, Miss Houghton."

"Karen."

"Karen. Would you like some more coffee? A brandy? What can I make right for you?"

"Everything," she laughed. "You suppose we could have a little more champagne? I'm afraid I'm an addict. Marcus's told me I'm the only addict whose French connection is the widow Clicquot." She laughed again and then remembered what was probably her Southern manners. "I mean if it's not an imposition," she said.

He said he was a sucker for widows and orphans, and motioned for the waiter.

"I was thinking," Karen Houghton said to him quickly, "I'll be leaving for New York pretty early in the morning but I thought we could maybe have it sent to my suite. Well, I mean, if you'd like to."

It occurred to him, sitting on the couch: go slow. She was sitting beside him, a cushion away, half facing him, feet tucked under her hips, a cigarette burning, a glass in her hand. She sat like a neatly withdrawn invitation. And Kelley had never had to crash any gates. The theory that women didn't know what they wanted, he'd long ago decided was absolute bull, and beyond that, he wasn't after what was easy but merely what was simple—a straight, natural coming-together. He'd had too many women to require any less; and if he felt a little hook of irritation right now, that was okay too. He was also relaxed. He'd talked about the airline; he'd learned she lived alone, that she enjoyed her occupation, that she'd been on the cover of twenty magazines, that she liked to go to parties, that she wasn't in love. And again he had the instinct that there had to be more. Some door he hadn't opened, some gate to the secret garden.

Now she leaned back again and sipped at her wine. "Tell me something," she said. "I mean something you've never told anybody else."

He shrugged. "That could cover a whole lot of ground. How about my laundry mark—you want to know that?"

"You think you're so tough," she said.

"No, I don't think."

"Meaning you know."

"I mean I don't think about what the hell I am. I just do it as it comes."

"Do what?"

"Do anything that comes. Anything I have to." He shrugged. "Or want to."

"Easy as that. No chinks," she said flatly. "In your armor, I mean."

"I didn't say that."

"Then tell me—" She smiled. "I'm giving you a tough question. Tell me what scares you."

"What *scares* me? Christ. I don't know." He shrugged. "Being . . . locked up. Locked in. Time after my father died, I went down to work in the mines. I'm talkin' Kentucky coal mines. I'm talkin' *down*. Couple of thousand feet. I'd get down there, I'd have to stick a fist in my mouth. I thought I might scream. Six-one, eighteen, big toughie. Gonna scream. I felt buried. *Buried.* I thought, This is it, this is what they want to do to me, they'll bury me alive and then they'll bury me dead. I lasted maybe a month. I had to get out of there and as far above the ground as I could possibly make it.—Which is why I grew up to be a submarine captain." He looked at her; she seemed to sit closer to him now, head against the pillow. "And a Texas rancher. *Rich* Texas rancher."

"I don't care if you're a grifter." Serious.

"You don't."

She was watching him with brown velvet eyes. He realized that he had, in fact, told more to this improbably beautiful woman than to anyone he'd ever met.

A finger reached up and traced the brow above his eye. "You've got a scar there."

"Mmm."

"Little chunk out of your eyebrow."

"Mmm hmm."

She'd moved even closer. The finger moved very slowly to his mouth. He sucked on the side of it. Looked at her eyes. Reached over and kissed her, finding her mouth very open, very hot. His hand slid downward to the bowl of her beautiful silk-covered breast and then the lady went rigid, pushed him away, got up, crossed the room, stood glaring at him, running her fingers through her hair.

Leaning back, he shook his head. "What's that all about?"

"It's no heavy mystery," she snapped, "it's called no."

"Yeah, I was getting that impression," he said.

"Good. Then why are you looking at me like that? No one ever said no to you before?"

"Not often. No."

"Oh Christ. You're so damn cocksure of yourself."

"No," he said slowly, "I just pride myself on never attacking without provocation."

"I wasn't provoking you."

"When's your birthday, Karen?"

"You mean what's my sign?"

"No I mean when's your birthday? What day?"

"May third."

"Fine. May third I'll buy you a dictionary, you look up 'provoke.'"

Still across the room now, she lit a cigarette.

He squinted at her. "May third what?"

She hesitated. "Fifty-two."

He laughed dryly. "Oh Christ, you're nineteen. A nineteen-year-old Southern—" he almost said "belle" and then it hit him. "Virgin. You're a virgin, right?"

"That would appease your ego, wouldn't it."

"No. You've got the wrong idea about me, lady."

"And what am I supposed to do, anyway? Everybody's always clawing at me. Always."

"Well . . . let me give you a few tips, honey. You don't want to be clawed, you don't tease the bears."

She sat now, propping her elbows on the desk, her fingers through her hair. She looked up at him hopelessly. "I just thought—I just thought I could relax with you a while. I was just . . . relaxing."

"Whatever you say."

"You're angry."

"No." He shook his head. "I'm sorry. I'm really sorry I upset you. Listen, I don't know about you, but I think I better go home right now and cram for an exam." He rose from the couch.

"Oh dammit," she said. "Oh dammit dammit." Kelley saw her eyes getting shiny with tears.

He walked over to her, lifted her chin with his hand, and puzzled at the beautiful teary little face.

"You hate me," she said.

"Of course I don't hate you. You're a sweet, very bright, very beautiful lady. A little—you'll forgive the expression—fucked up, but you're not very hatable." He rubbed gently at the tears, then licked his finger. "Virgin tears," he said. "They're good luck."

"Oh dammit," she said, closing her eyes.

He kissed her very quickly and chastely on the cheek.

Sometime in the middle of the night it rained, briefly and loudly. Kelley woke to thunder and saw he'd been asleep with the light still on and the operations manual resting on his stomach. For a moment he thought about the eerily beautiful Karen Houghton and wondered if he'd dreamt her, wondered who she was—Orphan Annie, Artful Innocent, Angel as Tough Cookie; cock tease. He turned out the light and put the handbook on the floor. At least he understood how to fly the Dakota.

The day dawned nasty—dark and overcast, a dry hot wind coming in from the desert. Spinnaker fussed over his plane as though he were sending his daughter off with a couple of Hell's Angels.

"Now you'll get more revs out of her in the cool air, so you'll need about three hundred extra feet for take-off." He turned to Kelley. "And if you tell me to relax one more time, Slick—"

"What?"

"Just let me see you in the co-pilot's seat. Chained."

"You don't trust me."

"That does sum it up."

The take-off was shaky. The port engine fired, missed, fired, missed again, and then finally caught with a bang that could have doubled as a mortar attack. The starboard caught quickly.

"Parking brake."

"Off," Charlie said. He nosed up the throttle. They were skimming the runway.

"How's she feel?"

"Like I'm piloting ten tons of Jell-O."

And Kelley could see it from the co-pilot's seat. The wheel still flaccid, the pedals in a flap. "There's a tall lady in front of me with a big hat. You want to trade seats?"

"I got it," Charlie said.

Kelley saw that too. The pedals hardening, the wheel getting stiff.

"Control," Charlie said.

The ground speed was climbing. 90 . . . 95 . . . 97 . . . 100. . . .

"Rotate," Kelley said.

Charlie responded, pulling back on the yoke, lowering the tail, which should have raised the nose, which should have made them fly.

"She should have left the ground at a hundred," Charlie said.

"Planes don't read."

"What?"

"Planes don't read instruction manuals. They don't know what they're supposed to do."

"You gonna tell me relax?"

"No," Kelley said. "I'm gonna tell you shut up and drive."

They were up.

She was smooth. She was flying; she was A-okay.

And then suddenly she wasn't. Something was off. There was too much lift and then a downdraft hit them like a brass-knuckled fist, slamming them downward in a tight right spiral, the Dakota bucking and yawing as she went.

"Yoke!" Kelley said.

Charlie pulled it up, but the plane kept aiming like an arrow for the ground. Nose angle, forty degrees; bank angle, over a hundred degrees.

Kelley yelled, "Up! Give it max. Put your nose up. Higher. Higher. *Higher,* goddammit!"

"But—"

"*Higher!*"

The draft kept pushing on the plane, the altimeter readout spinning like a top. Kelley reached over and yanked at the yoke, slamming the controls up to maximum power. The engines reacted.

"They'll conk!" Charlie yelled.

"We're gonna *die* either way!"

The Dakota hung in there, bucking its fate, the airspeed jittering around on the dial, the engine screaming under maximum power.

And then they were out of it. As quickly as the whole thing started, it stopped. It had hit like a bolt of invisible lightning—an air-burst dropping straight down from a cloud, spreading half a mile and attempting to murder any low-flying plane. A wind-shear had pushed Bill Turner to the ground over enemy jungle. And Kelley had learned how to navigate a goddam motherfucking shear.

Charlie readjusted the straining controls. The Dakota seemed to shudder as though she were shaking off a terrible dream and then climbed again smoothly.

For a very long moment neither of them spoke.

Then Kelley started whistling "Yes Sir, That's My Baby."

Charlie said nothing.

Kelley said, "Your first wind-shear, eh?" Then he said, "You can't duck 'em, fuck 'em, you follow me, Charlie?" He gestured with his pencil, jabbing at the sky. "Up, max, and hold it."

"You're good," Charlie said, "aren't you, you bastard."

"Shit. We were goddam lucky," Kelley said.

8

LYING ON THE bed, naked, still damp from the shower, an ashtray balanced neatly on his stomach, a bottle of Cutty resting on the floor, he found himself occasionally laughing out loud.

He'd bought three planes.

He kept thinking of the lady he'd flown this afternoon. He was half in love with her, a fat ugly bitch but with guts of gold. It was going through his mind the way she'd felt when he'd flown her. He'd taken her down on an empty blacktop ribbon in the desert, Charlie yammering, "You can't *do* that," Kelley assuring him, "I just did."

He reached over slowly and swigged from the bottle.

He'd bought three planes.

And landed a quarter of a million in the hole.

Which also made him laugh.

What the hell, he decided, he'd get it.

Or not.

His telephone rang and he yawned and stretched before he grabbed the receiver.

Charlie said, "You're buying me dinner."

"So I said."

"Well . . . I've got a date."

"Good. You want to hit me for *two* Double Whoppers or you want to be alone?"

"You'll meet us for a drink. You'll come to room sixteen-thirty at seven. Okay?" There was something peculiar in his voice; Kelley asked what it was. Charlie said flatly: "If you'd flown through a wind-shear and then with some maniac who landed on a *road,* you might sound a little bit peculiar yourself. See you later, okay?"

Kelley knocked twice; Charlie opened the door of the duplex suite and the first thing he saw was a view of the city through a wall full of windows—like a neon Fourth of July, every kind of color blinking and exploding. The next thing he saw was the woman on the couch. She was one of those great Eurasian beauties, the best of both continents, exotic and delicate, her long straight hair spilling to the shoulders of a white satin dress.

"So you're the big winner," she said with an edge. There was no trace of accent, only a trace of contempt —or amusement.

Kelley didn't feel like responding to either and didn't. He said, "That's an interesting view," and gestured at the window.

Charlie said, "Burke—"

"Genevieve," she said, "and if you'd like a drink, Mr. Kelley, there's a bar in the corner." She was already holding a highball. Kelley walked over to the bar, poured himself a Scotch and looked up at Stryker. Stryker had a cigarette in his mouth and merely squinted through the smoke-screen.

"We've certainly heard all about you," she said. "I expected you to come flying in here with a red cape and an S on your chest."

Kelley looked at Stryker, who still wasn't talking. "Why do I get the feeling that three could be a crowd?"

"Four," a man said.

Turning, Kelley gaped at the dusty old man who'd accosted him in the bar last night. At the moment he was dressed in a red silk robe but he seemed to be the kind of person who attracted lint.

"Well, I can see that Charlie didn't tell you anything, which is exactly what I told him to do, so I better introduce myself. I'm Colonel Hollis and it seems as though you've already tangled with my wife." The old man sat down beside her on the white linen sofa and patted her pale hand affectionately. "Jenny thinks I'm just about to make a mistake and she's a clear-spoken woman. Now I like that in a woman. Too many of these women, they get a fella whirlin' so he don't know where he is. They say yes, mean no, and that's worse'n if they're doin' it the other way around. Now, first of all, fella, I'd like you to do me the favor of settin' in a chair. I can figure you're as fast settin' down as you are on yer feet and I don't like lookin' up at dark young giants, it makes me feel old, not short, mind you, just old.

"Now," he continued when Kelley had a chair. "I heard you got plans. Have you got 'em writ down?"

Kelley nodded.

"That's good, that's fine," Hollis said. "Did you write 'em in English or in gobbledegook like the banks like to see 'em?"

"I guess it must have been in English," Kelley said, looking at Stryker, who was looking at a wall.

"Well, that's banks fer ya," Hollis went on. "Anything has to do with human personality, they don't understand it. Which is how it oughta be. You can't bank on human personality. You can gamble on it, but you can't bank on it. As to you, young fella, to some you'd be a mighty interesting crap-shoot. Army says you're insubordinate. Are you insubordinate?"

"I'm impressed," Kelley said. "You checked with the army."

"Son, it's not my habit to offer a man a half a million dollars on the cut of his jib. Well now, I notice that got a slight rise. Not much, but a movement. See what I do is, I'm a gambler on people. Downstairs at them tables, all you got goin' is a fixed set of odds. Every time you roll the dice, you got one in twelve chances of any particular number comin' up, but the point is that *every* time the dice are bein' rolled, *a* number comes up, you see what I'm sayin'? You're not gonna roll the dice, get an earthquake, get an elephant, you're gonna get a number. Now, you start shakin' people up, you get almost anything. Shook this here up," he gestured at his wife, "shook her up real good and I got myself a bride."

Genevieve Hollis sipped at her drink; her face was as placid as an ivory mask.

Kelley said slowly, "And what are your terms?"

"Oh yessir, Mr. Kelley, I got 'em. You can bet. For that kind of money, I'd want to have a say."

"What kind of 'say'?"

"Say half of the business," the old man chortled. "We split down the middle."

"Who runs it?"

"You do. Unless I don't happen to like what you're doin'. Then I do. I told you I'm a gambler, Mr. Kelley, but I also like to feel I got control of the risk. Set the thermostat on trouble, if you see what I'm sayin'. Decide on exactly how hot it's gonna get. So you just let me look at them papers overnight and—"

"Forget it," Kelley said.

The old man squinted.

Charlie, who'd been standing at the window, turned around.

"If I run an airline, I run an airline," Kelley said. "If you want to invest in it, fine. Limited partnership, fine. You want more than that, sorry, you'll have to keep shopping."

"I see." The Colonel nodded, passing a hand on his liver-spotted face.

Genevieve Hollis came to life with a small spiteful smile.

"Well," Hollis said after a time, "well boy, you got yourself a tough row to hoe. You get big enough, the big boys'll go fer yer throat. Won't let you get away with that cut-rate nonsense. You get fellas like ole Rip Chambers at Federal—man'll rip yer balls off and steal yer other eye. So you get yerself in trouble, and I'm bettin' you will, you come back here, we'll renegotiate the deal. You can always reach me through Charlie."

Kelley stood. "I'll be happy to keep that in mind."

Stryker walked him to the elevator. Silently, to start with. Then he said, "A man could do worse, I suppose, than listen to a guy who's got four hundred million."

"All I need is two hundred thousand," Kelley said. "He probably earns that much while he's sleeping, and I'm not gonna roll over for it." He looked up at Stryker. "And what's your 'roll'?"

Stryker looked hurt. "Hey listen, man, the Colonel comes in last night, talks about this one-eyed guy wins a fortune, walks away from the tables. So I figured how many pirates could there be, so I tell him I know you and he asks a lot of questions, so I start to make a pitch. I tell him about the airline. That's all. Now you want to get mad about that, you can call your airline The Flying Fuck and then you go take it."

"Right," Kelley said. "Except I think the old bastard was pulling my daisy. He says, are you insubordinate? He says, will you take my orders? I think he's playing people-games. Little side bets with the Dragon Lady."

Stryker chewed his lip. "That's not beyond the realm of the possible," he said.

"Right." Kelley rang for the elevator. "Now—you want to have dinner?"

"Can't," Stryker said. "Colonel wants to mosey on

back to the homestead. Let me ask you something though. If you start things up, will you hire me?"

"*When* I start things up, I won't be offering money like the Colonel's, or even like the majors."

"That wasn't the question."

The elevator came. It was empty; Kelley got into it and leaned against the door. Then he said, "I tell you what the question is, Charlie. The question is, what can you get for your house?"

Stryker said nothing; he was looking at Kelley as though he'd been hit.

Kelley said, "Think," and let the elevator close.

He got back to his hotel room at a little after two, having lost a few hundred and bedded the best of the available offerings that swarmed around the tables—ladies on vacation from everything, ladies in calculated heat, ecstatic in the knowledge of well-placed coils and the total approval of Helen Gurley Brown. The lady he'd chosen was a teacher from Maine. "A second-grade teacher and a first-class lay," was exactly how she'd put it; and then gone teary when he'd left to go home.

His phone was ringing as he climbed from the shower. When he answered it, he heard a click and a buzz. Hanging up, he fiddled with the radio dial, got a Dylan record, and turned off the light, lying there cigarette and drink in his hand. Sleep was impossible. He pulled at the drink and stared at the pattern of moonlight on the ceiling. His mind raced with images. Someplace—it seemed to be quite far away—there seemed to be a dull and persistent knocking, a sound so faint he wasn't certain it was there. He hollered, "Who is it?" A woman said, "Maid." He looked at the phosphorescent dial of his watch. No way. It would have to be the teacher from Maine, wanting a little post-coital discussion, a few tart recriminations to last her through the night. Wearily he got up and crossed to the door, cigarette clamped in the corner of his mouth, towel at his waist.

He almost dropped both.

He said, "I thought you were leaving for New York."

She said, "And I did. I left and came back. Do you want to let me in?"

Kelley stepped back and let Karen Houghton come slowly through the door into the dark room with Dylan's raspy voice.

"I'm sitting on the plane and I'm thinking, this is stupid, this is absolutely totally stupid, I don't even know what the hell it is I'm saving." She looked at him in the dim moonlight that came through the window. "All I could think about was what I was missing." She shrugged. "So I landed in New York and turned around and came back."

He said, "Are you sure?"

She said, "Christ. I spent eleven hours on a plane. Am I sure?"

He laughed.

"If that's *at* me, goddammit, you can go straight to hell."

"That was joy," he said. "Also a little bit of nerves. That's quite a responsibility you're imposing on me."

"You *are* laughing, aren't you." She looked at him, her eyes grown large in the dimness of the room, the moonlight making yellow ribbons in her hair. "I'm making a fool of myself and you really don't want this."

"Karen, Karen." He took her in his arms. "I just want you to stop looking like the sacrificial virgin."

"Is that how I'm looking?"

"A little." He kissed her, and her mouth was ready for him, open and warm; a giddy little shiver ran through her body and her hips canted towards him.

"Fast learner," he said, still kissing her, lifting her quickly off her feet, like someone in a movie, and taking her to bed.

"Are you sure?" he said again.

"Will you stop acting as though I'm made of eggs?"

"An unfortunate analogy." With quick fingers he undid the little hooks and eyes at the neckline of her dress and stripped down the zipper. Tenderly, occasionally calling out her name, he took slow loving care of everything she offered; the breasts, the most delicately ripe he'd ever seen. From time to time she'd take in a long deep breath and let out a little purr, and her breath against his neck would make him struggle for control because he wanted it to be as easy and right as he could possibly make it.

For a long time afterwards she lay in his arms, her hips making tiny reflexive pulses. When he left her, she murmured, "Ooooh," like a kid that lost hold of its balloon. Laughing, he kissed her on the tip of her nose. "As MacArthur once put it, 'I shall return.'"

She said drowsily, "Can I ask you a question?"

"Mmm hmm." He handed her a lit cigarette.

"Is that just you or is it always like that?"

"You'll have to make your own comparisons," he said.

"For you then, is it?"

"No," he said truthfully.

"Good. I just hate to think of you being that beautiful with any other woman."

Kelley said nothing.

Karen rolled over and looked at him searchingly. "Did that—did that . . . *mean* anything to you?"

"It was lovely," he said. *"You're* lovely."

"That's not what I mean."

He sighed, already feeling the familiar chasm opening before him, the natural separation that became a rift that became a gap, the woman floating away on some ice floe of her own creation, her hand extended frantically for rescue. "I know," he said gently. "And the answer is I *don't* know. And you don't either. All we know is it was fine, but let's don't hitch any wagons to a moon."

She stiffened and pulled herself away from him quickly. "You really do know how to sweet-talk, don't you."

"Is that what you want?"

"And all you want is action, is that the way it is?"

"Oh Christ, babe, don't do this." He tried to coax her back to softness with his hand. "Just don't go all insecure on me, huh? We made love. We didn't fuck, I really made love to you, but it's not instant glue."

"And you don't feel—"

"Oh Karen, there was something so sweet about this. I'm gonna kill you if you kill it."

"Kill what?"

"I don't know. Whatever it could be."

"Could it be something?"

"I don't know."

And now she was crying. "You're so warm and then a switch gets pulled and you're cold."

Kelley didn't say anything. For a time he just held her, stroking her hair, feeling the beat of her heart against his chest.

"Have you ever—" She stopped.

"Go on."

"Been in love?"

"Never."

She rallied slightly. "A virgin."

"Exactly," he said. "And you ought to know you have to be gentle with virgins. You ought to understand that they're new at this business and need a little extra-special touch of understanding."

"Oh," she said.

"Here I travel eleven hours to be with you and this is how you act."

"It's true," she said, sniffing. "I only want you for your soul and here you go spilling out your miserable body."

"I'm sorry," he said. "I won't do it anymore."

"Don't you dare," she said, "not do it anymore."

In the morning he lay there watching her sleep, his own particular Sleeping Beauty, the bright hair fanned on the pillow like rays of some extravagant moon. She was not, even now, the woman of his dreams. When he dreamed about women they were dark and Gypsy, and still he felt a sharp sting of excitement. It wasn't, he decided later, so much that her beauty dazzled him as that it puzzled him—as though even in a chilly and random universe there had to be a purpose to adamant perfection, that perhaps if he could find it he'd know something urgent.

Waking, she watched him slowly for a while. He came to her eagerly, but, "No," she said, "I have to catch a ten-o'clock plane." Again he conceded. He would not rape a woman, even in his bed, though a few years later he would rape this woman with unexpected fury on a cold tile floor.

At breakfast she explained she had a shooting this evening. Checking her watch, she said, "And Marcus'll kill me. He'll tell me I look as though I'm haunting a house."

"Stop that," he said. "You look beautiful."

"That's because I know where you are. By this evening I won't."

"Fine. I'll be in Phoenix."

"Really?" she said. "Why?"

"Karen," he shook his head slowly, "forget it. I'll be

broke for five years. I'll be working maybe twenty-six hours a day and I'll *still* be broke."

"That still leaves the nights."

"And your champagne taste."

"I won't touch another bottle of champagne till we launch your first plane. How's that for a promise?"

"I don't want you to keep it."

She looked at him. "Yes," she said firmly. "You do."

And again he was caught. "Did anybody ever get drowned in your eyes?"

"Do you feel yourself sinking?"

"A little bit, yes."

"Good," she said. "I want you dead or alive."

He drove her to the airport. In white jeans and a white shirt, she was a red flag. One look at her and ground agents and baggage handlers became men with real missions. At the gate she kissed him with sufficient heat to raise a 747 and left him in turbulence, wondering how to get the damn thing to land.

He walked to the counter and bought himself a one-way ticket to Phoenix and an open-date ticket from Phoenix to New York. A few hours later he was standing on a minor Arizona airfield looking for a lead on Hitch Ryan.

"You have to have *heard* of him," Kelley said to the fourteenth pilot who had never heard of Ryan. "You'd have to have *seen* him."

"Hey, Rob," the guy turned to a greasy mechanic. "Guy says he's lookin' for Hitch Ryan. Says he runs some kind of crop-sprayer here. Says he's a dead ringer for Redford."

The mechanic managed a greasy laugh and continued to scrape the points off an engine.

"Tell you what," Kelley said. "You see him, you tell him I'll be staying at the Biltmore."

Kelley checked in and sat around the pool of the

Arizona Biltmore admiring the women in the Pucci swimsuits, listening to guys making million-dollar deals over jacked-in phones. Poolside beer went for three bucks a head.

"What line are you in?" a guy who was a land broker asked him at the pool.

"Airline."

"Yeah? What airline you got?"

"None."

The guy laughed. "The Flying None."

Kelley tried to figure how to hit the guy up, but a man who sold desert for a thousand an acre wasn't ripe to be hit.

"Blue sky," the man told him, "that's all you got goin'. Myself, I sell sand, but I sell it to a big buncha cretins in the East. They think, Arizona! They think about the sun, they think about Barry Goldwater, they think good climate, retirement at leisure. But I never mislead 'em. I call it—get this—Pioneer Village. I tell 'em the highway's called Donner Pass. You like that?"

"And Christ how the money rolls in."

"You got it." The man looked up from his Miller's and gazed across the pool. "You ever see one of those movies in the fifties—guy gets a lethal dose of radiation, comes back, his face scared you shitless for a week?"

"I guess."

"Well he's here."

A man headed towards them with exactly that face. Someone had clearly tried to put it back together and hadn't quite made it. He appeared to be smiling or maybe he was screaming. He stopped at the deck chair. "Kelley?" he said.

The real-estate magnate said, "Hey-I-gotta-go," and went off like a rocket.

Kelley said, "Yeah. Do I know you?"

"Not me," the man said. "You used to know a guy named Ryan."

"Uh huh. You a friend of his?"

"No. I'm Ryan."

"Oh shit. Sit down," Kelley said.

"Well, I don't know about that." Ryan grinned at the averted faces. "People got a heavy investment in lunch."

"What happened?"

"What the fuck does it look like happened?"

"Like we live in fame and go down in flame."

"'Bout says it." Ryan stretched himself out in the chaise. "And all the king's horses and all the king's men."

"Looks more like the work of the horses," Kelley said.

Ryan laughed. "Couldn't even get a job flying cargo. Like, you know, they figured I'd curdle the freight."

"So that's why you're flying cargo," Kelley said.

"Something like that. And then there's the money." Ryan turned and studied him. "Is this just a visit for old times' sake, or you want to talk business?"

They went to Kelley's room, where Ryan sat discretely at a distance from the mirror. "Way it works," he said, drinking his beer from a bottle, "I drop it on the desert. Far enough out you can spot any stake-out. Low enough down, you can dodge any blips. You keep changing drop-zones. Easy as shit. And if somebody happens to pick the shit up—what the hell do I know?"

"Yeah. Sounds good," Kelley said. "About the money. How much?"

Ryan looked at him. "I don't know about your attitude, Kelley. I mean, you sound pretty crass. You gotta think of this as kind of a Berlin Airlift for fried-out junkies. Or dropping leaflets. I guess you never dropped leaflets, did you. 'Attention, citizens of

Dum Luk, Uncle Sam's about to bomb you to fucking smithereens so get outta here.' Right? Except the leaflet's in English. You know how many fucking Vietnamese peasants even read Vietna*mese?*"

Kelley sipped his beer. "Listen—you know what Turner used to say? He said we've got three zones over here: the drop zone, the landing zone and the twilight zone."

"Yeah. He used to call you a third-zone native."

"How much?" Kelley said.

"Say fifty a run. They give you five percent down because, face it, things happen. You stiff them, you're dead. You get caught, you're on your own."

"Jesus. Aside from *that*," Kelley said.

"Okay," Ryan shrugged. "But aside from that, you get your bread pretty quick."

"And you're happy in your work?"

"Is this psychological counseling or you want to do a run?" Ryan looked up. "How the hell'd you know what I was doing anyway?"

"You wrote to Kuralsky."

"Yeah," Ryan said. "In the hospital. Never answered me, the prick."

"Try the Ouija board next time."

"Oh?" Ryan shrugged. "Well . . . some guys do get all the luck. These guys I work for, they can use another pilot, so that's why I wrote him. You want it?"

"What I want is a hundred thousand dollars."

"So you make two runs."

"I don't think you follow me. I want it from you."

Ryan looked up at him. *"What?"*

"You heard me," Kelley said. "Only thing you've got nothing wrong with is your ears."

"Only thing *you've* got nothing wrong with is your balls.—Why would I want to give you my money?"

Kelley thought it over. "Well . . . goddamned if *I* know," he said. "On the other hand, what'll you do with it in stir? On the other hand, what're you doing with it now? On the other hand, you'd own a tenth of an airline, be the chief pilot, fly a bunch of people to Utica. Does that sound wonderful or not?"

"What do you mean by 'fly a bunch of people'?"

"Sit in the front of the plane, go vroom."

Shaking his head, Ryan got a cigarette out and lit it. "No. I couldn't cut that."

"Fine," Kelley said. "Listen, I don't give a shit what you do. You want to go kill yourself in some fucking desert, fine. Only let me have the bread before you go."

For a moment Ryan sat there and studied him fixedly, then he started grinning; the grin widened till he threw back his head and laughed till his eyes got shiny with tears. Then he caught his breath and said, "Jesus, man, Jesus," rubbing his eyes. "Know what Jefferson told me? Told me, 'Never look back, Kelley might be gaining on you.'"

Now Kelley laughed.

Six months later, he was standing in the Rose Garden of the White House, accepting a Distinguished Flying Cross. At the press conference afterwards, he announced the formation of Blue Sky Airlines.

"Three planes, three pilots," he said to the press. "We're gonna do a lot of distinguished flying."

9

WHEN HE PULLED himself slowly from the cobweb of a dream, he imagined for a beat he was back in Can Tho, waking, wary, with the taste of grass and the attitude of danger. Deal with it, he told himself, open your eyes; but he waited till the atmosphere clicked into place:

Empty bed.

Fifth Avenue.

Now.

Friday.

He looked at the Tiffany clock. Friday morning at a quarter of eleven. The hour confused him. Had he slept that late? He remembered the party at Marcus and Candy's; a couple of joints and he'd told himself bedtime stories till dawn. A hell of a night. He sat up slowly, a slight frown creasing his forehead, and reached for a cigarette. Lighting it, he leaned back slowly on the headboard and squinted at the room which Karen, once again, had left looking like a war zone, the red silk gown still crumpled on the floor like another bloody victim. Idly he wondered what had happened to the maid. She'd probably quit. He'd have to ask Frannie to rustle up another.

Karen, he discovered, was nesting in the kitchen. She was drinking black coffee and from the looks of the ashtray, she'd already smoked about a dozen cigarettes.

He said, "My God, you're getting worse than I am."

She said, "I've exceeded your wildest dreams."

He looked at her squarely. She was pale and slightly haggard in the light, dressed in what he thought was a St. Laurent suit, the red tweed jacket lying on a chair. He looked at her again, more searchingly this time, but still felt nothing; she was simply someone he used to know.

He made a fresh pot of coffee and glanced at the paper. The weather was making page one of the *Times* with blizzards that were taking on dimensions of a dreamgirl: thirty-four inches, nineteen inches, thirty-two inches. The upstate airports were all blanked out.

Karen said, "I thought I'd fly to Palm Beach."

Lighting a cigarette, he shrugged indifferently. "Who is it this time? A ski bum?"

She smiled. "In Palm Beach?"

"*Water*-ski bum. What difference does it make?" He was sorry he started it. The point was—exactly—what difference did it make?

But then again, it couldn't be quite that simple. Her hobbies, he felt, had a justification. He hadn't been around. From the very beginning, even when they'd met, even in Vegas, each of them had clearly been in love with someone else; he with an airplane and Karen with herself. And still, or at least for a while, it had worked, or he'd thought that it worked. Till the thing about the kid. He'd occasionally speculated how she must have felt, thinking during sex about his unwelcome seed, about its possibly ruinous effects on her ability to model a bikini for *Harper's Bazaar,* so that finally she'd gone out and had herself fixed, like a cat, not even telling him, just doing it, wanting to remain the baby in the family. The night he'd found out, his fury had erupted, untamed and destructive; he'd wanted to punch her face in and instead he'd taken her coldly on a cold floor. He'd repented in a while and tried to see it her way, accepting her appeal that he was too involved with business to really be a father, that he was acting like "some kind of fucking Neanderthal" as Karen had put it, that it was, after all, *her* body. But he couldn't look at *her* body after that without knowing how purely and completely it was hers. After that, it had gotten very quiet between them. No further arguments, no further scenes. They'd asked no questions and told no lies. Karen spent the money and Kelley wrote the checks. It had a certain fearful symmetry about it.

She said, "And I'm off. I suppose you won't be going to the house if I'm gone."

"The Island?" he said. "No. I'll stay here.—What happened to Conchita?"

"Who?"

"Conchita, Cuernavaca, whatever her name was."

"Esmeralda," she said. "I fired her. She tried on one of my dresses."

"I see." He looked up at her, shaking his head. "Christ. Fifty lashes would have done it, don't you think? I mean here we are living in a million-dollar sty—"

"I wasn't aware this was living."

"I see. Well, get used to it, kiddo. It's as good as it gets."

She picked up her jacket. "So I'll see you, I guess. I'll be at the Imrys' if you need me, okay?"

Kelley just nodded. And thought, what the hell could he possibly need? He poured his coffee. The front door slammed and he thought about the two little birds flying south. Karen and Candy, flocking to the sun.

Running a hand along the rasp of his jaw, he tried the refrigerator, looking for food.

The milk had gone sour.

There was very exotic mold on the bread.

There were eggs, but the box said "November 21." He didn't know what happened to a seven-week egg, but to hell with it, he thought.

He took his coffee and the newspaper into the study. It was dusty but in order, the one room in eight that was decidedly his. His desk, his books, floor-to-ceiling shelves of them, covering the range of his eclectic curiosity, everything from oceanography to poetry. That, and a painting that Karen didn't like—a picture of a somber black-hatted man stepping through a doorway in the middle of a pale, unpromising sky and finding nothing but the rest of the sky. To Kelley it was both ironic and amusing and no more surrealist than everyday life—a guy going rapidly from nowhere to nowhere and looking so totally serious about it.

He sipped his coffee and looked at the man. He'd have to start dealing with the Serious Men. Twenty-two million was Serious Money, and he had to pay the loan back on March 31. As McDermott had put it, "You default and you're dead." Well . . . he'd been at death's doorway before. And if living well had been Karen's revenge, then for Kelley there were times when survival itself had seemed to be an almost gaudy victory.

He'd made up a list. During the night he'd gone through the Rolodex files in his mind and come up with a short list of possible sources, a roster of men who had money to burn and a reason to burn it.

But first on the list, of course, was the Colonel; the likeliest prospect of the six, count 'em, six.

He looked at the clock. It was time, it was way past time, for the call. He'd decided to make his approach straightforward, a "whaddaya know, Sam, they're at it again." The tone ironic, the lion discussing the flies on its tail.

Sitting at his desk, he dialed the familiar number in Dallas. When Hollis's secretary came on the line, he said, "Hi, Roseanne." His voice, he thought, sounded tinny as hell. The Tin Lion. Off to see the wizard. "It's Burke Kelley. Is the old bird around?"

There was a startled pause and then, "Oh my goodness, I guess you haven't heard. The Colonel had a stroke about—well, let me see now—it was just at Thanksgiving."

No, he thought quickly, Hollis was alive; he had to be alive or the news would have traveled. "How's he doing, Roseanne?"

"Well . . . he's home-bound now, Mr. Kelley. Doesn't like that a bit. He used to come into the office every day and good lordy, the man's near to ninety years old. And right to that day he was still making all kinds of rascally deals."

"Still fine in the head though."

"Oh, feisty as ever. If I get one phone call a day from him, I have to get ten." She lowered her voice and said confidentially, "I think he's real angry that things're goin' on nice and smoothly without him."

And exactly, Kelley thought. That was Hollis to the end. A man who wouldn't ever believe it was a pie till he'd stuck in a finger. Fine. Okay. So why not treat him to some lemon meringue? "Well," he said slowly, "things aren't going too smoothly up here. Reason I called was, I wanted his advice. I figure I'll be down there in a couple of days. Is he up to a visit?"

"Well now, I surely will ask him, Mr. Kelley. It'd right cheer him up to know you want to talk business. I'll get back to you later."

He hung up the phone and glanced at the paper that he'd brought to the desk. Full-page ad, back of section one:

FEDERAL'S PUT CALIFORNIA ON SALE
$449 $149*

> From now to March 1, we'll fly to California for
> the lowest fares going, and we'll fly you in style.
> Because you deserve it. Because you demand the
> experience and quality—

He dialed the office and asked for Dukovic. "I
demand some experience and quality," he said. "Have
I got the wrong number?"

Duke said, "Jesus, Kelley. Haven't you heard?"

"Heard what?"

"About the crash."

"Oh Christ." Kelley sat, heart pounding. "What
crash?"

"Not us, not us, I'm sorry," Duke said. "I didn't
mean to scare you. A seven-twenty-seven—"

"Out of where?"

"Out of *here,* for God's sake. They think it was a
wind-shear."

Kelley took a breath. "How many dead?"

"Everybody. One-fifty-three plus a crew."

"And the ground detectors?"

"No. They showed nothing," Duke said. "The radar
and the wind gauges didn't pick it up. I had one plane in
here with a cockpit detector and I sent it to Chicago.
Then Ashe came in here with—"

"Hold it," Kelley said. "Can the rest of it wait?
I've got the chopper in town. I'll be there, half an
hour."

"Good. We got a few other killers to discuss."

Zeedee, in the lobby, talking to the doorman; Zeedee, in the kind of backwoodsman clothes that cost two
thousand dollars; Zeedee, looking up, saying, "See? I
told you," when Kelley crossed the lobby. "Joe here,"
he said, "just said you didn't answer. I said, 'He's

coming down.'" Zeedee smiled at his wisdom. "I ran into lovely Karen on the street." He followed Kelley out into cold morning air. "Hey—you need a lift? I got a car around the corner."

Kelley looked at him. "Really up and at 'em this morning. Busy, bright little fella."

"It's the vitamin C," Zeedee said. "Does the trick. —Wanna ride with me or not?"

"You want to take me to the heliport?"

"Anywhere you want."

They got to the car, a little navy-blue Austin. Kelley saw the other man sitting in the back and could smell the thing coming. On the other hand, to walk away now would look dumb.

"Kelley, this is Chook," Zeedee said when they were seated.

The guy in the back was a bantam Latino, a hard-face guy with a pencil mustache, sleepy kind of eyes that could pick out an insult at four hundred feet.

Kelley said, "Hi."

Chook looked for the insult, couldn't find it and shrugged. He was dressed in a smooth brown leather jacket and brown twill pants. He now lit a brown cigarillo with a solid gold lighter—a Must de Cartier—and settled back in the seat.

"So. You're in big trouble," Chook said.

Kelley, facing forward, couldn't figure out if Chook had a gun at his head or was just shooting the breeze.

Zeedee, at the wheel, sporty in his red-and-black lumber jacket, grinned. "Man there likes to get right down to cases." He glanced in the mirror. "Like I'm telling you, Chook, you gotta do some romance. You say, 'Hi, honey, how's it goin? Want a drink?' You got that? *Then* you can say, 'Let's fuck.'"

Kelley said, "You missed the turn-off to the Drive."

Zeedee said, "Shit. I got a sense of direction—"

"And timing," Kelley said.

"Okay, are we fucking here or fucking around?" Chook said. "I thought we gonna talk."

"Floor's yours," Kelley said. Get it over with, he thought.

"Two million," Chook said, "by the end of the month. I go down, pick it up, come back, make a sale. The two gets you twenty."

Kelley said nothing. Then he said, "In used dollar bills, I suppose."

"You're in big trouble," Chook said. "You gonna go down. You wanna go down makin' jokes, or get serious? You wanna get serious, you know where I am."

Kelley said, "Listen, I appreciate the offer—"

"Hey! He 'appreciate the offer,'" Chook said. "That's white of him, right?"

"Stay cool," Zeedee said. He looked up at Kelley. "I tell you, man, you *are* in very big trouble. So is Chook. So am I. So we're all in a heavy kind of daisy chain here. See, I buy from Chook and Chook buys from Alvy or whoever the hell, but no tickee, no laundry, you see how it goes? So now Chook's told a shipment'll be ready on the first, and his baker, his bread-man, you see, disappeared. So Chook gets the deal or he doesn't, you see? If he *doesn't* get the deal, then *he's* out of business, and *I'm* out of business and two'll get you twenty that *you're* out of business. Or invest the two million and everybody's well." Zeedee finished and grinned.

Kelley said, "Christ." They were now on the Drive. Another two, three minutes, he figured, it's done. "First of all," he said, "there is really—" he was about to say, "some shit I will not do," but he remembered Chook's eyes and said, "a misunderstanding. I do need the money but I don't need the grief. Not this kind of grief. Okay? Not ever."

"Ah! it's the *grief* you object to," Zeedee said. "Is that right? 'Cause we're not getting *in*to any grief. What we're talking here's coke. Okay? Not smack. So we're not talking poor little kiddies on the corner, what we're talking here's rich little kiddies on a toot."

"No, what we're talking here's jail," Kelley said.

The Austin pulled in through the heliport gate. Zeedee pulled over and idled in the lot.

"Like I said," Kelley turned now and looked back at Chook, "I appreciate the offer." He got out of the car and looked flatly at Zeedee. "Zeedee—the man with the golden head. Thanks," he said, closing the door, "for the ride."

10

FRANNIE CAME IN with a notebook and some coffee. She was wearing a pretty green sweater and skirt and she looked, Kelley thought, like a piney forest. Sitting on the couch, she crossed her pretty limbs and flipped through her notebook.

"First of all," she said, "the entire company is hot to see you, but especially Duke. Something about the computer messing up? He says you talked about it yesterday."

"Right. Go on."

"Let's see. Colonel Hollis's secretary called. She said, 'y'all come,' and 'plum tickled' and 'rat welcome,' and I *think* the English translation was 'tomorrow.'"

Kelley just nodded. Good. Then tomorrow his troubles could be over. Or beginning in earnest. He lit a cigarette and swiveled in his chair. "Did you get to take a look at the auditor's report?"

"Can I bum one of those?"

He lit one for her. "I thought you'd quit."

"I did. Till I looked at the auditor's report. I finished it, I wasn't sure if I should eat it or burn it. What I did was, I locked it tightly in the safe."

"Good," Kelley said. "And if it tries to get out of there, hit it with a club. Seriously, Frannie. That report isn't in. You never saw it in your life." He looked her in the eyes.

She nodded gravely. "I think I understand."

"Uh uh," he said. "Don't think, Frannie, and the *last* thing you want to do is understand. I tell you what you can do. See if you can track down Lester Quaid."

She looked at him as though he were nuts; or worse.

"Relax," he said quickly. "Jesus, I don't want to sell him the company. I just want to quietly know where he is.—Go on. Any outside calls I'd want to take?"

She continued to watch him for a couple of seconds, then looked at her notebook. "Yes, there was one. McCarren. Something about you requested an appointment?"

"Who the hell's McCarren?"

"Claire," Frannie said.

He remembered green eyes; the girl with the dark urchin haircut telling him, "I'm not girlie, I'm tough."

He got her on the phone and was surprised at how pleased he was at hearing her neat husky little voice. He asked about the party. "Did you ever get fed?"

"Barely," she said. "You said lamb chops at ten? It was pigeon at midnight."

"Squab," Kelley said. "That was Zeedee's extravagant imported squab."

"Well . . . I don't know. It tasted like they caught it on the windowsill or something. Then Zeedee got around to wanting to show *Casablanca* on the Betamax and that's when I left."

He wondered idly if she'd gone home with Cubbitt, the disgruntled yachtsman. He said, "Of all the gin joints in all the world, if you want to come to mine I'll send the chopper to get you." She laughed, and he put her through to Frannie to fix up a time.

He hung up the phone and then sat for a moment trying not to think, as he'd told Frannie not to think. He wondered if there was such a thing as an insanity plea for stock manipulation. Because that's what he

was doing by suppressing that report—keeping the
stock price up artificially to buy himself a little more
time to get a loan.

Or maybe it was more like a crime of passion. This
guy tried to screw my airline, your honor, and I really
went nuts . . .

Duke was sitting hunched at his desk on the phone, a
jeans jacket hanging on the back of his wheelchair, the
sleeves of a turtleneck sweater rolled up. "Jesus
Christ," he was saying to the phone. "Forget it, man.
I'm calling the Ghostbusters in. No." He hung up and
looked balefully at Kelley.

Kelley said nothing; he sat there and waited.

"We have ghosts," Duke said. "We're a very literally
ghost-ridden line." He sipped some coffee from a
plastic cup. "Yesterday, I did what you told me, okay?
The computer tells me the flights are booked full, I
count the actual heads that are getting on the planes."

"Hit me."

"I never hit a cripple," Duke said. He put down his
cup. "Yesterday alone, eighty-six percent of our definite reserved-seat computer-booked passengers never
showed up. Allow me to repeat that astonishing figure
—"

"Don't," Kelley said. "You mind if I steal a sip of
your coffee?"

"Go on. The only disease I've got is raging para-
noia."

Kelley grabbed the cup. "You got a calculator
handy?"

"Yeah. In my head," Duke said. "That's exactly a
quarter of a million dollars we were just suckered out
of. That's yesterday alone."

Kelley took it slow, sipping the coffee. He was
thinking: times thirty. He was thinking: maybe six
million dollars a month. He was thinking: okay, and for

how many months? He was thinking: that mother-fucking son of a bitch.

He picked up the telephone and started to dial, then hesitated. "Shit. I forget the kid's name."

"Whose name?"

"The Whiz Kid. The genius. The kid that looks like a teenage giraffe."

"The computer kid? Heidigger. Bernard Heidigger."

"Ber*nard?*" Kelley said. "Okay. I believe it." He dialed Heidigger, told him the problem, told him to check the computer and report. Replacing the receiver, he squinted at Duke. "You ever do something that's perfectly logical and feel like you're crazy?"

"I don't know what you're talking about."

"We're talking about sabotage. We're sitting here talking about sabotage as though we're starring in a fucking thriller."

"It happens," Duke said.

"I know it happens, that's not the point. Maybe I'm in the wrong movie. Maybe it's a Bruce Lee movie, right? Listen—you ever hit a guy below the belt? That's a straight question. In combat. In a barroom."

"No," Duke said.

"Well I have, okay? One night in the street, a guy comes at me with a large pistol, his family tree gets a large surprise. I consider that fair. But now you start redefining self-defense. Where do you draw the line? What I'm saying is, I'd rather kick Chambers in the balls than—what? Book mythical people on Federal. Stall my goddam planes on his runway. What else has he been doing?"

Duke shook his head. "Nothing we can prove he was doing on purpose."

"I'd like to prove *this.*"

"Only what'll you do with it?"

"Put it on my tombstone," Kelley said. " 'This man

was sixty percent murdered.'" He laughed. "Could be true. Six million a month out of ten-million losses. Yesterday I didn't want to think about it much because I thought it was a cop-out. Maybe it's not."

"We'll find out," Duke said, "how long Mr. Chambers has been kicking our balls."

"And then we have to try and stop it," Kelley said.

Duke said nothing.

Kelley got out a cigarette and lit it. He blew a contrail of smoke at the ceiling and watched it disappear. They both knew the odds of stopping this cutie were approximately zilch. The computer could be fed by another computer—by any other computer in the world—with any kind of false or misleading information. And how could you separate the false from the true?

Kelley rubbed his jaw. "Go on. You said you had a list of disasters. Something about Warner."

"No, that's not a disaster," Duke said. "That's just another Warner story. I'll give you that and then I'll give you the disaster."

"Jesus," Kelley laughed. "Go on."

"Okay. So Ashe Warner comes in here this morning. It's possibly ten minutes after the crash, the plane is still burning, the marketing department has a hot idea. We ought to take some fast ads on your wind-shear detector. Something subtle and dignified, he says. Just a small discreet announcement that only Blue Sky has detectors in the cockpits. I said we only had them in a *few* of our cockpits, the rest're in the factory, he said it didn't matter. We do have detectors and they are in the cockpits, so we're legally correct."

"Hold it," Kelley said. "Where'd we *find* this guy?"

"Through your friend Rosetti."

"Ah, Rosetti. Who's suddenly the new adman for Federal."

Duke cocked his head. "You serious?"

"Yeah. Hard to tell though, isn't it?" Kelley took another long pull of the coffee. "So what did you tell him?"

"Warner? You haven't let me finish the story. He decided that you—as inventor of the world-saving item—ought to pose for the ads."

"Something subtle and dignified."

"Oh absolutely."

"How about a shot of me tap-dancing on the graves of the people who died this morning? Caption: Why die? Fly Blue Sky."

"Right. And you only think you're kidding," Duke said. He stole back his coffee. "You want me to continue?"

Kelley just nodded.

"You're behind on the fuel bill. You're three months behind and it's—"

"No. Not possible."

"Well . . . you better tell that to Araco Fuel. Their rep gets on the phone with me—"

"Jesus. McDermott let the *fuel* bill slide?"

"That's how they tell it."

Kelley sat silently and stared out the window. He had a great desire to get up and push his fist through the window, but forget about the fist, he wouldn't have the money to replace the window. "I'll take care of it," he said. "We'll call Ashe Warner. See if McDermott's murder would be legally correct." He looked up at the doorway.

Frannie came in with a sandwich and some coffee and handed them to Duke.

Kelley said, "You part-time waitressing or what?"

Then he looked from Frannie to Duke, back to Frannie . . . who'd been wearing that green-stuff yesterday too.

112

"Never mind," he said, rising. "Some days you don't see the forest for the trees."

McDermott wasn't in. His secretary said he had a dental appointment. Kelley left a note: "Pay the fucking fuel bill or lose some more teeth."

11

THE FIELD WAS icy. The plane had gone down about six hundred feet beyond the end of the runway, where a fuel tank exploded. The air was still pungent with seared flesh. Kelley looked on as Emergency Service teams in black slickers picked their way slowly through the ice and the foam and into the burnt-out carcass of the plane. He shivered. The wind pushed hard through the field. On the runway behind him was a cluster of trucks and emergency vehicles, jacks, cranes, everything an airport could hurl at catastrophe to make it disappear. The television news crews were there in their glory, grabbing little shots like the one of the teddy bear lying in the snow. Catch this, folks. In between the pitch for effective mouthwash and bolder-looking whites.

Kelley turned to leave. A cop stood behind him, blowing on his hands. "Gotta be a lousy way to go," the cop said. "Locked in. See it coming."

"They didn't," Kelley said. "See it coming."

Which is why they'd gotten into it and died.

He headed for his car now, and wondered why the hell he'd come out to this scene, what angle on death had been added to his store.

As he crossed the tarmac, a television team was approaching at a trot. Busy little folks. People whose job was to pile inanity on top of disaster. ("Will you tell us, Mr. Kelley, what's your opinion of this great tragedy?" "Well, in my opinion, it's a great tragedy.") Then they'd go on and have some fun with the survivors. ("How does it feel to lose your husband, Miss Jones?")

The reporter moved in now—a nice-looking fellow with neat dark hair and a cashmere muffler that was blowing in the wind. "Any comment on the story of your auditor's report?"

"What?" Kelley said.

"Would you like me to repeat the question?"

"No I wouldn't like you to repeat the question, I'd like you to explain it."

"That your fourth-quarter losses were an all-time record."

The camera was going, picking up every little furrow and twitch. Kelley looked at it levelly. "I think we've got enough real disaster today without dealing in false ones. If you guys will excuse me—"

He got into his car, turned the ignition, and lit a cigarette. He mustn't appear to be running from the scene. He turned on the radio and slowly pulled out. Sonofabitch, he thought. Who could have done it? Who could have leaked that story to the press? Now in addition to everything else there'd be real hell to pay. The stocks would tumble. The rating on his bonds would go down to a C: Danger of default, and potential investors, with the possible exception of the Colonel and Quaid, would be running for the hills. And there would be Kelley on the six-o'clock news, Mr. Morally Superior. "I think we've got enough real disaster today—"

"I'm in a great deal of pain, Kelley," McDermott said. "I had root canal work done and I

115

shouldn't, I assure you, have come back at all. Now I *do* come back and then I find abusive notes on my desk—"

"Oh knock it off, George." Kelley sank wearily down on the couch in McDermott's office, which was stuffy and hot. "I'll give you a Bronze Star for coming in here with a toothache but I still want to know why you haven't paid the bill. We use twenty million dollars' worth of gas every month and you've allowed it to sit there for three and a half. Now I want to know why."

Sighing, McDermott took a long sip of tea from his silver-plated mug. "Chapter ten," he said flatly, "of the bankruptcy laws. If three little creditors bring you into court, you're automatically bankrupt. You don't have a say. I've had letters from suppliers threatening to sue you over five hundred dollars. Caterers, stationers, printers. All the things you never think about at all. So I decided to pay off the little bills first and let the big ones hang."

"But you could have paid something on the fuel and you didn't."

"No. I didn't."

"So we're back where we started."

"I decided you ought to have the cash on hand."

"Oh shit," Kelley said. He was trying to be patient. "I don't need it in my hand, George, I need it in my tanks. If they cut off my fuel, if they put me on a basis of COD, I'm sunk. So I think you better pay them today. Can you pay them in full?"

McDermott shook his head.

"For two months then. Can you pay them the forty?"

"If I did, it would leave you only twelve days of cash."

"And I think you better do it. Now. Today. Send it by messenger. And then I want to see you go home and go to bed because I do have to tell you, George, you look like shit."

Claire McCarren was in Frannie's office, the two of them laughing. They both looked up when Kelley came in still angry, and it stopped him. Or maybe it was Claire McCarren's green eyes, bright and knowing. Or the way she looked up at him: quizzical smile. She was wearing a cashmere turtleneck dress the color reminding him of hot chocolate, and she sat with her cropped head tilted to the side. She was hard to scowl at.

"You been here long?" He looked at Frannie. "What else did I miss?"

She said there were messages waiting on his desk.

He looked at them quickly while Claire looked around. *The Wall Street Journal* had called. Twice. So had the *Times*. There was a memo from Frannie. *Lester Quaid, 113 Avenida Atlantica, Rio. There till the end of July.* "Want a drink?" he said to Claire.

She was looking at a couple of ads on the table. The last of Rosetti. "No thanks," she said vaguely. "'Blue Sky's Smilin','" she read out loud. "You like this stuff?"

He poured himself a Scotch and then sat in the club chair. "I told Rosetti it was cornball shit. Rosetti said, 'Exactly! That's why it's great!' Frank started talking in exclamation points about five years ago and we suffered a breakdown in communications. Frank told me 'cornball' was the magic word."

She had a brown leather briefcase open at her feet.

Kelley said, "You got any magic in there?"

"Layouts," she said. "Just plain old layouts. And for God's sakes don't be polite about them, please. If you hate them—"

"Claire?" He shook his head at her quickly. "Just do them. If I hate them, I'll throw you out the window."

117

She laughed. "Scout's honor?"

"Absolutely. Go on."

What he liked was, she didn't seem to shift any gears; she didn't turn into the Lady Executive, earnest and pitching, she was just Claire McCarren, saying to him, "Well . . . what you need is some ads that have balls but no corn." Not saying it tough, just saying it because it was the accurate thing. She'd done her homework. She knew the figures. She knew that Federal was out for his blood.

"What I've got," she said, "is a two-step attack. Step one is an advertising campaign. Let people know that even when they're getting a bargain on Federal, it isn't any bargain. Step two is a war campaign. If it keeps getting tougher, I think you better damn well acknowledge it's a war and you're fighting to survive it." She shrugged and said, "Listen—what've you got to lose?"

"You're right. Only everything."

"Well . . . there you go. You're Rocky," she said.

"I'm quite rocky, yes."

"I mean you're the underdog scrapper," she said. "Americans are really kind of schizzy, you know? We worship winners but we love underdogs. You *are* the underdog, so why not use it? It's absolute truth in advertising."

"Hold it. Just hold it," Kelley said. "I don't know about the truth. You want to go into the Absolute Truth business, try another planet. You look at the papers, I mean over the years, I've been called about every kind of animal there is—everything from maverick to predator hawk. In Federal's truth, I'm a hawk and a spoiler."

"Oh sure," she said, shrugging. "And Edison spoiled the candle-dipping business."

He laughed. "You want to paint me as a symbol of progress."

She said, "And you'd rather be a spoiler and a hawk."

He said, "Absolutely."

She said, barely smiling, "However, you haven't thrown me out any windows."

"Yet. You haven't finished yet—have you?"

She laughed. He liked the way she looked at him, eyes meeting his, really seeing each other. Nice. A girl in a hot-chocolate dress. A mind behind the eyes. A girl he could talk to.

The buzzer on his desk rang insistently. Kelley just sat, very still. He said to her: "You want to pretend we're not home?"

The thing rang again. This time he went to it. Frannie on the phone, telling him a letter had arrived from Araco. He asked her, "What's in it?" She said, "I don't know. But just sitting on my desk here, it killed a few plants. It arrived by messenger."

Kelley didn't like the sound of that either; he told her, "Bring it in," and she came in holding it as though it were a letter-bomb.

He opened it quickly.

Standard letterhead from Araco Fuel.

Signature, LeRoy Barron, Treasurer.

His eyes moved up and then ran down the page: ". . . repeated attempts . . . outstanding bills . . . $72,000,526 . . . demand in full . . . future deliveries COD . . . We sincerely regret . . ."

He handed her the letter. "Get him on the phone. If he won't take the call, hang up, try again, say it's the hospital and his mother's dying, but get him on the phone." He turned back to Claire.

"And you'd like me to powder my nose," she said, rising.

"No. Not yet. It could take her a while. Or forever. We could grow old together waiting for that phone to ring."

She watched him alertly through the haze of his smoke. She smiled. "The year of living dangerously, huh?"

He nodded. "Trouble is, the more years that go by, the less fun it gets to be. It's not such a hot-shot adventure anymore. I feel like an old gunfighter."

"Well . . ." she said slowly. "At least a lot of them lived to be old."

"Wild Bill Hickock."

"Sure. For one."

"Ran a circus at the end. Wyatt Earp tended bar. Freddie Laker's doing spot commercials for telephones."

She said, "You don't really see that in your future."

"Hey—I don't *see* the future, do you? I see a brick wall, I see I'm heading towards it at ninety miles an hour and that one of us'll smash up the other one to dust, but I don't see *which*. Do you?"

"Poor wall," she said soberly. "Never had a chance."

He laughed. "Make fun of me," he said. "Go on." The buzzer once again was ringing on his desk. He picked up the phone and said, "Hi, name's Kelley. I used to run an airline and now I'd like to talk about the dust in your sink."

There was dead silence.

"Frannie?" he said.

"No sir. It's Bernard Heidigger, sir. You told me to report about—" the voice got low, "the s-o-b-a-u—"

"Sabotage?" Kelley said.

"Yes sir. It's definitely sabotage, sir."

"You know where it's coming from?"

"No sir. I don't. But it sure isn't hackers. Whoever it is, they got a sexy machine. You know what I mean, sir?"

"Kind of computer maybe Federal's got?"

"Yes sir. Or any big company, sir. I'm trying to figure out a way I can stop it."

The buzzer rang again. "Go to it," Kelley said, and punched line three.

Frannie said, "I've got Lee Barron on one."

Kelley nodded at Claire, who got up and walked out. He took a long breath and then jabbed at the button.

"Okay—" he said before Barron said a word, "I know you're angry but the check is on the way."

"You can bet every button I'm angry," Barron said. "And I don't like to be dodged either. Your McDermott's been in more conferences this month than the fucking UN."

"I'm sorry," Kelley said. "The truth is McDermott's had some medical problems and I've been out of town. I learned this morning that the check was overdue and I ordered it sent to you by messenger today."

"You mean the check is in the mail," Barron said dryly.

"I mean you should have it in about any minute."

"In full?"

"In part. It's forty," Kelley said.

"I want payment in full."

"Hey come on now, Lee. Come on. That's not the agreement we've had and let's not change it now. When you get this check, I'm behind twenty million, not thirty-two. You'll get another twenty on the first of the month plus five towards the balance. And you'll get another five for the next four months. That's the level best I can do now, Lee. The only other thing is to leave it up to you. You can cook the goose but then you can't get the eggs."

Barron was silent. You could practically hear him calculate the risk. If he drove the airline into bankruptcy now he'd be lucky to collect a few cents on the dollar. On the other hand, if Barron heard the six-o'clock news, if he even caught a rumor of the deepening pit, then he'd try to play it safe and the ballgame—right this second—was over.

Barron took a breath. "You can pay me the balance in *three* months," he said. "Not four months, three."

"If that's a deal, you've got it."

"It's a deal," Barron said. "But if I don't get the six-point-six on the first and if you get behind again—"

"I understand," Kelley said before the threat hit the air, "but we won't have to cross that bridge, I assure you."

He hung up the phone and then sat there wearily rubbing at his eyes, trying to figure was it fraud or theft or a little bit of both and what did it feel like in his "heart of hearts" as the lawyer had asked him. He got up and paced. The floor of his office was a treadmill now; he'd be running like a bandit for a couple of weeks. He looked at the drink he'd been leaving untouched beside the chair across the room. He needed it now, a little taste of victory, a few voices from the cheering section.

Frannie came in and found him sitting on the chair.

He built her a shrug. "The bad news is we've got two weeks to live. That's also the good news."

Frannie took a breath. "You want McCarren again?"

"*Rocky*. Did you ever see *Rocky?*" he said.

"Three times."

He nodded. "Yeah. Send her in.—No," he said. "Give me a couple of minutes."

He looked at the brown leather briefcase on the couch. Claire had left it open. Whatever was in there, he wanted to like it.

Only what if he didn't?

He'd rather find out in the honesty of solitude. Besides, she'd meant for him to look at it anyway. Besides, it was the season for sneaky business.

He lifted the layouts out of the case and put them, like cards in an unknown hand, facedown on the table.

He sat on the couch and turned the first one over.

She hadn't been kidding. It was ballsy stuff.

He flipped some other ads.

There was one headed WAR-FARE that simply had a
price-list to twelve major cities with the logo: BLUE
SKY—THAT'S THE TICKET.

An ad for the financial pages that said BUY WAR
BONDS.

An ad that said DOGFIGHT.

A recruiting poster, BLUE SKY WANTS YOU.

He looked up to find her standing in the open
doorway.

"You cheated," she said.

"Never trust me," he told her, "I'm known to do
that."

"Well?"

"I want to take this to Ashe Warner. I don't think I
want him to quit on me yet so I want to have Ashe be
the one to take you on. Meanwhile, let's do it. Get
some fast mechanicals and let's go to town. First
possible insertion." He paused. "And I'd like you to
think about Paris. I'm planning to open up a route
there in April. You better get a separate contract on

that because if April never comes, I don't want you to be stuck without getting a commission."

"I'll chance it," she said.

"Why should you?"

She looked at him, the green eyes level. "Hey—don't question *every*thing," she said.

He looked at her slowly for another long minute, then rose abruptly and reached for her coat. "Come on," he said, "ladybug. I'll fly you back home."

_____**12**

SHE LIKED WATCHING him; the sun-browned hands on the instrument panel, the black eyes scanning the blacker sky. There were stars around them, distant headlights on an endless road. They'd been silent for a time but it was comfortable silence. A couple of times he'd looked up at her and smiled—the way you smile at someone when you're sharing a sandy blanket at the beach, or sitting in front of a fireplace reading. That look that's just saying, "you're here and I'm glad," taking it for granted.

And thinking about it, she was suddenly angry. He was taken property, he was married to The Fabulous Karen Kelley, the popular darling of *Women's Wear Daily;* he was Burke Kelley on a Boys' Night Out, giving her a couple of beach-looks in a cockpit. Watch it, she told herself. Stay on your toes.

He said, "You okay?"

"Uh huh," she said. "Fine."

Lighting a cigarette, she tried to remember what she knew about his marriage. For a time, she remembered, they'd seemed to be the hottest couple since the Jaggers, photographed everywhere, the lovely ex-model and the dashing young ace. They'd dashed around the beaches and the islands and the slopes, but that had been—when?—in the early seventies? Occasionally now there were pictures in the *Times,* "Mr. and Mrs. Burke Kelley" at this charity function or that opening; Kelley, unsmiling, squinting at the lens as though to say to the photographer, or maybe to the reader, "Don't you have anything better to do?" Karen sometimes with another escort. Karen, in fact, seen rather often with Zachary David. And Kelley shows up at Zeedee's for dinner. Who knows what goes on? Evenings in Byzantium, Claire thought dryly. Love in the rarefied circles of the rich. She could only assume he had one of those remote and sophisticated Liberal Arrangements, with liberal allotments of ladies on the side.

Well, okay. Not this one, she thought.

The man is dynamite and clearly labeled: DANGER! PROCEED AT YOUR OWN RISK! GET THEE TO A NUNNERY, DIRECTLY TO A NUNNERY! What else? Just keep on joking, she thought. If you happen to be living through one of history's more prolonged Comedy Hours, keep cracking wise.

On a recent trip home, her father had told her she was getting "just a little bit too New York." She'd said, "That's like getting too thin or too rich," but her father had given her a flat-eyed look and said, "Jokes are the epitaphs of emotions."

Boom!

The line had hung in the air. For the first time in her life she'd felt the sting of her father's disapproval.

He'd said something else. Her mother had asked if there were any interesting men in her life and Claire had said lightly, "No, thank God," and her father had turned and looked at her again. She'd said, "Oh for heaven's sake, Dad, I'm kidding. Not joking— kidding." And then gone on to describe Tom Cubbitt, trying to make him as interesting as possible, saying he'd proposed marriage, which was true, saying she was thinking about it, which was not.

Her father had said to her the following morning, driving in the car on the way to the airport, "About this fella, this Cubbitt fella—tell me some more."

And what could she say? There *is* no more. He's a good-looking jock. His attributes consist of being large and golden. And rich. His interests are jogging and boats. He jogs every morning. He jogs in bed. He once rolled over and said to me, "Well! That was quite a workout, wasn't it?"

"So." Her father looked up from the road. "For one of the more articulate members of the family, you are mightily quiet over there, young lady. Seems to me you aren't exactly in love."

She shrugged and said she didn't expect to be in love. She said, "You don't know what it's like out there, Dad. It's a desert with strange predatory animals. You find yourself something that doesn't bite your hand, you're in absolute heaven."

"Bullshit," he said. He drove in silence. She turned on the radio. He turned it right off. "I want you to listen to *me* now, Clary. I'm not asking you to go get bit, but I'm asking you not to be a chicken-livered coward. It's one thing to protect yourself, I'm all for it, it's another to protect yourself clean out of living." He smiled. "Now you let that settle in your head, and then you can turn on the radio again."

Well . . . it had *un*settled her head. Everything he'd said was so right—and so wrong. He didn't understand the turf of the city. He didn't understand there was all that glitter, but no gold. Nothing but a limping parade of lightweights—the Bright Young Comers, the Bantam Jocks, the Sharp Insiders with nothing inside, self-makers, health-kickers, rabbits in a magic act; now you see 'em, kid, now you don't. It was Wonderland and every woman was an Alice. She'd wanted to tell him it wasn't that easy, to stop judging her by the standards of a simpler world that had gone out of business. And what would he think of this business right now? The fact that Kelley had asked her to dinner and she'd promptly accepted. Would he call that "a little bit too New York?"

Kelley said, "You better put out your smoke." She looked up quickly. "We're there." He pointed. "See the pretty city?"

Manhattan glittered, like a diamond bracelet squandered on the ground.

They had dinner at Des Artistes, a pretty little restaurant just off the park, with leaded windows and huge bowls of flowers. He ordered a rack of lamb with wild rice and to start with, Scotch salmon and a bottle of Moët.

When the wine was poured, they touched glasses and he toasted her, saying, "To absent friends."

It surprised her, the tone of melancholy there. "I expected you to say, 'To extraordinary luck.'"

He looked at her evenly. "I just did."

She laughed. There were things about him that surprised her. She'd expected him to be a wheeler and he was. What she hadn't expected was the deadpan humor, or the suddenly boyish face when he laughed, or the weary puzzlement she felt he was feeling. "Like an old gunfighter," he'd said.

Now he said quickly, "And to present laughter."

He asked her where she came from and she told him from a little town on the prairie.

"And you come from a large happy family," he said.

"You got me," she laughed. "I think I'm the only person I know who adores her family. Not just likes, not tolerates, adores. My father is one of those big bear-y men. He's like a tree. He's *there,* you know what I mean? My mother's a doctor."

"A doctor?"

"A country doctor, you bet. I've got a couple of brothers. Raymond's a farmer and a big environmentalist. Avery's a writer for the Washington *Post*."

"And you, I take it, are the black sheep."

She laughed. "That's closer to the truth than you know."

He studied her quietly. "Well. Sure. Dragging the family name through the mudholes of Madison Avenue."

"Actually," she told him after a pause, "McCarren isn't the family name."

"Oh?"

Was he looking just a little upset?

"McCarren was a boy I married one year."

Now he was frowning. "And divorced the next?"

"You sound disapproving."

"And you sounded . . . I don't know. A long way from the prairie."

The waiter came, wheeling a cart full of food.

"I guess you don't know about the prairie," she said. "You lose a husband, you bury him, cry, you get back on the wagon."

"You lost him?"

"Not carelessly," she said, "I assure you. He died of a tick bite. And if life can have such a nasty sense of humor, then I really think it's better if people do too. I loved him, and that was a long time ago." She paused. "And I didn't mean to get so serious. Or angry. Or whatever I was getting."

"Both," he said. "I think."

They were silent for a moment, focused on the food. "Okay then, so what about you?" She looked up. "I mean while we're on the subject."

"Of marriage?"

"Uh huh."

"Well . . . we could put it I got what I asked for. The

most beautiful girl in the world," he said ironically. "And I think that wraps up the subject for the moment."

"Do you have any children?"

He grinned at her now. "We're doing this, right? The vital statistics? No. I don't have any children. Do you?"

"One of my vitaler statistics, I'd say. His name's Mark and he's eight. And he's funny and he's smart and he's cute and he's . . . some kid, my kid." She felt herself smile.

"You like him."

"That's it."

"Listen—you want to bring him out to the field? Have me give him the Junior Birdman tour?"

She looked at him thoughtfully. "You surprise me, you know?"

"Why?"

"I don't know, but you got yourself a date. Can we do it in June? The thing is, he's staying with my parents this semester. Just till I get my business off the ground. My father, by the way, will be absolutely thrilled to know I've got your account. He's afraid I'll become, as he puts it, a huckster of the vicious."

He laughed. "Are you in jeopardy?"

She shrugged. "I don't know. It's a tricky kind of line. I mean someone defined advertising once as 'the art of selling the unnecessary to the unintelligent.' And a lot of that's true. I mean face it—does the world need another designer toothpaste? And then you take a look at what's happening out there. Kids killing kids over radios and bikes, and what was the latest one? Designer sunglasses? Somebody's doing a magnificent job of selling some totally atrocious values." She stopped. "I'm sorry. I don't mean to sound earnest."

He nodded. "You always do that?" he said. "Caption yourself? You say, 'I'm being angry, I'm being earnest,' and then you apologize."

She felt herself flushing. "Most people don't like it."

"Well," he said, "listen—'most people' are assholes. I tell you something. I can't talk to 'most people' anymore. Most people, I'm not even sure if they're people. You ever get the feeling? You're talking to a guy, it's not a guy, it's a suit?" His gaze had gone sideways and fixed in a squint. "Hey listen, I want you to look up slowly at the guy by the mirror, he's just sitting down."

She followed his glance. The man appeared to be six-foot-four, white-haired and florid.

"You know who that is?"

She shrugged and looked back. "Add a cowboy hat and it's Lyndon Johnson."

"Add a pilot's cap and it's Rip Chambers. Alive and well and—"

"President of Federal?"

"That's who it is. I thought you'd like to look at the enemy's face."

She squinted again. "I can't see the whites of his eyes from over here . . ."

"You want to hear a story? Called 'Why's His Name Rip?'"

She picked up her wineglass. "Why's his name Rip?"

"I thought you'd never ask. Okay. Here we go. He was a paratrooper in World War Two. Okay? You know what a ripcord is?"

"What opens the chute?"

"Okay. So you jump from the bay, count ten, and then let 'er rip. Only Rip liked to wait, kind of skydive a little on military time. So he counts up to thirty while the jumpmaster's standing there and having a heart attack and hollering, 'Rip! Rip! Rip!'" He paused for a moment. "You like that story?"

She shrugged. "It's okay."

"Sexy?"

"A little."

"Okay. It's a lie. I once met a guy went to grade school with Chambers. Even in the seventh grade he was Rip. But old Rip tells the story at a Wings Club dinner—I mean, he's the speaker—and he tells the story like it's, 'hey folks, and ain't I the hotshot shit.'—You see what I'm saying?"

"He's a phony."

"He's an ego-tripper. Of the worst kind. He's a very large man who doesn't fill his own boots. And what he's doing right now is defending his ego. Not his airline, his ego. Like Johnson, okay? Johnson got his ego involved in the war, and the rest, as they put it, is history, right? Same thing with Rip. He's overcommitted. Federal's hurting." He laughed. "I'm the guy with the two broken hands and I'm saying, 'but you oughta see the other guy'—right? Shit.—Am I sounding earnest?" he said.

"I like it."

"See?" He looked at her slowly. "'Most people,' I couldn't say that to, Claire. Most women—forget it. I'd talk about the wine."

"Is that what you'd talk about?"

"Hell, I don't know. If you were most women . . . ? I'd tell you you have about the best face I ever looked at in my life."

"You use that one often?"

"Probably," he said. "Like the wolf who cried wolf. Then along comes the best face, and where are you?"

He was giving her that sexy beach-look again.

And again in his car as he turned on the heater.

"Okay," he said, blowing on his hands, "what next? It's too early for bed, so what do you want to do?"

She wondered exactly what he meant by "bed." If he'd made that assumption. If he had, she decided, he wouldn't be wrong. Her body had voted Yes so long ago the polls had closed and the news was undoubtedly on television now. But her head was still in charge of this risky business and her head voted No. Not now and not ever. He was too practiced. It was too easy. She would not be another notch on his gun. A little wine, a little music, a short flight of fancy and "I'll fly you back home."

He was looking at her now, looking slightly amused. "Hey," he said softly, "I didn't ask you to name the capital of New Mexico, lady, I just asked you what next? You tired? You want to say good night?"

They went to the Café Carlyle and heard Bobby Short singing old Cole Porter tunes. He got to the one about "flying too high with some guy in the sky," and Kelley looked over, and the line came up, "is my idea of nothing to do," and he shrugged, two-handed, and she thought, right there, that minute, he could have her for the price of that shrug.

It was snowing slightly by the time he started driving her down to the Village—like powdered sugar being sifted from the sky.

When they got to her building, he walked her to the door and then stood for a moment looking down at her face. He put a hand on her arm and he said to her, "Well." Then he said, "If I'm not here next week, if you have any questions, call Frannie." Then he said, "Have a good sleep," and walked off.

That was it.

Alone in her apartment, she stood in the hallway for a moment and thought how it was pretty silly of her to plan how she wouldn't go to bed with him when he wasn't even interested.

Not even a little.

And she had to laugh at herself because the real joke was, she was half in love with him.

Three-quarters, she thought as she hung up her coat.

Seven-eighths, she conceded on her way to the kitchen.

Which was all the more reason she was glad to avoid it. ("Waiter, do you have any sour grapes?"/ "No."/ "That's good, I didn't want them anyway.")

Well . . . so look at it this way, she thought. You sure didn't need it. It would mean something to you and nothing to him, and in the morning you'd have to dust yourself off and pretend it didn't happen, or that it did happen but only in the socially acceptable manner, casual, cool, without any meaning. And then you'd have to go through the whole Chinese torture of having to listen to a phone that doesn't ring, of not being able to concentrate on work, not being able to think straight because your mind isn't your own anymore, you've lost it, start to put an ad in the paper, *Lost: One mind. Last seen in the vicinity of Burke Kelley.*

The buzzer rang loudly. She ran to the door and against all caution, opened it wide, and he was standing there with small dots of snow in his hair.

She said, "If this were a Hitchcock movie, it wouldn't be you, it would've been some kind of crazed killer."

He said, "I'm crazed." He said, "The truth is, I've never talked to anyone else in the world the way I've talked to you today and I've never felt like this with anyone. I never felt seventeen when I was seventeen and I feel seventeen. I don't even know if you're in love with Tom Cubbitt. But listen—I'm going to Dallas tomorrow, and—" He stopped. "And I'm sounding like I'm *six*teen, right?"

"And you're just gonna stand there gawking in the door?"

"No, I don't think so." He moved past her and into the room, and she closed the door, and he turned and she came into his arms, and it was the most natural thing, she thought, as though they'd known each other for years and been separated and come back together, kissing hello at the airport.

They made love on a big brass bed, no fumblings, no questions, just a sweet straight urgency. He'd either forgotten it could be like that, or he'd never known it could, or he couldn't remember which. It didn't matter. Seeing her smile, looking into those green eyes, knowing who it was, not just knowing her, he thought, *recognizing* her, as though he'd been carrying her picture around, and now here she was. When he entered her he said, "Coming home now," and she said, "We've missed you," and then they were flying someplace. She was a magic carpet, taking him somewhere—home; by a wildly scenic route, iridescent, moonshot, getting lost on the way. He went out of himself; if you'd asked him, he wouldn't know his name or address. Or galaxy. And then they were kissing again, lying on their sides, looking at each other, their eyes wide open, smiling with everything, eyes, mouths, limbs.

She looked up at him, soft green eyes. "You know what you said?"

"No," he said. "Probably something like 'Gaaah.'"

She giggled. "No. Before that. You said, 'Coming home now.'"

"Did I?" He kissed her. "That was eloquent of me.—C'mere."

"I couldn't get closer if I tried."

She was curled right into him; pieces of a puzzle that locked and fit.

"Come with me," he said.

She looked up at him again and laughed a little bawdily.

He squinted. "To Dallas."

It was her turn to squint. "I have work to do, Kelley."

"On the weekend?"

"Mmm hmm. If you want to get your radio commercials on the air. Did you look at them?"

"No. Do you like them?"

"Uh huh."

"Okay, so do I."

She laughed. "I think it pays to be sleeping with the boss."

"Hey," he said sharply, "don't do that, okay? That's not what this is." He watched her. "Or is it?"

She said, after meeting his eyes, "Time will tell."

He wanted to tell her not to see it like that, to just see it and believe it, but maybe she was right. Time, in its infinite wisdom, would tell. "In the meantime," he said.

"What?"

"C'mere."

She looked over at him, lying on his back, eyes closed, drifting, not drifting away, not yet, his hand still on her, his fingers making small circles on her hip.

She thought, you want to talk about a gift from the gods, what they gave you is a present without any future. You can take it if you'll take it for exactly what it's worth. If you do that, you don't even have to get hurt. If you always keep your luggage packed in the hall and never, never take your running shoes off, not even in bed.

She wasn't sure she could do it, but listen, she told herself, you sure better try.

He looked at her sleeping. He'd felt her, in the last moments, pull away. Not physically, just pulling into herself, which was okay too because she hadn't been obvious or clumsy about it. But now in her sleep she was his again, her arm thrown lightly on his shoulder, looking happy about it. Which was more than okay.

He watched her for a while, trying out the sound of "I love you" in his head just to see how it hit him.

What was interesting was, it didn't hit him as wrong.

13

HE WOKE ALONE in a room that was sunny with the smell of coffee and bacon in the air. He woke feeling good. For the first time in weeks he'd slept without dreams and awakened knowing where he was and why.

He closed the door in the neat yellow bathroom and noticed the man's bathrobe on the hook. He gave it his back, taking a long and luxurious leak. He decided he could let it bother him or not. He decided not to but it bothered him anyway. He splashed at his face, ran Scope through his mouth and came out to the kitchen in slacks and a shirt.

She turned from the stove in a terry cloth robe and cocked her head at him. "I didn't realize we were dressing for breakfast."

He wanted to go over and hold her and didn't.

He said, "I thought it was a formal occasion. Our first breakfast."

She said, "Um hmm," and turned back to the bacon. "I'd actually figured I'd bring you this in bed."

He said impulsively, "I think I'll go back and we can start this again."

She looked at him again. "Would you like to?"

He nodded, saying nothing, and crossed the kitchen, and took her in his arms; pulling her towards him, he kissed her, feeling her lips go softer, opening to greet him.

"Where'd you go?" she said softly.

"To the bathroom," he said. "I have absolutely no right to be jealous but then, there I was, pissing and pissed.—Tom's bathrobe," he said.

"That's truly unimportant."

He looked at her slowly. "I don't know. The guy wears a monogrammed bathrobe."

"So?"

"So a guy in a monogrammed bathrobe has a major advantage." He shrugged. "He wakes up in the middle of the night, in the usual cold-sweat identity crisis, he looks at his robe, he says, Oh! I'm Cubbitt, he goes back to sleep."

"Jesus, you really are goofy," she said.

"And jealous. And I'm not coping with it well."

"So now you want to talk about Karen's bathrobe?"

"Sure. It's got somebody else's initials. Karen wakes up, thinks she's Christian Dior."

Claire started smiling.

Kelley smiled back. "It's irrelevant," he said, "but it's not unimportant. Is that what you said? 'Unimportant'? It's not."

She said nothing to that one.

"I read you," he said. "So you go ahead and be just as silent as you want."

"And what do you read?"

"You want to get serious and you don't," Kelley said. "Except you already are. And relax. So am I.—I don't know where that takes us, but that's where we are." His eye caught the morning paper on the chair. He saw the headline at the foot of page one: AUDITOR'S REPORT CASTS DOUBT ON BLUE SKY'S CONTINUED SURVIVAL.

He took the paper and went into the living room. Sitting on the couch, he opened it and read:

According to the annual auditor's report, Blue Sky Airlines appears to be living on borrowed time now as well as borrowed money.

Financial experts see no way out for the cut-rate carrier whose staggering losses and looming debts make slim any chances for long-range survival.

"Clearly, what they need is a fast infusion of outside money," said a Wall Street broker, "only no one with any kind of brain in his head would invest any money. . . ."

It socked him in the gut.

He told himself, shit, you expected it, right? He told himself, sure, but it's sort of on the lines of expecting to be shot. Guy points a gun at you, heels back the hammer, and nine times out of ten you still die of surprise.

Hollis would be reading this item this morning.

Him, and a couple of million others.

The market would open on Monday with a dive.

And Barron would bust him in two weeks flat.

Claire came in and handed him coffee. "I'm sorry," she said.

He shrugged at her. "Welcome aboard the *Titanic.*"

She sat down next to him. "What can I do?"

"You? I don't know. You want to be the girl on my burning deck?"

"If it comes to it."

"No. I wouldn't want that," he said.

"Then what do you want?"

"I want to have met you twenty years ago, Claire."

"I was nine years old."

"Stop bragging."

She smiled.

"Stop smiling."

She did. "Now what?" she said.

"Now I want to tell you exactly where I am. Okay?"

"You're in my living room," she said. "You're sitting on my couch. That's all I need to know."

"Bullshit. I don't want blind faith, I want to talk to you, and I want you to listen. If something doesn't change, I'll be bust in two weeks. I want you to know that."

"I know that," she said.

"So I want you to know you're not picking any winner."

Claire shook her head.

"What's that supposed to mean?"

"Message not received."

"Hey, look—don't get bubble-headed on me," he said.

"Then don't talk to me in garbage like winners and losers. I don't know what that means. I don't care what it means. Some of the world's winners are some of the world's more desperate rats. I think you'll fight hard because you're fighting for something that actually matters. And that's *all* that matters."

"How I play the game."

"All right. Say that."

"I don't know that you'd be happy with how I play the game." He was watching her eyes. "I'm not a nice guy, Claire. And maybe I don't deserve a nice girl. Maybe if you knew me better, you'd agree."

She was watching him too. "If I were twenty," she said, "I'd tell you you were wrong. But I'm almost thirty, so the best I can tell you is, I *hope* that you're wrong."

The *Daily News* had the headline too. BLUE SKY AIRLINES: "COLOR IT RED," AUDITORS SAY.

His doorman was reading it when Kelley came in. The guy looked up with a chilly nod, a "Good morning, sir."

In his own apartment, he kicked off his shoes and went into the study. The answering machine had a couple of blips that meant two messages. He rolled back the tape.

"Uh, Mrs. Kelley? This is Marianna at the Halston Boutique? We have that mousseline gown that you want. Um. We look forward to seeing you. Bye."

"Hey—lookin' good on the tube tonight, man. I like how you tell 'em they're full of it, you know? Like right in the eye. Only you and me know who's full of it, right? Like Zeedee, this morning, he say to me, Chooky, it ain't over yet. So now I think maybe you call me, okay? It goes, seven-oh-oh, two-three-two-five."

He clicked the thing off. He thought about calling Zeedee: "Get your goddam monkey off my back," but he thought, what the hell. Zeedee, clearly, had problems of his own. He telephoned the office and booked himself a seat on the noon flight to Dallas. And yes, they could book him a suite at the Mansion.

He went into the kitchen, which was just as he'd left it, with yesterday's coffee cups sitting in the sink and yesterday's newspaper sitting on the table. He emptied the old coffee grounds, made a new pot of coffee, and spilled all the spoiled milk down the drain.

In the study, he picked up the box of grass and locked it in a drawer.

Then he telephoned Margaret Stryker at the upstate farm.

"How is he? Awake?"

"If he is," Margaret said, "he'll sure want to talk to you. Hold it. I'll check."

He waited, drumming his knuckles on the desk. He sipped at his coffee.

Stryker came on, his voice sounding thin and thick at the same time. He said, "Christ, I go away for a couple of seconds and look what happens."

"What?" Kelley said. "Is something happening?"

"Well, I tell you, not much around here. Any news down there?"

"Nothing much," Kelley said. "Yeah. I met a girl, Charlie. I take that back. I met *the* girl, Charlie. I want you to meet her."

A very long pause. "I don't know," Charlie said.

"But you'll think about it, right? I'll come up next weekend. Aside from that one, I'm flying to Dallas, pay a little visit to our mutual friend. You want to give me odds?"

"I don't know," Charlie said. "He thinks he's King Tut. He wants to be buried with everything he's got. I think he's made a yacht reservation on the Styx."

"Bought a condo in heaven?"

"I guess so," Charlie said. "See if you can get me to his real estate agent."

Kelley sipped his coffee. "How's Margaret?"

"Holding up."

"And the kids?"

"Growing up. Fast. Too fast, I'm afraid."

"Let me ask you something, Charlie. And I want you to give me a no-shit answer. You know me, Charlie. I'm about to fight a battle that's already lost. But there isn't any reason you have to do it with me. I can put up your stock the first ten seconds of trading on Monday. You'll come out with a—"

"No."

"Take a little more time. The subject is whether your kids go to college. The subject is—"

"Closed," Charlie said.

He hung up feeling unhappy with the answer. He wanted Charlie to be free of it, out of it. And that too was selfish; he wanted the weight of other people's lives to be lifted from his shoulders. He just wanted to fly, crash if he had to, but take no one with him, no one he cared about.

And then there was Claire.

The timing was really too lousy for words.

She was half out the door when the telephone rang, the answering machine already coming on, "This is Claire McCarren, who isn't at home—" She clicked the thing off and said, "Lies, all lies. I'm here."

"Mizz McCarren?" The voice hit the *Mizz* in a way that annoyed her—a guy being snide.

"Yezz?" Claire said. It went over his head but amused her anyway.

"This is Ashe Warner. I'm head of marketing for Blue Sky Airlines—"

"Yes," she said. "Of course."

"And I seem to have a message here from Burke Kelley. From yesterday, I guess. I left the office early but apparently he wanted me to see you this weekend. So how about tomorrow. Say, quarter of two."

"Good," she said. "You want to come up to my office?"

"No," he said flatly. Hesitating suddenly, giving it some thought. "And neither of us wants to make the damn trip to Newark." He seemed to say Newark like the way he'd said Mizz—like the gender and the city were both, let's face it now, quite second-class. "Okay, so we'll make it at my place," he said, and gave her the address. "I'll have your ads sent from Newark and I'll read them in the morning and we'll see what you're about."

I'm about to dislike you tremendously, she thought. "Fine," she said pleasantly, and hung up the phone.

The Mansion in Dallas looked more like a large villa than a small hotel, more like the places he'd stayed in Monte Carlo; or maybe it was only the Riviera colors— the terra-cotta walls against the bright and unlikely greenness of the trees.

He arrived, feeling restless, in the late afternoon, telephoned the Colonel and was told by the butler that the Colonel was resting and couldn't be disturbed. He'd left instructions that Kelley should appear around noon on Sunday. Would that be all right?

Well, it would have to be, Kelley told the butler.

He hung up the telephone and dialed another number, one he knew well. He listened to it ring about half a dozen times and finally, accepting no answer for an answer, decided that Miranda Clawson wasn't home. Too bad. There were no other women he could think of whose company could even remotely amuse him. Not on this weekend; not after Claire. There were couples he could call, maybe get invited to a party at a ranch—men in their mink-cuffed crocodile boots, ladies in diamonds—or go the other way—a down-home cookout, everyone in jeans, and fascinating talk about soybean futures and pork-belly pasts. . . .

He rented a car and drove, alone, out to Big D Texas, a New West mock-up of an Old West town, with funky saloons and Wild West showdowns staged on the street—the American drama of good guys and bad, and everything settled with a virtuous gun and a virtuous woman.

He ate ribs, drank beer, and watched all the black-hats tumble to the dust.

That night he fell asleep and dreamt about walking on a hard-dust street with a pistol in his holster and Claire on his arm, and suddenly Chambers opens up from a rooftop, Rosetti behind him. Rosetti saying, "Listen—eleven million bucks, man, I couldn't turn it down."

14

You could drive around Dallas, Kelley thought wryly as he drove around Dallas, and see why Texas is the state of things to come. The values of the city are power and speed and cost and size. You move from the city to the outer suburbs and the values are the same but expressed more naively and more eccentrically. The heavy powerful speedy winners present their architects with color photographs of Loire Valley castles and Turkish palaces and say, "Do me this." The American Dream, reaching backward to baronies, dukedoms and fiefs.

The Colonel's mansion was set behind a locked-up wrought-iron gate. You leaned out the open window of your car and announced yourself politely to a small black box. If the box liked you, it buzzed in your ear and the gate unlocked itself. The modern American version of the sentry. Hark, who goes there? Click. Buzz.

He followed the landscaped road to the house. The trees were olive trees imported from Italy. It was a long drive and a lot of olives till he got to the motor circle opposite the ranch-style mansion itself. The walls, Hollis told him, had been formed out of genuine Mexican lava; the red tile roof had been built, Hollis told him, from handmade tiles.

The butler, a dignified Mexican of possibly sixty, let

him into the landscaped terra-cotta hall and then asked him to wait. He disappeared into a large room at the left that Kelley knew was the study and came out again quickly. "Ma*dam*," he said, hitting rather hard on the *dam*, "is aware that you're here."

"I'm here to see the Colonel."

"Ma*dam*," said the butler, "would like to see you first."

"Not exactly." Genevieve was standing in the doorway. "You may go now." She waved a hand at the butler, or possibly at Kelley, he wasn't sure which, a feeling compounded when she said to him flatly, "I don't like your being here. You get yourself in a ditch and you're asking for a sick old man to pull you out. I have no respect for you."

She stood in the doorway, arms across her chest, a white gardenia in her heavy black hair. Her Oriental features, still delicate and fine, looked a little bit lacquered, a little bit taut. She looked like one tough fortune cookie now.

Kelley said, "Well . . . either way, Genevieve, I have great respect for *you*." She appeared to be blocking the doorway to the study. "When Sam kicks off, you'll throw yourself screaming on the funeral pyre. Now that's really guts.—Is he in there?"

"No. He is not." She narrowed her eyes. "He's in the garden right now. I'll come out with you."

"Don't miss a trick," Kelley said. He watched as she moved ahead of him, slim and graceful in a blue silk dress.

The garden was the size of a football stadium. That was the side garden. The back garden was for barbecues and generally big enough to spit-roast a dinosaur.

Hollis looked small and sunken in his chair. It was a hot day, about ninety, the sun beating down, and he sat with a heavy red blanket on his lap, a blue flannel bathrobe wrapped around his bones and his liver-spotted features raised to the sun. A tall black man leaned against a tree looking dreamy and bored.

The Colonel seemed to rouse himself at Kelley's approach; he blinked hooded eyes and tried for his usual tough-bird pose. "The bastards won't let me have a bourbon," he said. "So I want you to have one and then we'll get together and we'll work something out." He winked broadly, or believed that he did. It appeared to be more like the death-twitch of a lizard. He turned to the black man. "You listen to me, Harold. You get the man a drink now, and none of yer darkie dawdlin' about it."

Harold was cool. He might decide to break a man's head for those words, but he'd do it, Kelley thought, with an admirably delicate and weary restraint. Harold took his time about parting with the tree.

The Colonel said to Genevieve, "Go on. You too. Now scat. This is man-talk. We want to do some talk man to man."

Kelley sat down in a wrought-iron chair.

Genevieve didn't look happy about it.

"Go on," Hollis bullied.

"Half an hour," she said. "Then I'm coming back. I don't want you to tire yourself out."

Hollis laughed faintly. "Like tellin' water not to get itself wet. Now what I'm getting *tired* of is tellin' you to go. Gwan. Now. Off with you. Scat." He fluttered a hand.

Genevieve looked at Kelley for a second with eyes black as guns and then turned with dignity. Hollis looked up, watching her retreat. "Goddam woman never did know her place. Won't let me have a pork chop. Grapes. She gives me a plate full of grapes. Now I shoulda told Harold to bring you a cigar." The Colonel got a gleam in his dead-bird eye. "You ask fer one, hear? You tell him you want yourself a good panatela."

Kelley took his jacket off and tossed it on the grass. "I don't know about it, Sam. I don't mind killing you. You want to know the truth, I've dreamt about it often, but not with a cigar."

"A Remington."

"Mostly."

Hollis enjoyed it; he cackled dryly.

"I'll let you have a drag on my cigarette, though."

"Wait'll Jenny's inside." The bird eyes squinted towards the edge of the lawn. "'Nother twenty paces. You can start lightin' up."

Kelley did as he was told.

Hollis said, "And how's George McDermott these days? He still doin' his job?"

"I don't know." Kelley took in a long drag of smoke. "Last week he almost drove me straight off a cliff, Sam. Would that be his job?"

Hollis raised his eyebrows as though he were lifting up heavy bundles. "George's job is to protect my investment. I remember it rightly, I seem to own a sizable chunk of yer stock. I let you borry that money . . ." He gazed into space. "She's gone. You can let me have a piece of that smoke."

Kelley handed it to him.

"I don't remember when."

"When what?"

"When you borried."

"It was seventy-eight, Sam. I was in a hole then too and my answer was expand. I was four feet of airline in a six-foot hole and I figured if I grew I could climb right out. And I was right, wasn't I?"

Hollis just grunted. "And I give you McDermott to make sure you was."

"Bullshit, Sam. You didn't give me McDermott. You sicked him on me. You just can't stand to make a deal without conditions. And the more galling the conditions, the better you like it. You want to see how much

149

dirt a man will eat. That's how you get your kicks. All right, so you got 'em. And for thirty million bucks, you got convertible debentures and now you own *fifty* million bucks' worth of stock. I didn't do badly by you, Sam. And give me back my goddam cigarette too."

Harold came back with a small silver tray: a single shot glass and a bottle of bourbon. No soda or ice. He put it on the wrought-iron table near Kelley. "How it is," he said slowly, pointing back at his tree, "I be right over there. Lady just told me I should fracture your arm you try to hand him a drink."

Kelley looked up. "You gonna do that, Harold?"

"Shit no. I'm just tellin' you what I been told."

"He wants a cigar."

"I don't know," Harold said. "Be cool. Give it time."

Kelley said, "You hear that, Sam? Be cool. Harold thinks Jenny's gonna fracture his arm."

Harold said, "That is the God's honest truth," and went back to his tree.

Kelley poured a drink and set the bottle on the table, out of Hollis's reach. Then he raised the glass, "To extraordinary luck," and drank it in a gulp. Then he poured another shotful and held it.

Hollis's eyes remained focused on the glass. "Well now, so what do you want of me?" he said. "George's been tellin' me you're off into two dozen fool schemes at once. You want my advice? Sell out. Let whatsisfella Quaid buy yer stock. You can walk away clean. You can start another goddam airline if you want."

"I want this one," Kelley said.

"Stubborn. Shoulda knowed you wouldn't take my advice. What you really come after?"

"Another fifty million."

The old man laughed; it sounded like wind over dried-up leaves. "Well now, could always count on you fer humor."

"What're you saving it for, Sam? Even if you lost it, what difference would it make?"

"Well . . . I got my two girls to take care of."

"And I've got fifty-five hundred employees. I've also got a part of the public that needs me."

"The public," Hollis said. "Now that's a hot hoot. Don't court me with 'the public.' I'm inclined to go along with that Vanderbilt fella. Said, 'the public be damned.' It's a damned nuisance, too, and it's dumber'n a cow. You take a dog now, you feed it, you pet it fer a bit, you got a real friend forever. Take a cow, feed the damn thing fer twenty-three years, it wouldn't know you from a post and it wouldn't lift its tail to switch a fly off yer corpse. So you want to go tell me what yer doin' fer the public, let me ask you what the hell they been doin' fer you. Where they been when you need 'em? They been helpin' you out?"

Kelley said nothing.

Hollis said, "Hmmp," and was silent for a time, as though he'd run out of air and was waiting for some more.

Kelley handed him the drink and then looked at him slowly with his head to the side. Hollis took a sip and then closed his dark eyes as though he'd just tasted life. "All right," he said suddenly, "I'm too damn tired to argue anymore. Better call over Harold. Tell him to take me back into the house."

Kelley felt a cold stone drop in his gut. But all he did was shake his head and say softly, "You're dumber'n a cow, Sam."

Hollis looked up. "Yer damn right I am. I'm gonna give ya yer money. Now how's that fer dumb? I'm gonna play one more round with you, boy. Just fer my amusement."

Hollis sipped again.

Kelley waited for the hitch.

The Colonel handed him the half-filled glass and then

licked at the sticky smile on his lips. "Condition is, you fail, you never start another airline. Sign a paper that says that. I got lawyers that can think of ways to hold you to it, too. Would you do that? Are you that damn sure of yerself?"

"Sure," Kelley lied.

"You'll get the papers next week. And now you'll get Harold here and take me back home."

Genevieve was standing at the door to the study. Smiling; looking pleasant.

Bad sign, Kelley thought.

She said: "You'll come in now and have another drink?"

Kelley just nodded. No fly had ever gotten sweeter pitches from a spider, but still he was curious. He followed her in.

In Hollis's study was a large Van Gogh in a heavy gilt frame. It was a picture of peasants toiling in the field; and now they were frozen—sentenced to hang on a damask wall. It was a room just loaded with French antiques, with a pale green carpet and a pale green couch. Two of the walls had been furnished with books, possibly chosen for their green leather bindings. The large French windows peered out at the garden through green satin drapes.

"So," she said slowly, "you worked out a deal?" She was standing at the liquor tray, about to pour a drink.

Kelley said he didn't care for any bourbon, and lit a cigarette.

"I don't like smoking in my house," she said sharply.

"Fine. We'll go back to the garden, okay?"

"No," she said. "Let's get it over with here." She sat behind the desk and apparently enjoyed the position immensely. She took on the air of J.R. in drag. "Did my husband promise you money, Mr. Kelley? Yes or no."

He gave her a look from under highly raised brows. "Whatever Sam did—or did *not* do, Jenny—is between him and me."

"And don't call me Jenny. My name's Genevieve."

Kelley just nodded. "Yes sir," he said.

She ignored it. "You're right. It's between Sam and you. That's exactly where it is. It doesn't go any further."

Kelley waited, saying nothing.

"Let me spell it out large and very clear, Mr. Kelley. When Sam had the stroke, he signed everything to me. He can talk about money, he can talk until everybody's green in the face, but that's all. Am I clear? It's like the weather, you know. He can talk but he can't do anything about it." She smiled. "Does that answer any lingering questions that could weigh on your mind? Deal's off," she said cheerfully. "Whatever it was."

She swiveled in the desk chair and gazed at the garden. "A man named—I forget his name—it was something like Kopple, I think. He's a lawyer for Lester Quaid . . ." She swiveled back to Kelley.

And brace yourself, he thought, here comes the shot.

"As you know," she said, "Quaid has been after your stock now for quite a little while . . ."

"And you sold it," Kelley said.

"Let's say I got an offer I couldn't refuse. Your Blue Sky stock has been tumbling for a year, as you undoubtedly know, but he bought it two months ago at last year's price."

"All of it?"

"No. Half, Mr. Kelley. Just enough to whet his appetite for blood. And of course he's got an option to buy the other half. And of course he'll have to buy it at the same kind of price."

"When?"

"When he gets enough stock to take over."

"So you win either way."

153

She smiled at him slowly. "That's the only kind of gamble I believe in, Mr. Kelley." Pivoting now, very slowly, in the chair—a Southern Lady in the old porch swing. "Because," she said finally, "I've really worked very, very hard for my money and I want every cent of it."

Kelley looked around. He looked at the million-dollar painting on the wall, and the diamond on her finger, and out through the window at the seven-acre lawn. "I see," he said thoughtfully. "And what were you planning to buy with it, Jenny?" He grinned at her lazily. "Happiness?"

She did stop moving in the chair.

Claire's impression of Ashe Warner: he was George Hamilton. Hamilton in one of those movies from the sixties, the dark winter tan and the slick black hair and the smile that knew about the tan and the hair and the Hamilton connection; about thirty-five.

He stood in the doorway grinning with a Diet Pepsi in his hand. Gray flannel slacks, loafers, a pale yellow turtleneck sweater.

"Want one?" He gestured with the Diet Pepsi.

Claire said, "Sure," and he went off to get it, leaving her, rather abruptly, in the hall.

There were no ashtrays in the living room.

There were no books.

There was nothing made of wood.

There was gray wall-to-wall industrial carpeting with small yellow diamonds (did he dress to match his rug?) and a gray leather sofa that was shaped like an L, and a few glass tables and a big potted tree. A stereo system that looked as though it might have been sculpted by Brancusi played Little River Band, "Take It Easy on Me."

The stats of her ads were on one of the tables.

"So—okay now." Warner, coming at her with the

Diet Pepsi in a Baccarat glass, handing it to her, relaxing on the opposite angle of the L. "So," he said, "I gather you've met Mr. Kelley."

All she did was nod.

"And he seems to think you might have some possible ideas."

"No," she said.

"No?"

"He definitely thinks I have some definite ideas."

Marvelous; the little flicker of surprise, the eyes going, Watch it, or maybe they were telling her, I Do the Jokes. "I see." He was nodding, and suddenly, bang! the old Hamilton grin. "Real gutsy," he said. "I like that."

"Good."

"But don't push it," he said. Still grinning. "A little goes a very long way."

She looked around the room again. "Less is more?"

"You got it." Ashe Warner sipped at his pop. The record dropped. The next selection was Elton John. Warner reached over and picked up the stats. Underneath them was a copy of yesterday's newspaper, open to the item on the auditor's report. "Okay," he said. "Apparently he liked some of these." Another big grin. "No, *de*finitely liked." He selected a few of them and tossed them on the floor. Picture of an airline dinner on a tray: WOULD YOU REALLY PAY $200 FOR *THIS*? and another one: BLUE SKY—THAT'S THE TICKET. "I assume he meant these."

"Uh-uh," she said. "The other stuff."

"Oh?"

"The air war."

"Uh oh." Warner shook his head. "Well, too bad now. This is kind of cute. Not that I think it'll do us any good, but it won't do us harm. This air-war stuff though—forget it."

"Why?"

"Hey—Because nobody cares, that's why. If the airlines want to have fights with each other, that's the airlines' business. Nobody cares. But you're trying to turn it into some kind of cause. Save the Baby Seals. Support the Red Cross—"

"It's not Save the Seals. It's Save Yourself Money."

"Oh. Hey now. Is that what it is?" Again he shook his head. "Well . . . I tell you now, you could've fooled me. I figured you were saying there's a war and we're losing. We're a big bunch of losers.—You believe people want to associate with losers?"

She tilted her head at him. "Tell me something, Ashe. Is Blue Sky a loser?"

"I'll tell you something, Claire. If it loses, it is."

"Is that the way you see it?"

"It's the only way there is."

"No. I'd say it's a question of perspective. You can look at it that way, but a lot of people won't.—Did you look at the radio commercials I did?"

He nodded. "And I wondered what the hell you've been on. You'll get seven celebrities to do testimonials? Come on now, Claire. These're first-class guys."

"And winners. Would you say they were winners?"

"And they wouldn't touch us with a pole. I was gonna say, not for a few million dollars. But yeah—for a few million dollars? Possibly.—You know what kind of radio budget we've got?"

"I want sixty thousand dollars."

"Times seven, you mean."

"Times zero. I've checked about the rights to the music. On a sixty-day basis, we can get it pretty cheap. And I'll get you those guys and I'll get them recorded and I'll do it in a week."

Ashe Warner laughed. "Oh yeah. Oh yeah, real gutsy," he said. "You got three problems, lady. One—I think your concept is a major disaster. Two—I don't have an extra sixty in the budget. And three—you couldn't do it if I let you have a year."

"And then," she said carefully, "there's one other problem." She looked him in the eye now. "Kelley said do it."

Warner said nothing. She almost—not quite—felt sorry for him too. Portrait of a man with his dick in the wringer. Only why would he always have to put it on the line? There'd been too little time for her to handle him with velvet, to say to him, Why don't you think about it, Ashe. She had to get the war campaign on the air.

"Look," he said, "why don't I show it to Rosetti. Kelley respects him, and maybe we can work out a softer kind of version—"

"Rosetti works for Federal."

"Well, not yet. He's still in transition."

"From rat to vampire. No," she said. "This is what Kelley wants to do."

"Well then, you'll have to wait till he's back."

"Tomorrow."

"Wrong. Rumor has it he's out hunting money. It could take him a while."

"Then I'll go to McDermott."

"Yeah. Okay. You do that," he said. "McDermott seems intent on busting us anyway."

"What's that supposed to mean?"

"That? Means that." He pointed at the item on the auditor's report. "You think that walked into the news by itself?"

According to Varig, there were plenty of seats on the night flight to Rio.

Sitting on his private terrace at the Mansion, Kelley put the phone back down on the table and thought about his options. Option. Singular. He only had one.

The Wall Street analyst quoted in the *Times* had it figured correctly: "no one with any kind of brain in his head" would invest in Blue Sky. Making phone calls was futile.

He stared at the telephone and thought about making a phone call to Claire. Except what would he say to her?

He looked at his watch. It was twenty after two.

Miranda's phone voice was foggy with sleep.

Kelley said, "Rise and shine, my love. Morning bells are ringing."

She made a sound like "gmmmp," and then told him, hold on. He could picture her, lying under Porthault comforters, groping for a cigarette, squinting at the cloisonné Tiffany clock and deciding that her case for outrage was slim.

She yawned at the receiver. "How like a winter," she said, still yawning, "has your absence been."

"Is that a question?"

She laughed. "That's Shakespeare, darling. It's a sonnet. It's also the terrible truth. I haven't seen you all winter."

"That's what I'm calling to remedy."

"Goody. You want to have breakfast?"

"Winter," he said, "is what I'm calling to remedy. Why don't you come with me to summer for a while?"

"Now *that*," she said, laughing, "is pure poetry."

"Rio."

"By the sea-o."

"I've got two tickets on the ten-o'clock plane. That'll give you time enough to wash your hair and pack too many clothes and I'll pick you up at nine."

"Sold," she said quickly. No hesitation.

She'd once said, "I'd drop anything for you, including a piano on my own foot." He'd once flown to Nairobi to pick her up, because she'd called him, quite drunk, at two in the morning to tell him that her second husband had just left her, capital L, and there was a spider the size of a coconut in her bathtub and would he please do something about it because she was planning to slit her wrists and she didn't want any goddam spider sucking up the blood.

She'd been in his life for years, on and off, between and sometimes during her marriages. Miranda was forty the way Rita Hayworth had once been forty, with heavy, shoulder-length russet hair and that spectacular body. She and Kelley got along together well. "The reason I love you," she'd once said to him, "is because I don't love you." A convoluted statement he could well understand and a motion he could second.

She knew Rio and she knew Lester Quaid.

She'd be a good traveling companion.

Also, as Miranda once put it herself, "a good water-bed buddy."

15

ON MONDAY MORNING they had breakfast on the open sun-filled terrace of the Palace Hotel, with a view of the ocean and the mountains beyond, everything blue and green, the air smelling of tropical flowers and sea, Miranda in a bright green jumpsuit and a green straw hat, a hibiscus in her hair.

They drank Tequila Sunrises and dark Brazilian coffee and listened to the samba music floating on the breeze and finally Miranda said, "Tell me why you're here. Are you here on vacation or on the qui vive?"

"I'd answer that," Kelley said, "I honestly would. Only what the hell's it mean?"

"On the qui vive?" She lifted her eyebrows. "It means an opportunist alert for opportunity."

"Shit," he said. "I've been on *that* stuff all my life."

"And now?" she persisted.

He nodded. "Oh yeah. I need to get a small fortune in two weeks. After that, I need a *large* fortune in *ten* weeks."

"Or?"

"Fini, finissimo, finito, kaput. You think you're the only one that speaks foreign languages." He called for a telephone along with the check and again tried the number for Lester Quaid.

There was still no answer.

They were walking the palm-lined Avenida Atlantica, the sidewalks made of mosaic tiles, pictures of bright flowers and birds, the other strollers, like flowers and birds, in exclusive petals and costly plumage. Paunchy men and their leggy women. Miss Universe, having met Mr. Big, or the other way around, parading on the streets; conversations in French, Italian and Spanish; jokes in German, dealings in Dutch. Some of the richest people in the world came to Rio, he knew; and some of the poorest ones were already here. It was a city of fast times and fast money and hard times and hard money; it was, he thought dryly, the uneasy marriage of Jack Sprat—of those who could eat no fat and those who could eat no lean. It was a city of the big international hustlers, of go-getters getting it any way they could, a lot of money so fresh from the laundry you could still smell the soap. Money starched and crisp, not a sweat-stain on it. It glittered on wrists, flashed by in cars, flashed in smiles. And all of it observed by the mountaintop statue of Christ the Redeemer, presiding over Rio like the ornament on top of a huge Christmas tree—Jesus, arms outstretched in benediction, or maybe, Kelley thought, the man's just shrugging; two-handed shrug.

She said to him, "Where does Lester fit in?" She was looking at a diamond necklace in a window.

"I don't know." Kelley looked at his own reflection. Another hustler, he thought, right over here. "He controls a corporation called TPI—"

"Wait, don't tell me." She gave it some thought. "It stands for . . . Terrible Prick Incorporated."

"Cute," Kelley said. "I'm gonna leave it right there.

161

The point is, they wanted to buy the airline and somebody told me they're still in the mood."

"And you came here to sell it?"

"Christ no," Kelley said. "I came here to gamble. I want to get Lester to lend me some money. If I don't pay him back, he can have the airline for the price of the loan. And I tell you, kid, even in the shape that I'm in, that's the bargain of the century."

They turned off the side street and back towards the beach. Miranda shook her head at him. "It doesn't make sense."

"Sure," Kelley said. "It makes absolute sense. You ever see *Butch Cassidy and the Sundance Kid?*"

She shrugged. "So what?"

"Okay, so remember when the posse had them cornered? And Butch and Sundance are up on a cliff. It's a real high cliff over furious water, and Butch says, Jump, and Sundance says, I can't swim, and Butch says, Jesus, you stupid fool. The *fall*'ll probably kill you anyway."

She looked at him and shrugged. "You lost me there, Kelley."

"No I didn't," he said. "I'm right on that cliff. The thing is, the posse'll *definitely* kill me, so *probably* looks like a pretty good choice."

She thought about that for a while and said, "Oh."

It was nearly three o'clock when they got to the beach, the sun still high, the day still hot, the beach still the rumored Best in the World. Fine white sand, a spectacular view of Sugar Loaf Mountain, bronze Brazilian bodies, the high-strutting girls and boys of Ipanema.

Miranda was admiring the boys on display, the young body builders doing their weight-lifting numbers, their gymnasium equipment planted on the sand.

"Shall I leave you to your own plentiful devices?"

"Just browsing," she said, and grabbed him by the arm.

He rented a couple of canvas chaises. She wanted a beach umbrella—yellow, she said—and she unzipped the jumpsuit and stripped to a narrow yellow bikini, looking as ripe as any girl on the beach.

It took him a while to find a vendor with a beer. They were selling everything else, sweet cakes and soft drinks, sausages, biscuits, ice cream, shrimp, singing their wares in percussive voices, *"sorvete," "chouriço."*

He walked along the hot sand, barefoot, in bathing trunks, squinting at the sun. A couple of lookers trailed him down the beach, a pair of them, with long dark hair to their waists. They moved beside him, pushing their lips out, giving him the eye, giggling softly—what the Portuguese politely call "making charm." He bought them a beer and, against his protests, they followed him back to the yellow umbrella, where Miranda had attracted a circle of dark grinning young men. Kelley presented the groups to each other, *"Meninas— meninos"* ("Girls—boys") and hustled them off.

Sprawling on the chaise, he said to Miranda, "For a couple of old folks, we're not doin' bad." He handed her a beer and then looked at her sidelong. "Did I cramp your style?"

She wiggled her hand to indicate maybe. "I just saw speak-of-the-devil, by the way. I didn't wave him down and he didn't see me. He was sitting over there with his nose in a book."

"'The Atlantic Ocean: An Owner's Manual.'"

"Likely." She laughed. "Good old Lester. He does have a sharp-honed acquisitive instinct, doesn't he."

"Shit, are you kidding?" Kelley said. "Quaid discovered God about seven years ago. I heard he immediately applied for the patent and was totally pissed when they told him that God was in the public domain."

She laughed. "You mean the thing about the Reverend Devine."

"DeVane, I think. And it's not just a 'thing.' Lester discovered this guy and decided to market him like toothpaste. So now you've got DeVane as a national brand—three-hour television show, all those religious publishing companies—"

"T-shirts saying, 'I Walk with God.'"

"Are you kidding?"

"I think so, but I really can't tell anymore." She was rubbing her suntan lotion on his chest. "I ran into Lester at a party in Bel Air and he sounded sincere. Phony, but sincere."

"Well . . . so maybe he is," Kelley said. "He controls the entire DeVane Corporation. You make a few million out of God every year, you could get an epiphany. Give him your idea about T-shirts, why don't you? Ask for a royalty."

"I just might," Miranda said. "I just seriously might."

He smiled because knowing Miranda, she might.

Lighting a cigarette, he looked at the ocean and thought about acquisitive Lester Quaid, who was, if nothing else, the wave of the present.

And maybe, Kelley thought, I'm the wave of the past . . . receding even more quickly than the future.

The sun was hot and the ocean out there looked mountainous and rough, with high-rolling breakers that crashed against the sand. Signs warned swimmers to stay close to shore. There were very few swimmers and fewer surfers—some young Cariocas with dark hard bodies and flashing white teeth, teenage Tarzans, a couple of them now coming in from the surf, talking and laughing. One of them was making a gesture with his hand, pointing it up to the sky like a rocket, then nosing it down. *"La bomba,"* he said. A wave like a bomb. The kid had a bleeding gash on his arm.

Kelley waved him over, pointed at the board, pointed at himself, and extended a handful of crisp cruzeiros. Miranda said, "Ah. The old man and the sea."

Kelley said nothing.

As he moved to the water with the board on his head, one of the boys hollered, "*Ay, coragem!*" which Kelley understood to be Portuguese for "courage." He also understood the sarcastic tone. He turned to them, grinning, constructing the clear international sign, and the boys started laughing. "Okay," one said.

The water was a welcome chill against the heat; it was also a wild cold-blooded animal protecting its turf. It tried to push him back as he submarined into it, lashing at him, trying to punch him in the arms, making him curse silently. Then he got out beyond the line of the breakers, resting on the board, waiting for the big one, the right one, the one that could lift him and fly him back to shore. No other riders were out this far. Not even the young with their immortality intact. He was alone out here, as alone as in the sky, and he felt just as free.

He saw the wave building now, huge and powerful, went out to meet it, grabbed it on the right beat, and then stood, in a balancing act on the board, feeling exultant, effortless, mindless, poised above disaster, riding the tiger, unfuckingbelievable, soaring like a bird.

He came down hard, the wave dumping him at the last minute, the board shooting out ahead of him, but it was fine, he was only a few easy strokes from the shore.

When he hit the beach, grinning, breathing rapidly, and picked up the board, his mind still flying, he noticed that a crowd had gathered at the waterline as though he'd been performing, putting on a show.

Well, let them have it.

Among the audience was Lester Quaid, looking

hefty and hairy in his modest high-cut American trunks, his chest half-covered with an open silk shirt, his chest hair starting to turn a little gray, his head hair a slightly improbable black and slicked straight back from his square-jawed face.

"Bravo," Lester said. "Mucho macho. Like I always said, you got more balls than brains. I'll buy you a beer to wash the salt from your wounds."

They stopped at the umbrella and picked up Miranda and then went to one of the beachfront cafés, taking a table underneath the shade of a wind-eaten palm.

Miranda ordered a piña colada. Lester ordered Choppa, the local beer. "From a bottle," he said to the Indian waiter, "Garaffa, compreende?—Otherwise, they wash their feet in it, I swear," he said to Miranda. "Special for the tourists."

"You mean," she said coolly, "for the filthy rich."

"These people are just very dumb," Lester said. "And they're taking over. We're busy being scared of a Russian invasion? Forget it. We're being invaded by spics. English is a dying language. Menudo," he said, "Five, ten years, he'll be president of the United States. You watch."

The beer came and Lester lifted his glass. "To good ole Yánqui know-how," he said.

Kelley said softly, "To spacious skies." He sipped the beer; it was excellent and cold. He thought about washing his feet off in Lester's, or maybe just kicking him straight in the teeth, getting sand in his molars, just for the hell of it, but then like all the other peons in the world, he was, at the moment, too poor to be proud. He lit a cigarette and opened with, "So what are you doing here, Lester?"

"Enjoying myself."

Miranda giggled.

Lester responded with a sharp-eyed look. "What's funny in that?"

"Nothing," she said. "But you sounded homesick."

"No, not a bit. Not a bit," Lester said. "Besides, I've got a little business on the side."

"How little?" Kelley said.

"Oh well, you know me," Lester modestly grinned. "I'm bidding for a million-acre tract of their land. This country is a goddam gold mine of farmland. There's more farmland here than in any other single country in the world. I mean available farmland. You want to control the world a hundred years from now? Control the food supply. And where'll that be? Not up north, buddy. Not up home. We're pissing away farmland like there's no tomorrow. So a hundred years from now, ya'll come down for a Quaidburger, hear? A little corn on the side." Lester finished his beer, wiped his mouth with his hand, and then looked up at Kelley. "So why're *you* here?"

"A little business," Kelley said, and waited for a beat. "Maybe with you."

"Oh?" Lester laughed. "So whaddaya know. So we got to you, huh? Did you bring your white flag? Hey—are you ready to kiss my ring?"

"Hey— what I'm ready to *do,*" Kelley grinned, "is to kick you in the balls. But in that case you couldn't talk business for a while. You want to talk business?"

"Always," Lester said. "Except now I gotta go see a man about a cow. I'll be back on Wednesday. I'm having a little informal shindig, so why don't you fall on by and we'll talk. Okay? Around nine." He rose abruptly and walked off, strutting in alligator sandals, his silk shirt flapping.

Kelley sipped his beer and tipped back in his chair. "There goes the orgiastic future," he said.

"A Quaidburger."

"Yep. A little corn on the side."

16

LESTER HAD A large penthouse triplex in a tall white tower—one among row upon row upon row, hotels and condos, high-rise palaces advancing towards the beach-front, lining it completely, and then stopping cold at the edge of a quarter-mile strip of the sand. Like lemmings, Kelley thought, about to make their final dash at the sea.

The penthouse commanded a remarkable view—ocean on the one side and Christ on the other. Floodlit now on the darkened mountain, he seemed to be flying, his arms extended like precarious wings.

The building itself had a wavy facade, like waves of the ocean, or else like a giant three-titted woman, and Lester's living room was two tits wide and wrapped in a terrace. There were possibly seventy people in the room. It was furnished in a sleek International Modern —Brazilian leather and indoor trees, and from some-where in the night came the beat of a samba.

Lester, looking large in a white dinner jacket and holding a tumbler of Scotch in his hand, was greeting his guests in the marble hallway. He was flanked by a pair of breathtaking blondes in identical white lace dresses. A matched set. Exquisite bookends, and Les-ter was the book they would have to take to bed.

He shook Kelley's hand. "Good," he said. "Good.

For a minute there, I figured you might've changed your mind." He gestured at the women. "Tweedledum, Tweedledee."

The girls just giggled.

"Nice digs," Kelley said.

"Yeah. How about this place?" Lester grinned. "You know who I got it from? Banji Savik. The richest Iranian second to the shah. He was up at the pool—I got a pool on the roof—so now listen to this. Some guys come over in a chopper and bang!"

Miranda said, "*Shot* him?"

"Right in the pool. I was staying at the Park, I got a line on the story from Alvy over there, so I came right over. I said, 'I'll take it,' while the pool was still red. Pool's open, by the way, if you want to take a swim. Enjoy yourself, kiddies."

Lester drifted off, greeting other guests while Kelley looked around and Miranda said, "You know who Alvy is, don't you?" and gestured at a man with dark mirrored glasses and a black silk suit. Kelley studied the face; it was lean and blank and the eyes were a carefully hidden secret. "I don't know," Kelley said. "I imagine he's the world's hippest real estate agent."

"Now guess again."

"I don't want to keep looking at this guy for too long."

"You're getting warmer," she said.

"A death-squad hitman? Come on, I give up."

"Alvy," she said, "is José Alvarado. He used to be the Minister of Agriculture for Colombia.—Are you getting any pictures?"

"Of popular Colombian crops," Kelley said. He squinted at Alvy. "A coke broker, huh?"

"Not just a broker. He controls about a third of what comes into the States. The feds in New York have been after him for years. I mean they *know* he's the candy-man for most of Manhattan but there's no way to touch him." She giggled now. "How come you look so amazed?"

"Shit. What *amazes* me is how come you know."

"Everybody knows, dear. Alvy shows up at every party in Rio. He's a specialty number. You know what I mean? I mean, there's a whole bunch of Lesters on the beach. You know. They want to show how they're hip and inside?"

"So Alvy comes around with his death-squad expression—"

"Exactly. And the atmosphere trembles with chic."

Kelley looked around. "Before I start trembling, I better get a drink."

The bar was set along the living room wall, champagne corks popping to the beat of the samba, the beat very quickly becoming addictive, beginning to fill you like the beat of your blood.

Miranda, in a slinky green-flowered dress, her hips going crazy to the tropical beat, asked him if he recognized anybody here.

Again he turned his back to the bar and looked around, sipping at the double Chivas in his hand.

What got him was the trees. The room appeared to be an indoor garden; a couple of parrots hung on their perches, jabbering brightly and breathing the smoke. There was a woman with a literal monkey on her back, its soft brown eyes looking over her shoulder as she gestured and talked.

He recognized a man whose name was McKeon, an American banker who was up to his jowls in Brazilian loans. Brazil had already defaulted twice, making it an even riskier investment than Blue Sky Airlines. Kelley thought wryly: Maybe I'll say Blue Sky is a country—a right-wing Latin-American country—and McKeon will feed me the money with a spoon.

On a leather loveseat was Franco Lascala, an Italian

businessman who'd once been kidnapped. Lascala now traveled with a female bodyguard, a woman who looked like the young Sophia Loren. A woman with magnificent pectoral muscles.

There were Arabs, Iranians, Turks, Japanese. The exotic playboys of the Eastern World and the girls they played with.

Then in the corner, there was Crystal Koulermos in silver lamé, surviving scion of the Greek tycoon. Crystal, the Richest Woman in the World, though three bad marriages had dented her fortune. Kelley had met her with Karen in New York and found her to be an uninteresting, slightly dumpy woman with a small, annoyingly breathy voice.

"Now *there*," Miranda said, "is the answer to your problems. She's available again and she's prowling the globe, and she's known to pay extremely well for a divorce."

"That's the catch," Kelley said. "We'd have to get married."

"So?" Miranda shrugged. "I'm telling you, lover-duck, you start right now, by Saturday, the latest, she'll be calling up Karen. She'll offer to pay her a few million dollars and poof! Karen's gone. You'll be married in time for your two-week deadline."

Kelley sipped his drink. He thought about Karen. Divorcing Karen had been something he'd thought about a couple of times. Never too seriously; never for long. It would be, he was aware, a terrific hassle. Karen would find herself a hotshot lawyer whose rapacity was equaled only by her own. The proceedings would be ugly and costly and dumb.

He must have looked thoughtful.

Miranda said, "Jesus. It was only a joke."

"I know," Kelley said. "You want to come see the pool?"

"Uh uh. I don't think I'm up to that yet. I think I'll

hang around. I'll try to get Alvy to take off his shades. I'll go up to him and say, 'Oh dear! You have a sty?'"

"I wouldn't do that," Kelley said.

He opened the door from the stairway to the roof and got hit with an amplified blast of the samba. It was coming, live, from someplace beyond a tall potted flowering hedge. From beyond the hedge there were squeals and laughter and splashings in the pool. Kelley looked up at the ripe full moon and a sky full of stars. And thought about the angle of a chopper coming in, of Lester's body, floating in the pool and then Alvy on the telephone: "Hi. Guess what?"

He turned the corner and was into a couple of Arabian nights. It occurred to him slowly, looking at the squealing splashing nymphets, that the low-flying chopper had struck the first blow in the battle for Lester Quaid's liberation.

A girl came up to him, naked and wet.

"Tudo bem?" she said smiling.

"Tudo bem." He couldn't take his eyes off her breasts. They were show-stoppers, dripping wet from the pool.

"You come here often?" he said in English for his own particular random amusement, his eyes still on her, the hardened nipples on the rounded breasts.

"Eenglayss?" she said pertly.

He looked at her face; it was simple symmetry, nothing going on; as beautiful, he thought, as a blank check.

And he thought about Claire.

"No compreende," he said, and moved to the bar. He got himself a Scotch and looked around at the scene. A five-piece combo was playing in the corner and trying not to get any drool on their chins. The squealers and splashers were all in their twenties; they

were all colors, from onyx to snow, and if you narrowed your eyes, it was a shifting kaleidoscope of rumps and legs and shoulders and tits, and the samba music echoing the beat of your pulse. There was a table with food—shrimp, pineapple—everything you'd grab and eat with your hands.

Most of the men on the roof were in clothes, a handful were naked, a few were in trunks. A man in a suit got yanked into the pool. A guy about twenty with a lean, muscular suntanned body, a religious medal hanging from his neck, a prodigious erection rising from his groin, was approaching the lady whom Kelley had rebuffed. He watched until they disappeared behind the hedge.

"Kellee," a voice said.

Kelley turned around and recognized Paul DuLac coming towards him, tall and thin in a white dinner jacket, a highball tumbler clamped in his hand. Kelley knew Paul from Ste. Maxime, where they both owned villas. They'd met at Cannes, where one of Paul's movies had swept the festival. As a director, he'd been called the French Fellini.

"Is this in your next movie?" Kelley said.

"It well could be so." Shaking his head, Paul lifted his glass. "*La vie en rose,* eh?"

"Long may it wave. What brings you to Brazil, Paul?"

"Seriously? I did have a notion for a film. Something I could shoot on the beaches of Rio."

"About?"

"Ah yes. About," Paul said. "About. That's very American of you. Americans expect a one-line synopsis. If you can't tell your heartbreaking story in a sentence, they don't want to hear it. About life, *copain*. How's that? In a word."

"I stand here humbly chastened," Kelley said.

"Bullshit. You stand there with your usual aplomb. Myself, I am getting—what's your word for it—roused."

"La vie en roused."

They were looking at the pool. A man with a belly like a pregnant woman was groping at a blonde.

"Look at this," Paul said. "Look at this show. It's the winter carnival."

"That, or the fall of the Roman Empire."

"So? Oo-la-la." Paul raised his brows. He had one of those arch bony faces; sardonic expressions were a thing he did well. "You mean that, I think."

"Sure. Why not? Orgies in the moonlight. Nero fiddling with somebody's twat."

Paul laughed. "You know what your problem is, Kelley?"

"No, but I bet you're gonna tell me what it is."

"Beneath that intricately polished exterior, there still beats the heart of a Huckleberry Finn."

"Hardly," Kelley said.

"Don't deny it so quickly. Huckleberry Finn was a shrewd young man. He was also an incorruptible dreamer. Before your country got rich and beautiful he used to be the essence of American soul."

"Of the nineteenth century."

"So? You're a nineteenth-century man. You would, I imagine, have been a pioneer. You would have made your money in a California gold mine and founded a city. And you don't like all of these players in the pool because you, *copain,* see money as a tool and they see it as a toy."

"Sure," Kelley said. "And after the palm reading's over, do you do the crystal ball?"

"Now don't get angry," Paul said. "If nothing else, I'm an educated student of character. In art, you understand, character is all. Plot—a real plot—is merely the reaction of character to circumstance. I give you the story of an honorable man who's in a terrible fix. But I tell you it isn't the story of the fix, it's the story of the man."

Kelley narrowed his eyes. "You're leading up to something, right?"

"In fact," Paul said. "I hear you're in a fix. I see the dramatic possibilities in this."

"You want to buy the rights to my story?" Kelley said. "Fifty mil and it's yours."

"I can see this scene." Paul gazed at the pool. "You and I discussing character and finance." He turned back to Kelley, shrugging. "I'm making a parallel, perhaps. As it is, my next project is to shoot in New York. Jean Roque is to back it. You remember Jean Roque? I brought him to your house on Long Island last year."

"And said you wouldn't touch his project with a pole."

"Ah yes. *Tant pis*. Portrait of the artist as a rich young man. Rich and choosy." Paul shook his head, grinning. "I too have financial reverses. Art is long but cash is rather short. I put my own money in the last film I made and I lost every penny. So now I do a stinker for Jean Roque's ego and then I come back and do a film for my soul. The thoroughbred has to do its hitch at the plow. Perhaps you, too, will take a similar route."

Kelley raised his hands. "I'm plowing right now."

"If the crop turns out to be not as expected, you should call Jean Roque. He's staying, I believe, at the Palmer Palace. I'm serious."

"Why?"

"He was asking about you. I suggest it only if your back's against the wall. And there's a fully clothed woman on her way across the roof, a magnificent redhead, and I think I'm in love."

Kelley shook his head at the approaching Miranda. "We were just playing Last One into the Pool."

"That's good," Miranda said. "I've always admired self-restraint in a man."

Kelley introduced her to Paul DuLac.

"As always," Paul said, turning to Kelley, "you have admirable taste."

"How French," Miranda said. "As though I were something he was just about to eat."

Kelley laughed.

So did Paul. "When in Rome," he said quickly, "I forget my manners."

They went back downstairs where the party was mostly gathered in the dining room. Lester, it seemed, wasn't anywhere around. But then neither were the ladies in the white lace dresses.

Kelley spent the rest of the evening getting drunk and watching Miranda do the samba with Paul. He was conscious of Alvy, the Colombian minister, watching him intently from the corner of the room, and then following slowly when he moved to the bar, moving up to him silently and watching him again. Almost like a heavy in a lousy movie. Made for TV. Everything overstated and redundant.

Alvy said, "My boy says you're not in the mood." He spoke without moving his lips very much. Maybe, Kelley thought, so they could lip-sync it later.

"If I'm supposed to catch what that means," Kelley said, "you better give me the script. What boy? What mood?"

"You were asked in New York."

Kelley thought it over. It didn't take long. Zeedee in the car saying, "I buy from Chook and Chook buys from Alvy . . ." Well well well, as Zeedee would say.

Alvy shrugged his shoulders. "It's okay with me. Only Chooky, you know, he's upset, he gets bad. You want to stay careful, I think cut him in."

"On what?" Kelley said.

"What you're buying here, man."

"Suntan lotion. A couple of postcards, Wish You Were Here. That's what I'm buying."

"We'll see," Alvy said. "All things considered, I think this is shit." He smiled. "I mean all things considered. You know?"

"I don't know what you consider," Kelley said. "I don't care."

"How about I just keep an eye on your moves? Would you care about that?"

"If I did," Kelley said, "would that stop you?"

"Hey—of course." Alvy smiled with his thin little mouth. What his eyes were up to was anybody's guess. He walked away quietly, a man who was starring in his own life story and didn't fit the part.

Kelley turned to the bar and got another quick splash. He spotted Lester and his ladies-in-waiting, only this time the ladies were resplendent in blue, and Lester was flying, ready to plant his initials on the moon.

Lester said, "I'll call you tomorrow, okay?"

At a little after two, Kelley wandered upstairs to take what appeared to be an endless leak. He did not like the looks of his face in the mirror. His eyes, he thought, looked bleary and bloodshot. He looked, he decided, as drunk as he felt.

He passed by a telephone sitting near a king-size fur-covered bed. He hesitated, looked at it, sat on the bed. What he needed was a little infusion of Claire, a little clarity, a little bit of light on his life.

What he got from the phone was the answering machine: "This is Claire McCarren, who isn't at home, but I'll be calling in later to pick up your message. So leave one, okay?"

He looked at his watch again and wondered where she was.

Then he said, "Tell her to call me at the Palace."

Then he said, "Hotel." Then he said, "Rio." Then he said, "Collect." Then he said, "Shit," and replaced the receiver.

He was still sitting on the bed when the girl came in. She was one of Lester's blondes, Tweedledum or Tweedledee, and she looked a little weary.

She stood in front of Kelley and then, saying nothing, she began to undress, slowly and prettily, throwing the blue silk gown on the floor, stripping down, braless, to small blue bikinis.

"Are you telling me something?" Kelley said slowly. "Or is this just the changing room?"

"Mmm. I have had," she said in British-accented English, "a hard day's night. Now I'd like a little bit of fun for myself. And I'd like to wash the taste of Lester from my mouth."

"So to speak."

"So to speak."

He took her on the king-size fur-covered bed, took her with an energy he hadn't expected at this late stoned hour, took her with the spillage of his own frustration and his own certain knowledge that he was here whoring just as openly as she. He, too, needed comfort, respite from the trade. He fucked her till their bodies were gleaming with sweat and they yelped together on the mink-lined bed.

Huckleberry Finn.

17

"LISTEN," LESTER SAID, "you're a man of the world."

They were sitting by the pool in the high-noon sun, Lester looking less than bright-eyed and bushy. The blondes were still there. The one Kelley'd been with (she'd said, "Call me Dee") was now swimming in the pool—smooth, powerful strokes. The other one, Dum, was now lying on a chaise, her fine full breasts staring upward at the sky with their round unblinking roseate eyes. Kelley was distracted.

Lester babbled on. "Tell you something," he said. "I know guys back home, they'd be pissing in their pants. My partners, for instance. Or how about DeVane? Can you picture the Reverend DeVane in this joint? Jesus. It'd punch his ticket to heaven. But you," he went on, "you're smart, you're okay. I got a feeling you been around the world once or twice. I hear you get a little bit exotic yourself."

"Is that so?" Kelley said.

"Your house in Oyster Bay." Lester grinned at him broadly.

There'd been nothing exotic in the house at Oyster Bay, but still, if it made Lester happy, why not?

"In other words," Lester went on, looking serious, "I don't expect to hear you've been talking in the States. As far as they're concerned, I'm a Carmelite monk. You understand what I'm saying?"

179

"Brother Lester," Kelley said.

"Exactly. What I've got is a fortune on the line. This Brazil shit is taking my personal dough. The corporate money, that's a whole other thing. Listen—these guys I'm in business with now, these are very fundamental clean-living guys. They screw once a week, Saturday night, unless they forget to, or somebody has a headache or there's a good movie on the tube. Like *Bambi* or *The Robe*. You follow what I'm saying?"

Kelley said he did.

"I can be ousted from my own company the same way you can," Lester said. "And these guys'd kick me out on the grounds of moral tupperware, or whatever the hell it's called."

"Turpitude," Kelley said.

"Hey, Dummy," Lester hollered at the girl on the chaise, "go get us some snack-stuff. Coupla beers, a little caviar sandwich, okay? With onions," he said, "don't forget the onions."

"You'll remind me of them later, I'm sure," the girl said. She roused herself slowly and wriggled to the door.

"Okay," Lester clapped his hands now at Kelley, "so tell me some tales."

Kelley made his proposition. Asking, to begin with, for forty million dollars.

"I don't know," Lester said. "I lend you the money to pay your March debts. You pay me back in three quarterly installments beginning in June. Is that right?"

Kelley nodded.

"If I don't get the first installment in June, I get the airline, right?"

Kelley nodded again.

Lester stared mystically out at the pool. "You know if I were Federal, I'd keep on fighting you at *least* until June."

"At least," Kelley said.

"So nothing's gonna change much from now until June."

"That's the bet," Kelley said. "And you really can't lose. If I pay you, you can still try to buy up my stock the way you're doing right now."

Lester looked at him slowly. "So you know about that."

"Uh huh," Kelley said. "It's a lot easier to get my percentage all in one lump, though. Isn't it?"

"And faster and cheaper," Lester said.

"There you go." Kelley yawned.

Lester looked at the pool again. Dee emerged, dripping, in a small yellow suit. "You know, you really do deserve to die," he said idly. "You know *how* to survive. You could turn around your airline just as good as I could."

"But it wouldn't be the same airline," Kelley said. "I'd be breaking a promise."

"To who?"

"To myself. To my staff, to the public."

"Oh well," Lester said. "Fuck 'em all but eight. Did they have that saying when you were in the army? Six pallbearers and two road guards. That's all you need for friends. You know what's wrong with you, Kelley?"

"No. But it's everybody's week to tell me. Go on. Spit it out."

"You want to be the fucking Statue of Liberty. You say, 'Give me your tired, your poor, your weak.' So then you get what you asked for. You get the tired, the poor and the weak. And then you're wondering how come you're losing the war? You're losing the war because you're siding with the losers, that's all. The People. I tell you, kid, 'The People' is a dinosaur. Its day is over."

Kelley nodded. "Could be."

Dee had toweled off and was sitting on the chaise. She met Kelley's eyes as she lit a cigarette.

"Some things are just worth betting on, Lester. Or fighting for, maybe.—You want to make a deal?"

"Sure," Lester said. "I'll draw up the contract. You want to act fast, we'll have a deal in a week."

Miranda had been sleeping when he'd left to meet Lester. She was still in bed, though sitting up and taking liquid nourishment—a cup of strong black coffee in her hand. She looked up at him and managed a hungover, "Hi."

Kelley just nodded and pulled off his shirt. He was sweaty and felt sullen. Miranda, at least, looked cool and clean. She was watching him slowly.

"Went badly, did it?"

"Uh uh." He peeled off his white cotton ducks.

"You got the money?"

"Uh huh."

"I see. Then why do you look so unhappy?"

"Forty million bucks," he tossed his briefs at the chair, "does not buy happiness." He headed for the bathroom.

"If you're going to pee," Miranda said, "can I watch?"

He stopped and shrugged at her. "Whatever turns you on."

"It's a sight of which I absolutely never tire." She followed him into the white marble bathroom and leaned against the door. "Look at that," she said. "No wonder little boys want to grow up to be firemen. You realize I personally could only put out a fire if it were on my own foot?"

"Pervert."

"I consider it a rather mild perversion, considering some of what's been going around. Speaking of which, how's Karen these days?"

He looked up from the sink. "You consider Karen to be one of my perversions?"

Miranda walked over and turned on the shower. "Ah, bliss. Hot water," she said. "You'll excuse me while I wash off my muskier scents. I can summon them up again anytime at all." She disappeared in a puff of smoke.

Kelley fumbled through his shaving kit and reached for some aspirin.

"By the way," Miranda said, "who's Hitch Ryan?"

"Ryan?" Kelley poured out some bottled water. "My general manager."

"Oh. Is that all?"

"All? I don't know what you mean by 'all.' He was one of my two original partners. Before that, I knew him slightly in Nam.—Why?" There was nothing but the sound of the shower. "Hey?"

"Is he sort of a scary-looking guy?"

"No, not really. Or not anymore. Karen used to think so. Karen referred to him as Creature Feature, which pissed me no end. But then Karen has the insight and kindness of a stone. No. He's okay. I left him in Paris making deals for the gate space.—Why?"

"I had a weird chat with Alvy last night. You do remember Alvy—the minister of coke?"

"I was gonna say, of Lester's alternative religion. Yeah, I remember him." He opened the shower. "Want some candy, little girl?"

She grinned and then grabbed him—put her arms around his neck and started chewing up his ear. "Oh boy oh *boy,*" she said, "you're delicious."

His body responded.

"Watch it," she said. "I can't do it standing up. I get wobbly in the knees."

He made a guttural groan. "Then don't start it standing up."

"Sorry. Shall I turn on a lot of cold water?"

183

"If you can't think of anything better you can do."

"We could talk. I could say something quite unexciting."

"Alvy. You were saying, Alvy."

"Oh yeah." Running the soap cake all around his chest. "Last night at the party he comes up to me, nodding his head, he says: 'Tell your friend I say, how's Hitch Ryan.' Wait a second. No. There was something. . . . He said, 'Tell your *innocent* friend.'" Soaping his cock now.

"Hold it a second."

"Happy to."

"Stop it. What else did he say?"

"Nothing. Not a thing. He just stood there and laughed. Like, Hah! Gotcha!" She waited. "Does it?"

He leaned on a wall. "I don't know. I don't know what he knows about Ryan."

"Mmm. You mean you and Ryan running smack."

"What?"

She looked startled—innocent and pink, with her bright red hair getting curly from the steam.

"Is that what he told you?"

"Who? Alvy?"

"Come on, Miranda. This is no time for games. Is that what he told you?"

"You're really upset."

Kelley said nothing, just tilted his head.

"Oh well. If you're gonna be serious about it. No. I heard it years ago. You and some scary-looking buddy flew dope so you could bankroll the airline."

"I see. You believed it?"

"Well . . ." She shrugged. "I thought it was sexy."

"Sexy. Cute." Staring at each other, naked, through steam. "You remember where you heard it?"

"As a matter of fact. It was down in Palm Beach. At Marcus and Candy's. I remember I was there with my second husband and the weekend is practically engraved in my brain because the bastard was chasing after Monica Chambers."

Kelley was startled. "Rip Chambers' wife?"

"And Rip was trying to console my ass. Jesus, what a hearty old fart the man is. Anyway, we're all having dinner one night and Marcus . . . just tells it. Basically, I think, to tell Rip to buzz off. Or that's what I think. I mean Rip was saying Federal had you by the hairs and Marcus was kind of saying, don't underrate him."

"Yeah. Well. Good old Marcus," Kelley said. "And Chambers, I imagine, ate it up with a spoon."

"Well, okay. So did twenty other people. The story got around."

"Apparently."

"So—that's it," Miranda said. "Are there any more questions?"

"One more question. Was Zeedee there?"

"Yes." She tilted her head. "Now can *I* ask a question?"

"Try me."

She put her hand on his cock.

18

THE FLIGHT BACK from Rio landed at Kennedy Airport at ten Friday morning. Miranda had decided to stay on in Rio, a decision reached after Paul DuLac had called and invited them both to have dinner. Kelley wished her luck. She and Paul would be an interesting couple.

On the flight to New York he'd paced around the plane, compulsively wondering what the hell he'd done. The deal with Lester was a double-edged sword and from where he was standing, it was difficult to tell whose throat it would cut.

He'd thought about going directly to the office, but decided the first thing he needed was sleep—a little knitting of the raveled sleeve—and he opened the door to his penthouse apartment thinking only of a bath and a bed.

He dumped his luggage in the chilly hallway and turned to see a tall slim boy in his twenties coming out of the kitchen with a bread knife in his hand.

For a frozen moment they stared at each other. The kid was in a green T-shirt and jeans. He had a cat-burglar body but still, Kelley thought, there was something in the eyes, in the way they peered from under clean blond hair, and something in the mouth, something that seemed to foreshadow sibilance.

Kelley said, "It's not a throwing knife, kiddo, you might as well drop it."

The boy just grinned. "Oh my goodness," he said. Sibilant. "I'm not a *bur*glar, I'm the maid."

"The what?"

"I'm from the Butterfield House Cleaning Service." He didn't seem to know what to do with the knife. "I got the key from a Miss, uh, Washington."

Frannie. Ever-efficient.

Kelley took his coat off. "Okay, what's your name?"

"Lonnie."

"How's it goin' here, Lonnie? The fight against grime.—Can I get in the kitchen?"

"It's wet," the boy said.

"The entire kitchen?"

"The floor. It's been waxed."

"How about the bedroom?"

"It's airing."

"Pardon?"

"The windows are open and the sheets're all stripped."

"I see," Kelley said.

He went into the bedroom and quickly exchanged the contents of his duffle bag. In the study, with the door closed firmly behind him, he opened the locked drawer of his desk, pulled out the tinsel-wrapped box of chocolates and removed the top layer. The two little baggies of grass were intact. He replaced the chocolates, replaced the tinsel, put the box in his briefcase, and left for the field.

One of his classier minor talents was for falling asleep—with lights, music, camera, action, anything at all. Unless it was at night in his own bedroom. Then, on occasion, it could get pretty rough.

With Frannie out to lunch, he took off his jacket and sprawled on the sofa. He had it worked out; he'd smoke a cigarette and then sleep until two.

There was knocking at the door.

Ashe Warner said, "Sorry."

Kelley said, "No. It's fine," and sat up, yawning out smoke. Warner was drinking coffee from a Blue Sky Styrofoam cup. Kelley wanted some coffee. He liked Warner's suit—a glen plaid number with a dark gray shirt and a black silk tie. Shoes so shiny you could see yourself in them. Warner flashed a quick irresistible grin against his Racquet Club tan.

"How'd it go?" Warner said.

"It?"

Warner shrugged. "Things."

"Oh. Those," Kelley said. "So what've the native drummers been saying?"

"You were hunting for money."

"Yeah. Okay. That's a logical guess. It's also a logical guess that I got it."

Warner suddenly grinned. "So you're not saying."

"Hey—I just said. My guess is I got it, but I never count a chicken before it's in the pot.—How's the ad-stuff coming?"

Warner was sitting on the corner of the desk; one of those pictures from a fashion magazine, *Yuppie at Work*. He lifted his shoulders. "I guess I gave your girlfriend a pretty rough time."

"Oh?" Kelley looked at him. "Which one was that?"

"I just meant . . . Miss McCarren." Warner took a breath. "I didn't like the ads, Kelley. If you'd've been here, we could've worked it out."

"So what happened?"

"So the lady worked it out for herself." Warner flickered his grin. "I suppose you've seen the paper."

"The print ads?"

"The advertising column in the *Times*."

"No. I'll look into it."

"Yeah." Warner shrugged. "It doesn't change my opinion, by the way. I want you to know I was acting out of very sincere disagreement."

Kelley nodded. "That's what makes sincere horse-races."

"Yeah. Okay." Warner finished his coffee and crushed the paper cup. "You want to level with me?"

"Sure."

"Should I look for other work?"

"I don't know what you're asking. Do I think we're gonna fold? When? I haven't thought about canning you, Ashe, if that's what you're thinking. Most of the time you're energetic and smart. I just wish you'd be a little less . . ."

"What?"

"I don't know. Whatever you've been too much of," Kelley said.

The word occurred to him a couple of seconds after Warner was gone: ambitious. "Less ambitious," he said to the wall.

"Beg pardon, sir?"

The Whiz Kid, standing at the door. He really did look like a giraffe, Kelley thought—a skinny giant with a fuzzy little thatch and those horse-brown eyes. "You want to come in here and eavesdrop," Kelley said, "I'm just talking to myself."

"Yes sir. I do, sir." The kid loped over and settled in a chair. He was wearing some dusty-looking double-knit slacks; the fly was open. Kelley waited for a time.

"You got something to say to me?"

"Yes sir. I do, sir."

Nothing. The kid watched a movie on the wall. Then suddenly, "The thing is I stopped it all, sir. The stuff with the computer?"

"The *sabotage?*"

"Yes sir."

"Sonofabitch." Kelley looked at him slowly.

Heidigger was almost looking at him now. "I think we better keep it a secret though, sir. Because the way it is now they won't *know* that I stopped it so they won't switch tactics. You see what I'm saying?"

"Roll it back," Kelley said. "Who's they?"

"I don't know, sir. Except for what I said."

"It's a big corporation." Meaning it could either be Federal or Quaid. The same two choices.

"Yes sir."

"Okay. Go on," Kelley said. "And could you not call me 'sir'?"

"Yes sir. It was really awesome, Mr. Kelley. I mean they had this all-out incredible system. Their computer pumped phony names into ours, and not just ours, sir, to travel agents' offices all around the world."

Kelley just nodded. "That's the obvious part. Go on."

"You mean *how* they were doing it, sir? Okay, that's the thing, sir. It really had me stumped. Turned out they had a program with twelve hundred names. Their computer would shuffle them—you see what I'm saying —like the way you'd shuffle cards, so we never saw a pattern."

"Hold it. They were using the *same* phony names?"

"Yes sir. The way I got into it, sir, I asked Duke if he could get me a list of who was flying on the next plane out. This was Saturday morning. You see what I mean? Because once I knew exactly who was flying on the plane—"

"You knew exactly who wasn't."

"Exactly, sir. Yes. So I started to phone 'em. Me and Duke and Frannie and myself. So I tried this guy, he's called Marvin Zlotsky, turns out to be the morgue. Another person didn't show up on that flight was the box office at Shea Stadium. And you know what her name was?"

"Okay," Kelley said. "She was Mrs. O'Shea."

Heidigger stopped with his jaw a little open. "Did you get that from Frannie?"

"No, I got that from the weirdness of my brain. Go on."

"So I put the names in the computer. I said to it, you seen these people before? And bingo. Mrs. Shea—there wasn't any 'O,' sir—Mrs. Shea has been booked with us for two thousand flights. For six months forward, sir, and six months back, which is all we keep the records. So I said to the computer, okay, if you deal with that lady again, automatically erase."

"Jesus. And you did that for twelve hundred names?"

"After I tracked them. Yes sir."

"You're a fucking genius, Bernard."

"Yes sir."

Kelley looked up at the window. What he knew at this moment was two major things. He'd been sabotaged at least going back for six months . . . and with the sabotage gone, he had a chance at the future. He turned to the kid. "Bernard," he said slowly, "gonna write you a bonus, but I'd like you to think about two other things. See if you can get me the proof of who did it—okay?"

The kid nodded. "I'll try, sir. And what was the other thing, sir?"

"Oh." Kelley nodded. "Zip up your fly."

McDermott was out but his ledgers told everything Kelley had to know. The hex was gone. The operating losses, for the last two days, had been falling with the certainty of Newton's apple. If it kept on going, in a couple of days he could start to break even—at least on a daily operational chart. Credit Heidigger for banishing the ghosts. And possibly Claire. . . .

He bought the *Times* at the terminal newsstand and took it with him to the Sky Captain's Lounge, a coffee shop affectedly papering its walls with photographs of Major Moments in Flight. He sat in a crowded little booth in the corner right beneath a poster of *Amelia Earhart, The Woman Who Flew the Atlantic Alone*.

He ordered what he always ordered—a beer and a burger—and opened the paper, preparing to skim it for the advertising column, but the thing that stopped him was the page-three story: WIND-SHEAR DOWNS 727. It had happened in New Orleans. Thirty-six dead and twenty-two injured.

He lit a cigarette.

The airline that crashed was one he'd approached about the wind-shear detector but they didn't want to buy. It was too expensive and they really didn't need it. And, practically speaking, it didn't make sense. Their insurance would pay for the three dozen deaths, but the cost of detectors would come from their till.

He thought about ordering a triple Cutty and really getting clobbered, but decided against it; he turned some more pages till he got to the line MORE DASH THAN CASH, and continued to read:

Blue Sky Airlines, fighting for its life, is putting on a classy heavyweight fight staged by the hitherto lightweight agency, CMI, the agency headed by Claire McCarren. The ad that had people talking all week ("There's An Air War Going On; If They Win, You Lose") was only the kicker in a stylish campaign that continues to agitate for public support. "The Air War Continues. Take a Stand. Buy a Seat." "In War, All's Fare." It's a hard-hitting message Ms. McCarren is pushing. The question remains, is it coming too late— or will Blue Sky Airlines be saved by the belle?

He looked up, grinning, and thought, That's my girl.

He thought about the phone calls she hadn't returned and thought, Or possibly Tom Cubbitt's girl.

Or possibly nobody's girl but her own.

"How 'bout that?" Frannie said, sliding into the booth. "Want to spring for some coffee?"

"I'll spring for a lunch."

"Sport," she said. "Sorry, but I've already eaten. How was Rio?"

He told her.

She didn't look happy. "I don't know," she said. "I started to think about it, Kelley. I was thinking, that whole bit with the computer—who is that helping? And I figured it's Quaid."

"Doesn't matter," Kelley said. "That's his problem now. If he thinks he bought a sure-thing bet for his money"—he shrugged—"too bad. What matters to me is the forty million bucks."

She nodded. "I know.—Mr. Barron of Araco Fuel called this morning. To remind you of the bill? He also called you several indelicate names."

"Shock me."

"A slick unscrupulous bastard?"

"Okay. That's fair." Kelley smiled. "But I said I'd pay him in another ten days and he'll get it."

"Can I tell that to Parke-Bernet? Your wife bought a twenty-eight-thousand-dollar lamp."

"*What?*"

"I got the bill today. Tiffany lamp."

"Nice."

"She doesn't know you're off salary?"

"Shit," Kelley said. "Even if she did she wouldn't make the connection. Go on. What else?"

"Claire's in California recording some commercials."

"Oh?"

"She's coming back on the eight-o'clock flight."

"Which reminds me," Kelley said. "Get the Beagle fueled up. Rent me a car at the Saranac Airport and a cabin at the Lodge."

"Going skiing?" Frannie said.

"Among other things, yes." He looked at her. "I want to see Charlie," he said.

He waited at the gate, checking his watch like any other amateur waiter-at-the-gate. The plane from California was listed On Time. It was two, then three, then four minutes late, and then the first of the passengers streamed through the door, half of them wearing California tans and coats too light for the Northeastern chill. He spotted Claire in her dark mink coat, untanned and urban. Way better-looking than anybody else. He waved; she waved back at him and moved to him quickly, smiling.

No words. She was in his arms. He felt fur, smelled perfume. He held her hard and closed his eyes when they kissed; they could have been anywhere.

"Hey." She was laughing.

"What?"

"We're in a crowd."

"I missed you."

"Mmm hmmm." A little sarcasm there.

He pulled back and looked at her. "What's with 'mmm hmmm'?"

"Nothing." She shrugged.

He picked up the suitcase she'd dropped on the floor. "You got any other bags?"

"Just that," she said.

"Good." He was heading through the crowd. "How long were you away?"

"Since yesterday morning."

"Uh huh."

She looked up at him, green eyes steady. "So what's with 'uh huh'?"

"Well I'll tell you," he said, "I'll explain my 'uh huh' if you'll explain your 'mmm hmm.'"

She laughed then and suddenly kissed him on the cheek. "Deal's off," she said.

"Come on now. Don't mess around. I'm leaving for Saranac in twenty-five minutes."

She stopped. "I've got a lot to talk to you about."

"Good. Then come with me."

"Now?"

"Why not? You're at the airport, you have a toothbrush. What else do you need?"

She said nothing for a moment.

"I called you," he said. "Late, I admit. Drunk, I admit. But I also called you early and straight the next day."

She nodded. "I know. And I called you right back. And a sleepy-sounding lady was yawning at your phone."

"Oh," he said slowly.

"I guessed it was Karen so I didn't leave a message."

"No," he said, grinning. "That was no wife, that was a lady. She's a very good friend—"

"You don't owe me explanations."

"Yes," he said. "I do."

"I don't want any then. It has nothing at all to do with you and me."

"Exactly," he said.

"And what *I* do has nothing to do with you and me."

They were standing at the door to the outlying field. "I like that," he said. "I do. I really like that attitude a lot, except why do I hate it?"

She shrugged at him. "You can't have everything, pal."

"Pal. You coming with me to Saranac, pal?"

She looked at him, tilting her head to the side. "Why? Because I'm here and have a toothbrush?"

"No," he said, "and don't go tough on me, Claire. I've had all the little hard-baked cookies in the world. I expect something of you and I expect you to expect something of me. Otherwise there's a whole airport full of girls with toothbrushes—pal—and you'd be surprised at how easy I can take it or leave it. Start again: do you want to come with me or not?"

She nodded slowly.

He loved the way she looked at the plane and then giggled, "It's Daffy Duck."

"It's a beagle," he said, "it's called a Beagle. See the eyes?" He pointed at the down-sloping cockpit windows.

"No. That's a duck bill." She pointed at the nose.

"That's a snout."

Inside, she looked around at the leather upholstery, the way he'd had it done, like a flying living room, two facing couches and the two big chairs. "There's a bar over there and a stereo," he said. "Raid the icebox if you're hungry. Walk around. You don't have to stay up in the cockpit."

"I don't?"

"Except during take-off," he said. "If there's funny noises and I start to get scared, you could squeeze my hand."

Up in the sky again, in the driver's seat, stars, moon, music, Claire, away from the eternal gravity of the ground; things looking up. For the first time in weeks, months, maybe years, he felt lucky and good. And then something else. He felt he stood a chance of being happy on the ground. Actually happy. Possibly at home.

Claire came back from the cabin with some Cokes.

"You said you had a lot to talk to me about." He reached for the glass.

"It can wait," she said, sitting, looking out the huge windows at the night. "I remember you're the guy who throws people out of windows."

"With a parachute," he said. "I am not a cruel man. You want to tell me what's the subject?"

She looked at him. "How I Spent Sixty Thousand Dollars of Your Money."

"Oh," he said slowly. "You buy any lamps?"

"Lamps?"

"Never mind. You did some radio commercials. You bought the rights to a song and Ashe Warner's having a major coronary."

"Oh. Then I guess you know all about it."

"No. I know you got the money from McDermott and you told him you had my approval on the stuff, so I couldn't exactly ask him, On what? So I just said, Yeah, I think it's really terrific."

"I asked you," she said, "to look at the stuff and you said you didn't need to, and I had to act fast because Stallone—"

"Stallone?"

She nodded. "Old Sly himself just did your commercial."

"Rocky."

"Rocky. Singing and dancing."

"On radio?"

"Well . . . so I lied about the dancing."

"Can I hear it?"

"Sure. Got a reel-to-reel recorder?"

"On board? No."

"Then I guess it has to wait."

He was silent for a while. "You really got Stallone?"

"I really got Stallone." She paused. "And Billy Martin and Sugar Ray Leonard and Muhammad Ali. And yes—really."

He looked at her, squinting. "How about Michael Jackson, Frank Sinatra, and Wyatt Earp?"

"That's next week," she said. "I just started. Give me time."

19

THE AFTERNOON WAS everything it should be, bright and cold, sun glinting off the snow, ice forming patterns like frozen lace on the branches of the trees.

Driving to the farm with music in the car, on a country road that was hilly and curved, passing frozen ponds, and clusters of fir trees and bare-branched maples, Kelley, putting speed on, felt himself catapulting back into time and away from the edge of his own very sweet and newfound contentment. The night had warmed him, awakened him again to new possibilities, his own long winter was turning into spring; he was getting, he felt, younger by the minute. He wondered if Charlie had felt that with Margaret. Tina, then Margaret. (Karen, then Claire.) Life beginning whenever it damn well decides to begin, making you eat your spinach before you get your dessert. . . . And then suddenly ripping the tablecloth away, and all the dishes get scattered on the floor.

As he reached the top of a snow-covered hill, there was an abrupt clearing in the woods and he could see, towards the left, the bright red barn against the snow-white field, and beyond it, the farmhouse, the Strykers' retreat. There was smoke coming from the chimneys and rising up over the cluster of fir trees surrounding the house. Charlie had bought the place in the seventies. "For my old age," he'd said.

Kelley pulled up at the side of the house, a sprawling 1860's clapboard with barn-red shutters and a big front porch.

He heard the sound of guitar music, plaintive and twanging, coming from the house. When Margaret opened the door, looking thinner but genuinely pleased to see him, he caught the delicious aromas from the kitchen, the mingling essence of roasting turkey and baking pie.

They embraced and she held him just a little too tight for just a second too long, and he knew things were probably worse than he'd thought.

She pulled back and smiled. Margaret had never been a physical knockout but her looks knocked him out—a sculptured face with a forthright intelligence and warmth in the eyes. Her long dark hair was twisted in a single braid down her back and her tall slim body looked regal even in a fisherman's sweater and an old pair of jeans.

"Well," she said, sighing, "I don't have to tell you how good it is to see you. Now come and see Charlie." Her tone remained bright.

They passed by a den where Charlie Junior was playing the guitar. The resemblance to his father verged on uncanny—a strapping twelve-year-old with bright red hair. He looked up and waved with the old "Hi, Green," and Kelley answered with the old "Hi, Red."

Old, Kelley thought. Five years ago, this kid had been seven. And fourteen years ago Margaret walked into the Blue Sky office, just out of college and looking for a job.

He followed her into the master bedroom. Charlie was sitting in a chair by the fire with a bright yellow afghan over his lap, and Kelley felt his own eyes narrow with pain.

Most of the bright red hair was now gone. And most

of that solidly muscular frame. Charlie, who was forty-three, looked sixty—balding and frail—and Kelley felt helpless and furious about it.

"How's it goin'?" he said.

"Just about how it looks."

It was hot in the room with a fire in the fireplace and a space heater going. Kelley took his jacket off and pulled up a rocker.

"No chemotherapy today," Charlie said. "I don't think it's the fucking cancer that kills you, I think it's the fucking chemical shit."

"That'll end," Kelley said.

"One way or the other."

Kelley said, "Shit."

Margaret said, "How about a drink or some tea? Or some hot chocolate? How about that? With melted marshmallows swimming on the top."

"Why be a ninety-pound weakling?" Charlie said. "Drink Bosco.—You ever drink Bosco as a kid?"

"Corn liquor," Kelley said.

Margaret went off.

"How's life?" Charlie said.

"Mine? Or in general?"

"In general. Tell me what it feels like to live."

"Worth the trouble," Kelley said.

"I know, man, I know."

"Better than I do."

"True," Charlie said.

They stared at the fire.

Kelley started talking. First about Claire, and then about the airline—the end of the sabotage, the bail-out from Quaid.

"So we're clear until June then."

"If Lester comes through."

"And we'll cross the next mountain when we get to it, right?"

"A sensible policy." Margaret came back with a wicker tray holding large brown mugs. "Our son," she said to Charlie, "has just gone to Annabell Norton's 'to study.' Does that strike you as intriguing?"

"Christ," Charlie laughed. "My son has developed a precocious interest in algebra, it seems."

"Weren't you interested in algebra at twelve?" Kelley picked up a mug.

"No," Charlie said. "I don't think I got interested in algebra till a girl sat next to me at a baseball game and put her hand on my crotch. I was fifteen, maybe. Christ, kids today, I think they're *born* at fifteen."

Margaret sat at Charlie's feet on a pillow and stoked at the fire.

"So now," Charlie said, "we've got a ten-year-old drunkard and a six-year-old"—he looked down at Margaret—"what do you imagine Rebecca's been doing?"

"Fornicating, counterfeiting . . ."

Kelley turned to Charlie. "Okay, what's the joke?"

"Tell it to him, Maggie, will you? I'm tired."

She frowned at him.

"Of telling the story," Charlie said. "Go on."

"We've got a new county sheriff," Margaret said. "Man named McGinty. He ran on a platform of 'Let's Keep It Clean.' He's afraid this county, with all the ski lodges and all the 'foreigners,' as he calls anyone who wasn't born in these woods, is gonna turn this place into Sodom and Gomorrah. Well, okay. So he pulled a few drug raids on a couple of bars and the county applauded but it doesn't stop there. He arrested a couple of kids for smoking in the bathroom of the public library. He arrested a couple of grown-ups for screwing in a car by the lake. I hasten to add there was no one around them for forty-three miles. And we know those people. That was Georgia and Ed. They've been married twenty years and they thought it would be silly and fun just to do it, but McGinty doesn't know about silly or fun. You see where it's going?"

"And then," Charlie said, "he arrested our son."

"Billy," Margaret said.

"Billy the Kid," Charlie added. "Billy took a can of beer from the house. He wanted to know what it tasted like and so did a friend of his, so they took it to the woods."

"And got busted," Margaret said. "Can you imagine it? I had to go to court and explain that we didn't keep our beer in the vault and that boys will be boys, but Sheriff McGinty's got his eye on us now. We're also, you understand, 'downstate radicals,' whatever that means. I've never been entirely *sure* what it means, except we come from Manhattan and therefore are capable of every other vice. Maybe we'll open a bordello in the barn or overthrow the government. McGinty isn't sure. Was it Dickens who said it?—'the law is an ass'?"

They talked about the rest of the Stryker children— Becky, who wanted to be an actress or an astronaut, she wasn't sure which; Billy, who'd very reasonably decided he couldn't yet decide, and Charlie Junior, who'd been born air-struck and had to be a pilot and, after that, the next wave of Blue Sky management.

Sipping the warm sweet stuff in the mug, Kelley thought there wouldn't be a new wave of Kelleys, and maybe there wouldn't be an old wave of Strykers, but there would—he could feel it—there would be a Blue Sky.

Stryker looked drained. Margaret got up—to baste the turkey, she said—and gave Kelley a quick little cue with her eyes.

When Margaret had gone, Kelley said, "I brought you a present. Don't move. It's in the car."

On the way down the path, crunching on the snow,

he thought about the hotshot Sheriff McGinty and the "downstate radicals," and Billy the Kid.

Opening the glove box, taking out the tinsel-wrapped gift box of chocolates, he thought about the risks of holding weed in New York. Up to eight ounces was a year in the slammer or a thousand-dollar fine. No judge in the world would put Charlie in jail, but with over eight ounces, the charge went from misdemeanor to felony and that could get tricky. So the answer was to split the little bundle in half. Besides, eight ounces was a lot of cigarettes and a lot of antidote for chemotherapy. When Charlie needed more, well . . . Kelley knew the way.

He opened the box, removed one baggie from underneath the candy—the one he'd opened and smoked from before—and shoved it in the glove box.

Margaret was still in the kitchen on the phone. Kelley said to Charlie, "Sweets to the sweet," and tossed a deck of rolling-papers on the box.

"Oh my God," Charlie said. "You did it. You're saving my life. It's the only thing that stops me from heaving my guts."

"I know," Kelley said. "And the law is an ass. But be careful, okay?" He'd remained standing.

Stryker looked up at him through heavy-lidded eyes. "I take it you're leaving?"

"Got a girl with me, Charlie."

"*The* girl."

"*The* girl. And I'd like—I'd really love to bring her over tomorrow, so you'll think about it, Charlie. You'll take two joints and you'll call me in the morning."

The High Point Lodge was on the crest of a hill, surrounded by trees that clung to the hillside as it dropped at a dizzying angle to the lake. The lake was frozen and glittered slightly in the afternoon sun.

Kelley had picked it because it was unpretentious and

rustic; a lot of the furniture, he knew, was antique and the food was superb and the prices, since he'd first discovered the place in the early seventies, had nearly quintupled. Still, it was a lodge—a place where people came to ski and not simply to be seen skiing, a place of roaring fires in oversize hearths, where the bar was run on the honor system till after dinner, and the nighttime music was a jazz piano, occasionally amplified with vibes and a bass.

He looked for Claire in the bar, the restaurant, and finally the big lounge off the lobby, where he saw the owner, a man about sixty with a taut skier's body and a weather-broken face. "You're lookin' for the lady," he said, "she's up top."

Kelley went back to the cabin and changed, got his skis from the ski room, and drove to the lift. He looked above him, on the high white ridge, and spotted her quickly in the copper-colored ski suit he'd bought her this morning. She was skiing down the mountain, making swift precise turns as she cut through the powder. Facing the sun, he cupped his eyes and watched her as she moved with confidence and grace and then came to a short neat stop about ten feet away from him.

"I'm dazzled," he said. "You can really cut it. You want to have a beer or go back to the top?"

She peeled off the ski cap and shook out her hair; her cheeks looked as though they'd been burnished by the wind; she was absolutely glowing.

"I don't know," she said. "I don't know about skiing with you. I don't think I'm your speed."

"How do you know what my speed is?"

She was slightly out of breath. "Based on the few other things I've seen you do, I'd guess it was—"

"Watch it," he said, "you say fast—"

She laughed. "Expert. Awe-inspiring."

"Ah. Then let's go."

He took her on an easy run to begin with, a trail called Surefoot. She was sure and skillful. He put on speed and she followed him with ease.

Then he tried another, more difficult run, took it three-quarter speed and again she kept up with him, staying on his heels, flying with him.

They made three more runs and then Kelley said, "There's one around here called Downfall." Claire shook her head. "I wouldn't try it."

"I wouldn't let you," he said.

From the top of the hill, he saw her down below, bright as a penny sparkling in the snow. He looked down at the trail—a nearly straight drop about four hundred feet and then a sharp turn right. He took a breath, and then skated off the curve of the hill, and then schussed with the wind beating on his face, biting him, letting him know he was alive, free and flying down the powdery hill.

He kept thinking of luck, lying beside her in the bed in the cabin with the fire crackling in the stone hearth and the snow falling softly outside the window.

Luck, subdivided into Time and Chance. (If Rosetti hadn't quit, if I hadn't gone to Zeedee's, if Claire had never met Cubbitt, who'd brought her, or further, if Cubbitt had never met Zeedee.) Things in their infinite randomness collide—

Or not.

It was all a kaleidoscope, wasn't it? Patterns form and dissolve in an instant. Claire and the bed and the room and the fire and the temporary lull in the ongoing battle were simply another of the random displays. You could put up a sign, DO NOT TOUCH, LEAVE THIS PATTERN, but the chances of the universe listening to that . . .

She stirred beside him, her eyes on his face, lovingly. "What are you thinking?" she said.

"That a live butterfly's sitting in my hand and I don't want to move."

"I see. You want to starve the butterfly to death?"

"It's true," he said. "Women are the practical gender."

He got up and crossed the cabin, went into the small kitchen for the tray of hors d'oeuvres that was left by the management, daily, in the icebox, and brought it back to bed. "Will that hold you for a while?"

He watched her attack the food with a particularly joyous gusto, and got back into the bed, pulling up the covers and leaning on his elbow.

"Want some?" she said.

Kelley shook his head.

"Still think you've got a butterfly?"

"Sure. Standard process of metamorphosis. Caterpillar turns into a butterfly, butterfly turns into a pig."

She giggled and pelted him with shrimp.

He nodded. "You want to have a food fight?"

"No." She giggled harder, "No, I don't think so," and hit him with a cheese ball.

"Watch it," he said. "I am slow to anger, but my wrath is tremendous." He picked up a cracker with some caviar on it and menaced her with it. "On your nose," he said flatly, and got hit with pâté. "That does it. You're in major trouble, little girl."

"I'll tell Mommy."

"Too late." He divebombed the caviar onto her nipple. "Jesus, I don't want to waste that," he said, and licked it all off, while she heaved with giggles. "You surrender?" he asked.

"Absolutely and completely."

"And forever?"

"And forever."

"Till death do us part?"

She looked at him soberly. "What are you saying?"

"I imagine I'm saying, will you be my old lady?"

Her look turned wary. "Define 'old lady.'"

"Wattled. Wrinkled. Brown-spotted—"

"Yuck."

"Don't 'yuck' me. You're speaking of the woman I love."

"Oh."

She was silent for such a long time that Kelley said, "Forget it. It was just an idea."

"A fleeting notion, is that what it was?"

"No."

"Then I think we've got a serious problem," she said. "I hate to bring it up, but it's known as 'you're married.' Unless that wasn't a proposal, of course, but just a kind of very long-range proposition."

"Uh uh. We have to get married," he said. "Don't we?"

"I think so."

"That's what I thought." He started messing around with her hair. "How about your kid?"

"Mark?" she said. "You were made for each other."

He nodded. "And how about making some more?"

"Kids?"

"Uh huh."

She smiled. "I was terrified I wouldn't get the chance."

"Shit. I can give you maybe six, maybe seven hundred chances a month. But I have to tell you something. Karen's gonna put me through the wringer for a while. She'll go for a couple of million bucks and every headline she can get. And I don't want to start that roller-coaster ride until the airline's on its feet."

"So what are you saying? We have to sneak around?"

"Comes down to it," he said, "we can do some remarkably classy sneaking. I don't know if it matters. What I'm saying is, I don't want to start with divorce proceedings till we get to the summer. Till I've paid off the first installment to Lester and done a little juggling. Otherwise she'll tie up assets I need. I can't have her killing the airline."

"I know."

"It's urgent to me, Claire."

"I know that too."

"I want you to know how urgent it is. I think it's my life. I don't know what I am without it. I don't know who I'd be."

"Don't you?" She sat up, facing him, hugging her legs, her tilted head resting on her knees, looking up at him from under that thatch of brown hair. "I mean think about it. Really. If everything fizzled, what would you do?"

"I don't know." He looked away from her and stared at the fire. "Start again, I suppose. I've still got my first Dakota in mothballs. But I don't know, Claire. I don't know if I'm too old to be small-time again." He shrugged. "But it's not gonna happen like that. I've got the money from Quaid. I can see my way out." He looked up at her and grinned. "And I think I'm getting hungry."

"You want to go to dinner?"

"Later," he said.

They drove back from dinner on a back road with the car radio on, the moon bright enough to read by, the snow glistening, the pine trees tipped with it, a forest of Christmas trees shining in the night. He felt reverent, he wanted to sing a few carols . . . "silent . . . holy." He was mellow and bright and wondered rather fuzzily if those were the words . . . "May your days be mellow and bright," he said aloud, and Claire said, "You're drunk."

"On you," he said. "Yes."

Her head was on his shoulder; she was champagne-happy, drowsy, cozy, as mellow as he.

There was a faint, very high hum in the air, the sound, he thought, of a fast wind, or the night singing back, or the wail of the less-happy lovers in the world. He turned up the radio, drowning them out.

The road was curving and his headlights picked up the trunks of the trees, caught the wide-eyed face of a startled doe who froze and then ran. And then suddenly the wail was too technical to doubt. He saw the cop-car roaring up behind him and indulged in the stupidest reflex of his life. He stepped on the pedal.

Claire came fully awake and sat up. She looked at him quickly, looked in the mirror and turned off the radio.

"You're crazy," she said.

"You're right." He slowed down and began to pull over. "One thing," he said quickly. "You never heard of Charlie Stryker in your life."

She looked at him quizzically. He lit a cigarette while the big heavy cop lumbered over to the window. A flashlight beam hit Kelley in the eyes and then traveled to Claire. Kelley saw the sheriff's badge on the jacket and the name-tag, McGinty.

"Okay, where's the fire?" McGinty said flatly.

Kelley said nothing, but apparently McGinty was a literal man. He wanted to know where the fire was and repeated the question.

"If there was one," Kelley said, "I wouldn't get there in time. I was only doing fifty."

"In a forty-mile zone."

"I didn't know that."

"Uh huh. So you're blind," McGinty said. "We got signs all around. Then we get deaf because you didn't hear the siren."

"The radio was on."

"Let me look at your license. See if it tells me how you're blind and deaf."

Kelley gave him the license. McGinty looked it over

with the aid of the flashlight, nodding disapproval. "You're city-folks, right? You come to the country, bring your anarchy with you, is that the way it goes?"

Kelley said nothing.

"Let's see your registration."

"It's a rental."

"Then let's see the papers."

Oh shit, Kelley thought. He looked through his wallet. He played that game about as long as he could and then shrugged and said, "I must have left them in the room."

McGinty glared at him. "Out," he said. "Now. Keep your hands nice and easy, get up against the—"

"Oh for God's sakes," Claire bristled. "I saw them in the glove box," and before he could alert her she'd punched on the button and McGinty's little flashlight was shining on the spot—on the neat little baggie with the French maryjane.

20

THE NIGHT TURNED into nightmare: busted, printed, booked. Watching helplessly as Claire was booked too, and then taken away. He used his phone call to call Ab Wagner, his lawyer, in New York. Ab listened quietly. "Jesus," he said. "Keep your mouth shut. I'll charter a plane and come up."

The local reporters started filtering in at a little after midnight, asking their legally unanswerable questions, but free to aim their cameras and lights through the bars. Cornered, Kelley had only one of two choices. He could look them in the eyes or appear to be cringing. He chose to do neither. He sprawled on the bunk, lit a cigarette, and opened a copy of *Sports Illustrated* that some other occupant had left in the cell. A photographer chortled, "The laid-back Kelley," and Kelley could imagine it captioning the picture. The story, he knew, would be everywhere tomorrow, in Sunday morning papers all around the world. This lousy joke. This head-on collision of time and place. And Claire, caught neatly in the crosshairs, he thought; he was thinking of Claire while they snapped his picture reading "College Football: What Lies Ahead?"

The arraignment was held on Monday at noon. Ab had brought a razor but the sheriff had opted not to let Kelley use it, on the plausible theory that he'd slit his own throat with a cordless Norelco; so there he was looking ominously dark and vaguely barbarian, which clearly had been Sheriff McGinty's intention.

He saw Claire for the first time in the small county courtroom that was packed with reporters. His eye cased the crowd, catching Cubbitt and Zeedee, the two blond playboys shining in the gloom. And how in the hell did they get there? he wondered. Had Claire called Cubbitt?

He turned back to Claire. Ab sat between them at the long oak table reserved for the defense—Ab, looking spiffy in a gray flannel suit, his white hair smoother than a pigeon's breast. Kelley leaned across him and grabbed Claire's hand and reporters started scribbling.

"Forgive me," he said.

"It's my own stupid fault for opening—"

"Don't be silly."

"My father's here."

"Where?" He followed her glance to a man who looked just about the way she'd described him—a big bear-y man with blond-and-white hair and a stolid expression. He was staring at Kelley with hooded green eyes under pale heavy brows.

"I called him," she said. "I just couldn't bear for him to hear it on the news, but I didn't know he'd come here."

The judge called for order.

"You understand," Ab whispered, "this is only an arraignment. What happens—"

"Just get Claire free," Kelley said.

"You've told me." Ab nodded. "And I told *you* to be cool with each other. Like no playing kissy-face or grab-hand, right? The story has to be she was up here on business or the law takes for granted that the dope was half hers."

Both Claire and Kelley had been charged with a hard Class A misdemeanor, Possession of Narcotics.

Ab pleaded not guilty for both and then went into conference with the judge and D.A.

Kelley walked out to the scrofulous hallway and had a cigarette; he was still under guard. Ab had told him to stay away from Claire, and further admitted it was he who called Cubbitt. "Let him play The Actual Boyfriend," he said.

Claire was standing with her father and Cubbitt, who tried to look Actual, his hand on her arm. Then Claire and Cubbitt were talking alone and her father was standing with his back against the wall, his arms across his chest, staring darkly at Kelley.

Kelley met the eyes levelly, trying to put into his own steady gaze all the now and forever inadequate apology.

The city papers had the story, page one. From the almost stately KELLEY AND COMPANION ARRESTED ON DRUG CHARGE to KELLEY, SKY HIGH, BUSTED FOR DOPE, with the subhead LOVENEST ENDS IN THE ARMS OF THE LAW. The same article referred to Karen as "the grass widow."

Karen had telephoned early in the morning and commented simply, "I hope you don't expect me to fly up to Iceland and sing a little chorus of 'Stand by Your Man.' My God, it's only grass."

Kelley said, " 'Only.' I'll tell it to the judge."

A bailiff was poking him sharply on the arm. They went back into the courtroom.

The charge against Claire had been dropped, completely; not even a fine. She was merely a business associate with no prior record, and by opening the glove box she'd proved, "de facto," that she hadn't any previous knowledge of the cache. Kelley was given a lecture by the judge, from which he extracted the memorable phrases "jet-set junkie," and "overage hippie," but the case itself was concluded with the maximum thousand-dollar fine plus fifty for the speeding.

Kelley went to shave in the courthouse men's room with Ab at his side.

"You're lucky," Ab said. "You had two things going. The D.A. doesn't want to hang you for grass because it's bad for the local ski-business here. And then you've got the thing about the judge's mother."

Kelley turned the razor off. "Do that again?"

"She flies Blue Sky. From Albany to Florida once every year. He told me about it. In glowing detail. He doesn't like jet-set junkies a bit, but *cut*-rate jets . . . now that's something else. He told me he's aware that a trial, at the moment, could finish Blue Sky, and forget about you, it would cost his mommy an extra four bills." Ab hung his jacket on the hook behind the door, turned up his shirt cuffs and splashed a little ice-cold water on his face. "Clean," Ab said. "If you don't get busted in the next twelve months, and I'm assuming you won't, you don't even have a record."

There were no towels. There was only one of those hot-air machines. "Goddammit," Ab said. "I'm supposed to hold my face under fucking machines?"

"Relax," Kelley said. "I'm gonna buy you a couple of chinchilla towels."

"Yeah, and you only think you're kidding," Ab laughed. "Next week you get the bill."

The reporters attacked them, beginning in the men's room and moving down the hall.

"Would you give us a statement, Mr. Kelley? A statement?" *"Hey, Burke—are you smoking it more and enjoying it less?"* *"What kind of 'work' were you doing with the girl?"* *"Nice work if you can get it, is that how it goes?"*

Kelley said nothing.

The reporters followed him out through the door and into the cold, brisk morning air. Claire was also surrounded by the press and flanked by her father and the glowering Cubbitt.

Zeedee had wandered up to Kelley and Ab. "I think I belong with the groom's side here."

Kelley looked at him flatly.

The cameras flashed.

Cubbitt broke away from Claire and her father and strode up to Kelley; he was punching his fist. "You sonofabitch," he said clearly through teeth.

Kelley said nothing; he kept on moving.

"You stupid prick."

Kelley still said nothing. The cameras clicked, taking everything in.

"I ought to kill you," Cubbitt said.

"Hey, look, you want to fight," Kelley kept his voice low, "we don't have to do it in the papers, okay?"

"I'll do it anywhere I want."

"Then how about pistols by the river at dawn, only cool it right now."

They converged on the car—a stretch limo with curtained windows that was waiting at the curb. Kelley and Ab got in front with the driver, a uniformed Asian who looked straight ahead, while everybody else piled into the rear with Zeedee in the jump seat. The car took off, screeching from the curb as though it were moving from the scene of a heist.

There was silence for a time.

"Hey, nice day for a funeral," Zeedee said, toying with the curtain. "You start to get the feeling we're riding in the hearse?"

No one said anything.

Zeedee said, "The mood in this place is like death. You got *away* with it, bozos. You ought to be laughing

215

your fool heads off. And *you*," he turned to Cubbitt, "were absolutely brilliant. Brilliant! Let's hear it for Tom Cuckold, the misspent knight."

"Knock it off," Kelley said. "Why the hell are you here?"

"I was asked," Zeedee said. "I was having another soiree last night. Tom was pretty loaded. Your lawyer calls up. Tom says 'Wha-wha-wha' to the phone. I had to pour him on the plane. And besides, I was dying of hot curiosity."

"You don't button up," Cubbitt said, "you could die of something else."

"Shit," Zeedee laughed. "Everybody in this car wants to punch out everybody else in this car so you make me the scapegoat. Up all your asses."

"*Son.*" Claire's father had a voice like a sergeant. "I was you, I'd be quiet."

Zeedee was quiet. Kelley had to turn and see it for himself: Claire's father, Ed Johnson, sitting easy in his two-hundred-thirty-pound frame, looking "Watch it" at Zeedee.

Claire met his eyes.

Kelley said, "Quiet little weekend in the country."

Claire started laughing.

Cubbitt said, "You think this is some kind of joke?"

Kelley said, "A really lousy idea, Ab. Having us all ride off in one car."

"One happy family," Ab said dryly. "I mistakenly thought it was good p.r."

"The only *good* p.r. is a dead p.r.," Zeedee said absently.

"Shit!" Cubbitt said.

The car made the turnoff and headed for the lodge.

"You're right," Ab said. "I feel like I'm locked in a phone booth with an entire kindergarten class. Now listen to me, kiddies. When we get to the lodge, I think Claire stays in the car. Possibly her father can do all the packing." He looked up at Kelley. "She has her own room?"

"Oh yeah," Kelley nodded.

"And of course she'll fly back to the city alone."

"With me," Cubbitt told him.

"Whatever," Ab said.

Cubbitt leaned forward. "There's one thing I want." He grabbed Kelley's shoulder. "I want you to make a statement to the press. I want *you* to tell them she was here on business."

The limo had stopped.

"Get your hand off me, Tom."

"Will you stop it?" Claire said. "Will everybody stop?"

Kelley opened the door now and stood on the path. There was snow underfoot and a good cold wind coming in off the hill. The cars with the reporters were still on the ridge, he could see them above. With a forty-second lead, he used up a second to take in a good deep breath of the air.

"I want you to give them a statement," Cubbitt said. Cubbitt was moving from the back of the car.

Kelley said, "Don't be an idiot, Tom." Claire's father had also gotten out of the car. Kelley started walking up the path to the cabin. He heard the rapid footsteps behind him and turned, too slowly, and right into Cubbitt's rampaging fist.

The blow sent him spiraling backward to the ground, as much from the lack of traction on the snow as from the power of the punch. He could taste his own blood; and there were the reporters, cameras extended out of Chevrolet windows, a few of them already coming at a trot.

Kelley got up, knowing that everything now was for the record.

Claire's father moved forward. "Are you gonna hit him back?"

"Someday," Kelley said. "Maybe in the great school-yard in the sky." He turned and moved quickly to the door of the cabin, the reporters closing in.

"I want to have a talk with you," Ed Johnson said.

"Hey, Kelley," a reporter raced to the path. "Ain't you gonna show us your Sunday punch?"

Cubbitt was standing there red-faced and pouting. "Ask him," Cubbitt said. "Ask him for a statement."

Kelley put his key in the door to the cabin; with the cameras clicking, the reporters literally breathing down his neck, he got in through the doorway with Johnson ahead of him.

The drapes had been drawn. They faced each other in the darkened room.

Johnson said, "You better take care of your face."

"You want a drink . . ." Kelley said, and pointed at the bar.

In the bathroom, he checked the damage to his mouth. There was a lot of blood coming from a gash inside that seemed to have been made by his own sharp tooth. Talk about biting the mouth that feeds you. He rinsed and spat till he stopped spitting blood.

Johnson was sitting in the big wing chair by the cold hearth, a Scotch in his hand, looking a little trapped in his neat brown suit. He'd brought the bottle and a glass to the table. Kelley poured a shot and sipped at it, feeling its medicinal sting, while Johnson watched him.

"I want to tell you I've had it in my mind," Johnson said, "to tear you limb from limb."

"Is that all?" Kelley asked.

"Looks like I gotta stand on line though, to do it." Johnson shook his head. "That Cubbitt fella looked like a bigger fool'n you."

"The papers won't think so. They'll make him a hero."

"I don't think we got us any heroes here today."

They both sipped their Scotch.

"I don't imagine it helps," Kelley said, "but I love her very much. I think we got caught in a freak accident, like getting hit by lightning."

"I see. Like you're telling me it isn't your fault."

"No."

"Good."

They were silent again. Johnson got up and paced to the window. "You want to tell the reason you had so much dope?"

Kelley shook his head.

"Good," Johnson said. "You have a certain dignity about you, I'll say that much for you. And you look at my daughter like a man who's in love, which speaks something for your taste. She tells me the reason you were totin' that stuff, and it passes for decent by a human measure. It's proper that a man should take a risk for his friend, but it's *not* proper he involves my daughter in the risk. And my grandson too. Because my grandson's involved."

Kelley said nothing.

"This 'lovenest' thing." Johnson shook his head. "I've been lookin' real careful at the two of you fellas. This Cubbitt, with his asshole friend from the city, and I tell you, I'd be happy to throttle you both. But I guess I have to reckon Claire's a big girl and it's the twenty-first century or whatever the hell. But you bein' married, that's two too much. So I ask you, as a father, you plan to keep draggin' her name through the news?"

"No," Kelley said.

"You plan to not see her?"

"No," Kelley said.

"Well now, it seems to me it's one or the other. What I think is, that story that your lawyer was tellin', the one about Claire comin' up here to work. I don't know how many fools'll believe that story, but back home in

Kansas we might have a few, and that's where my grandson's been goin' to school. So I'd like for you to leave it at that way for now—"

The telephone rang. Kelley hesitated; then he figured, what the hell. He could always hang up with a fast "No comment" or a faster "Fuck off."

It was the switchboard operator. A person-to-person long-distance call. "From Rio," she said, excited to be dealing with exotic locations.

"Christ," Lester said through extravagant static, "what the hell's going on?"

"News travels." Kelley glanced up guardedly at Johnson.

"Dope and a girl. Naughty," Lester said. "Naughty and extra naughty."

"Is that why you called? To deliver me a sermon?"

"I called, you sinner, to tell you the eyes of Texas were upon you. My partners called me up, choking on their breakfast, and they tell me it's off. They don't want to back any dope fiends today. Not to mention any dope fiend that's fucking around."

Kelley made a guttural sound in his throat.

"I told you," Lester said. "It's conservative money. It's the same company that's backing the reverend Reverend DeVane. The company that publishes the Ten Commandments. And you," Lester chuckled, "are a very bad boy. An evil empire unto yourself."

Kelley glanced over at Ed Johnson, who was sipping his Scotch and possibly thinking the same kind of thoughts.

"Nothing I can do about it, either," Lester said. "Like I told you, my bread's in the Amazon ranch, and the rest of it has to be decided by committee. They still want to steal your airline, by the way. *Cuidado, amigo.* You know what that means?"

"Be careful."

"You got it."

Kelley hung up and then refilled his glass. He drank down the slug and then filled it up again. He was back on the treadmill now with a vengeance. With eight days left, maybe ten at the most, to get twenty-seven million to Araco Fuel. Twenty-seven million for the next three months and twenty-two million to the short-term lenders. Out of revenues that just worked their way up to zero.

He sat down on the couch.

"Bad news?" Johnson said.

Kelley sat still and looked at him a while. Then he said, "You're right. I am bad news. I shouldn't see her till my life's straightened out."

Johnson stared back at him. "Funny," he said, "I kind of expected you to put up a fight."

"Well, I'm just an all-round disappointment today, aren't I? I'm not fighting anyone today. The only thing I'm fighting for today is my airline, or my life, which may or may not be the same thing. But in either case, I'm not involving Claire in the fight. Her stuff's in room twenty."

"Then I guess I'll get up there and pack." Johnson stood. "Claire'll be coming back to Kansas tonight. She wants to be with her son, explain this to him."

"Sounds right," Kelley said.

"Is there any message you want me to give her?"

Kelley thought it over. "No," he shook his head. "I don't think there is."

He went in and took a shower, stayed under the hot water for a long time and turned it on hard and cold at the end. When he walked into the bedroom, Zeedee was sitting there, lounging on the bed with a Cutty in his hand. "I thought you might like some company," he said.

"Now that you mention it, not particularly."

"Well, too late. The limousine left. Not a minute too

soon, you want to know something else. Another few seconds, I'd've socked Mr. Cubbitt."

"Is he always like that?"

"He's very tall," Zeedee said. "He tends to take that as a mandate. Besides, you don't know the entire story. She had a date with him. He comes to the city to be with her, she phones him, she tells him, 'No, I gotta work.' That does it for Tommy. He now spends his Saturday dick-deep in doubt. He keeps asking me, 'You think he's balling her now?' I say, *'Tom!* how the hell would *I* know?' But we do this routine, maybe six, seven hours while he's drinking my bourbon. Love," Zeedee grinned, "really eats it with a spoon.—You want to talk business?"

"Not yet," Kelley said.

Zeedee was restless. He paced around the airplane cabin like a cat, clomping around in his hand-tooled boots, fooling with the stereo, raiding the pantry. He came back to the co-pilot's seat with a smoked oyster sandwich and a bottle of beer.

"Nice digs," he said, resting his boots on the panel. "You know that? For a Kentucky shit-kicker, you know how to live."

"How about for anybody else?" Kelley said.

Zeedee wiggled his hand. "If you *really* had class, you'd relax a little more, take it easy, enjoy it."

"Like you."

"Like me."

"You enjoy it?"

"I don't know," Zeedee said. "But if I don't, then there isn't any hope for me, is there."

"Yeah. Poor babe. Too old to rock 'n' roll and too young to die."

"Exactly," Zeedee said. "What comes in the middle?"

"Middle age."

"No fun." Sighing, Zeedee looked through the cockpit window. There was nothing out there but soup-thick clouds. "Where are we, do you know?"

"Sure. About ten miles southwest of Troy. Or was the question philosophical?"

"Well, if it was, then the answer is 'nowhere.'"

"No," Kelley said, "it only looks like you're nowhere. You're always somewhere."

"Philosophical."

"No. I'm just used to flying blind." Kelley lit a cigarette and stared at the soup. "Let me ask you a question. Why don't you invest in this coke deal yourself?"

"So who says I haven't?"

"Oh."

"I only put up two hundred thou. I'm not rich like you are."

"Like hell."

"I'm not. Daddy left the whole thing tied up in bundles. I only get the income. Half-mil a year."

Kelley laughed.

"Oh shit, that's nothing," Zeedee said. "The guy does the TV weather makes that. Airline presidents, I'm told, make more."

"That a fact?"

"I read it in the New York *Times*. Or *Ripley's*. I forget. And besides, you got stock, man. Equity. Access to the company till. You come up with two million by the end of the week—like I said, you're in clover."

"You're something," Kelley said. "You think I just— what? Walk into the office with a Vuitton suitcase and walk out later with the two million bucks? Is that how it goes?"

"But you know how to do it. Don't you?"

"I suppose. I've got pretty clean books, though. I'd have to put it back."

"Oh Jesus," Zeedee said. "The man doesn't listen. You're gonna put it *back* times ten in a week."

"If," Kelley said. "If the shit hits the shore and does not hit the fan."

"Three years," Zeedee said. "Hasn't hit a fan yet. What you got here's a genuine covered operation. I mean this is international payoffs on a mind-blowing level. No one's gonna mess with it. And let me tell you *this*. If you back Chooky this time, you back him the next. You can solve all your problems. Am I right or am I right?"

Kelley said nothing. He grabbed Zeedee's bottle and swigged at some beer. "Just tell me something, will you? How'd you get the idea?"

"About what?"

"About me."

"Oh. You want to know, it was Chook's," Zeedee said.

"Chook?"

"He reads the papers like everybody else. You'd be surprised. The man reads."

"I'm surprised," Kelley said.

"He had troubles. Like I told you—his backer backed out. A couple of weeks ago, the last time he delivered—okay, you were there, it's the night you met Claire—he tells me his problems. So he knows I know you—"

"How?"

Zeedee shrugged. "I guess he's seen Karen at the house a few times."

"Go on."

"No 'on.' That's it. He says to me, how about Kelley?"

"So it didn't just come to you as sudden inspiration."

"Not exactly."

"Uh huh." Kelley thought it over. It didn't quite click. "How about the French ambassador?" he said.

"How about Marcus? Or Cubbitt, in fact. You know those guys too."

Zeedee shook his head. "Only *those* guys aren't in the news needing bread. And *those* guys never ran smack in their youth."

Kelley looked at him sharply.

"Well, shit. You ain't exactly a virgin," Zeedee said.

"And you told that to Chook?"

"Chook knew it. In fact, Chook told it to me."

"I see." Kelley didn't see it at all. There was something going on here that didn't add up. Or possibly it did. With Alvy in the middle. Possibly Alvy had once dealt with Ryan. Alvy deals with Chook . . .

Zeedee said, "So.—You want to think about it?"

"No."

"Then let me put it this way—*will* you think about it?"

"Yeah," Kelley nodded. "Unhappily, I will."

21

THE APARTMENT WAS in order. He'd stopped at a deli and bought himself a little fundamental food: eggs, bagels, bacon and milk.

He turned on the radio, sipping a Scotch as he listened to jazz and the crackling bacon.

He'd figured a way to get ahold of the cash.

He turned the bacon and cracked a few eggs.

So now he could talk about you have to crack eggs if you want to make omelets. Or about how the ends justify the means. Well . . . in this particular instance, they did. He sure as hell didn't have to care about the buyers. He could feed them their candy without losing sleep. Or as Zeedee had put it, "We aren't talking poor little kiddies on the corner, what we're talking here's rich little kiddies on a toot." And to hell with them. Fuckum. Let 'em eat coke. In fact, it was a fine revolutionary concept: Fly the rich so you can fly the poor.

Sweet Jesus, he thought, how's *that* for a smooth-talking sonofabitch? He could talk himself into almost anything, right?

He nibbled some bacon while he scrambled the eggs and toasted the bagels.

The bacon was greasy.

Shitty omelet.

He poured some coffee, lit a cigarette and put his feet on the table.

He hadn't been talked into anything yet.

He still had a problem.

The problem was . . . what? All right, get down to it, he told himself now. You don't want to do it and the question is why. The law? But the law had been paid to keep out. The moral law possibly? *What* moral law? Thou shall not deviate thy neighbor's septum? No, if he made himself think about it straight, it came down to something much less important than that. His own self-image, his own way of looking at himself in the mirror. He thought about himself, or possibly secretly prided himself—okay, admit it now—*prided* himself on being an edge-player. Walking the edge. But he'd walked that edge like a tightrope walker, knowing the ropes. And knowing—here it was then—knowing himself.

And the man who'd be doing this was somebody else.

He wasn't even passing judgments on the guy. It was simply the fact that it was somebody else.

Okay, that was it.

So now he could sit here, drinking his coffee, and think about the problems of tightrope walking in another man's shoes.

He finished the cup and he hadn't quite talked himself into it yet; but he hadn't talked himself out of it either.

He showered, stretched himself out on the covers, and telephoned Ryan. Or tried to. The Crillon said Ryan was out. *"Moment, s'il vous plaît. Je pense que—moment,"* the operator left him with French Muzak. Heavy accordions. *C'est Si Bon.* Followed by the samba from *A Man and a Woman.* Followed by the clatter as he hung up the telephone and switched on the Sony. The television offered him urban romance: cops

227

chased robbers; robbers got caught. He drifted to sleep. The house-phone woke him, nasty and quick, with a sound like a foghorn bitching at the whole unregenerate ocean.

The doorman said, "A Mr. Ryan to see you."

Kelley said, "You're home."

Ryan said, "You know how I *know* that I'm home? Less than an hour, I get six hard times.—*Jesus*." He dumped his suitcase on the floor. "And I'm using your phone while you're fixing me—"

"A double Cutty on the rocks."

"And a noose for your doorman."

"Another hard time?"

"I don't think he trusted my face," Ryan said.

"Yeah? No shit." Kelley headed for the kitchen. Ryan, on the phone now: "Amy? Yeah . . . No, I'm in town. . . . No, in *this* town. . . . No, right now I'm at the Dixie Hotel with three unbelievable Oriental hookers. . . . Of *course* I'll be hungry an hour later. . . ." Ryan, laughing. Ryan's voice getting sexy and low.

Kelley put a couple of cubes in a bucket and it went through his mind—about Amy the stewardess and Ryan the pilot. Back at the beginning, when Ryan had been pretty much angry and shy and Amy'd said to Kelley, "Burke—I have to quit. I can't take it anymore." Ryan's avoiding her. Ryan, "with the goddam scars on his face like they're chips on his shoulder. "He's a bastard," she'd said. Except, as she'd told him, for one single evening at the end of November. Amy and Ryan getting stranded on the road, marooned in a rented Pacer in the snow, and hours going by and Amy really freezing and Ryan, in the darkness, beginning to talk to her, voice gone husky and almost elegiac, holding her, giving her the heat of his body, and Amy, having never felt warmer in her life . . ."and then suddenly the tow truck comes, and that's it," Amy said. "And Ryan goes back to being nasty and weird." She'd been crying at that point, telling it to Kelley in the Wanderer's Bar, watering a perfectly decent martini. Kelley had written out a verse on his napkin. The following morning he took it to a printer and had the thing printed on a red satin heart, and then dropped it into Ryan's cockpit at take-off:

> *Roses are red,*
> *Amy is blue,*
> *Ryan is yellow,*
> *And what else is new?*

Ryan was hanging up the phone in the study. Portrait of Ryan: cigarette in his mouth dripping ashes on the front of a herringbone jacket; faded Levi's and elaborate boots; face with that Fucked-up Redford expression. That's where it was now. Ten operations and Ryan, on a general chart of devastation, looked more like the victim of a rather unpleasant motorcycle crash than of, say, Hiroshima.

Handing him a glass now, Kelley said, "Well, how's your beautiful wife?"

"Beautiful. . . . Wifely." Ryan looked around and then sat in the wing chair. "So how 'bout Karen? Cleaving to your side?"

"Try 'to the seaside.'"

"Oh?" Ryan laughed.

"Hey—if it really gets bad," Kelley said, "she'll spend the winter at the beach."

"Hey—she'll spend the *nuclear* winter at the beach. Believe it, man."

Kelley said slowly, "I do."

Ryan said nothing. Obviously, Ryan was here to say

something, but he'd say it in his own sweet elaborate time. Ryan seemed to operate in several modes. In One, he wouldn't talk and in Two, he wouldn't stop.

Kelley said, "I didn't expect you till Friday."

"Well . . . there you go. And I didn't expect you to be Public Enemy Numero *Oono*," Ryan said. "But that's life."

"So it is."

"Yep. Just a barrel of surprise," Ryan said.

"Are we fucked up in Paris?"

"Nope. Things were going very nicely in Paris. Very nicely indeed.—And then I called Amy and I heard you'd been starring on the Six-o'clock Follies."

"So you flew to my side."

"Not exactly," Ryan said. "No, not quite." He lit up a cigarette and yawned out a lazy contrail of smoke. "Thing is," he said slowly, "I got on that plane and you were still up in Podunk. Your balls, shall we put it, were still in their court? And at that point the visions kept dancing in my head. This weird possibility they'd send you to Attica. And *then* what'd happen? You see what I'm saying?"

"So you came to take charge."

"Oh yeah. Like Haig after Reagan was shot. 'I'm in charge! I'm in charge!' Except now—" Ryan said, "for the twenty-dollar question—who *would've* been, huh?"

"Okay."

"Okay?"

"Got a point there."

"Yeah. I do," Ryan said. "What you got in that office wouldn't get you through the night. What you got there is teams. You got the war guys and the Wharton guys. And the *Wharton* guys, you know what they did?" Ryan said. "They took courses. Intermediate Backstabbing. Advanced Bullshit. You want that in French? I don't trust those guys."

"You mean you don't like 'em."

"Same thing," Ryan said. "And with Charlie out of town, you got me and Duke against Warner and McDermott. And if I'd been out of town . . ." He allowed it to float.

They were silent for a second.

"So what are you thinking?"

"Name it," Ryan said, "I'm thinking it."

Kelley got up again and crossed to the bar. He was thinking . . . the leak about the auditor's report, the unpaid fuel bill, the fucked-up computer. He picked up the bottle. "So you think we got spies?"

"I think we got Junior Achievers," Ryan said. "I think they'd sell their mothers for a junior achievement."

"Money."

"Power. Executive Position. Establishment Strokes. You want to make 'em salivate, you tell 'em they'll be lifetime members of the club."

Kelley said nothing. He filled up his glass and gave the bottle to Ryan. They sat there and drank. Ryan said, How close are we to the edge? and Kelley held his fingers a half-inch apart, and then Ryan said mordantly, Now—. Here's the Plan. . . .

Kelley said nothing.

"But you have one—don't you." When Kelley shook his head, Ryan said, "Funny. I thought you'd have a plan."

"Why?"

"'Cause you're the sucker that's *always* got a plan."

"Okay," Kelley said. "Want to fly a little smack?"

Ryan looked stopped. Like a frame in a movie. For a second he appeared to be frozen in the air. Then he said, "Jesus. I forgot I did that. I really forgot." He was shaking his head.

Kelley said carefully and matter-of-factly, "You ever have . . . second thoughts about it?"

"No. You mean then? No. *Now?*" Ryan said. "Now I

got kids. Now I think smugglers should be roasted on a spit. But then? Not a thought. Not *one* thought, man. I mean, you gotta look at that crap the way it is. You got all of these scumbags rolling in their millions—and then you got the suckers screaming on the streets. And you look at both sides of that nasty little scene and the first thing you figure, there isn't any God. And then you got it dicked because anything's possible.—Right?"

"I don't know."

"Well, I'm telling you it is," Ryan said. "If it weren't, ole buddy, you'd still be in the mineshaft and I'd be in the grave. You got the wonderful thing about Anything's Possible, it cuts both ways—you see what I'm saying? Of course when I was doing my death-trips to Durango I couldn't quite see it. My vision got a little bit narrowed in Nam. Then I went through all the V.A. bullshit and I'm walking dead. I'm a fucking freak. I can't get a job. I can't even get *laid*," Ryan said. "And the one thing I didn't think was possible then was Amy. Kids. Job. *Life,* as it were. Life in These United States, we could call it. But anything's possible. Along comes Kelley, like the fucking cavalry—" Ryan shook his head. "You saved my ass, man. I honestly no-shit owe you my life. So listen—you want me to fly a little smack?"

"No. No way. Not ever."

"That's good," Ryan said. "Cuz if you asked me to, I'd tell you, get fucked in the ear." He reached for the bottle and poured another shot. "Any other questions?"

Kelley took the bottle, poured another double and lit a cigarette. "José Alvarado. Alvy, for short. Ever heard of him?"

"No." Ryan pulled at his whiskey. "He wasn't that baggage handler from the Bronx . . . ?"

"Now try from Colombia."

"Oh. You mean—no."

"I mean—"

"Yeah. Okay. I *know* what you mean. That was Mexico, man. Different cast of characters."

"How about Chook D'Aquino? Ring bells?"

Ryan shook his head. "What the hell are you into?"

"Nothing."

"Uh huh. I see," Ryan said. He chain-lit a cigarette and stared at the smoke. He was silent for a time; then, "Well, man, as long as you know what you're into . . ."

"But I don't," Kelley said. "And if you don't know Alvy . . ."

Ryan looked up. "Then what?"

Kelley shook his head. "Never mind."

22

"OKAY," CHOOK SAID. "So I hear you want to talk."

"I didn't say that." Kelley swiveled his chair to face the window. "I said I'd listen, only not on the phone in my office."

"You want to meet?"

"No."

"So what the fuck you want, man? You want to know the story but you don't want to talk to me, you don't want to meet. You got an attitude problem, you know about that?"

"Exactly," Kelley said. "I'll get in touch through Zeedee. *If* I get in touch."

McDermott looked up from the ledger on his desk. He said, "Well, I suppose congratulations are in order."

"For what?"

"For your narrow escape from the law. Have you seen today's papers?"

"'Duel in the Snow'? 'Beau Bops Foe'? Yeah," Kelley said, "I saw it."

McDermott sipped tea from his mug. "The afternoon papers have been kinder," he said.

"Uh huh." Kelley sat and lit a cigarette. "I've been wondering, George. Speaking of the general kindness of the press. About that auditor's report coming out. How do you imagine that happened?"

"I imagine the auditor did it."

"You think?"

"Well, it seems to be the logical choice. It certainly isn't in the personal interests of anybody here—"

"I don't know," Kelley said. "I don't know about the interests of anybody here. It might, for instance, be in some people's interests if Quaid bought me out. Can you possibly see that scenario, George?"

"Why is it always," McDermott said slowly, "that I get the impression you're accusing me of something?"

Kelley looked startled. "Is that what you were thinking? No, I was actually asking your opinion." He thought for a moment. "Let's try something else. I'd like you to remember who saw that report. Not just heard about it but saw it, had access to it. Who could have copied the exact figures and fed them to the press?"

"No one."

"Think it over."

"No one at all. I was here when it arrived and took the package myself. I read it, locked it up. I discussed its existence, but exact figures down to nickels and pennies? No. If you're getting into mystery stories, I put it in the safe. And the only other person who knows the combination is Art Kindler, who wasn't even here. He was home with his old war wound again. He's now in the hospital with it, by the way."

"Oh? I'm sorry to hear that," Kelley said. "So now tell me who you discussed the thing with."

"Listen, you're up the wrong tree," McDermott said. "I discussed it with Duke and with Ashe Warner. Your chief of operations and your marketing chief. It was, by the way, in the safe at that time, and the next day I handed it directly to Frannie."

"Thank you, George. Was there anybody else?"

"You mean aside from *Sixty Minutes?* No. I don't think so."

"Good. How's your teeth?"

"My teeth? Well, that's very nice of you to ask. I have another session coming up this afternoon and a final one Wednesday."

"It hurts a lot, huh?"

McDermott smiled. "Spoken like a man who has perfect enamel. Yes indeed. It does hurt a lot."

Kelley said, rising, "Then take the week off."

"Are you serious?"

"Sure. Stay till you leave for your appointment today. If a problem comes up, we can reach you at home."

"Well," McDermott said, "I don't know what to say."

"Say good night, George."

"Thanks," McDermott said. "Sincerely."

Okay then; so that was that, Kelley thought. And he wasn't too eager to think about it more, and he didn't have to; the phone kept ringing.

The Chief of Pilots, checking on the rumor that the pilots would be asked to take a ten-percent cut. Kelley said, "Where'd you get *that* idea?"

"McDermott."

"Well, I'm not cutting anybody's pay."

"Will you *listen?*" Eller said. "The pilots don't mind. They say if it'll help you—"

"It won't," Kelley said. "And if push comes to shove I'd rather have *them* get the money than the banks."

"Well, the offer still holds."

"Tell 'em thanks," Kelley said.

The maintenance department. Six more wind-shear detectors had arrived. "You want to go in for some overtime again?"

"Christ," Kelley said. "No." Then he thought about the wind-shear accidents—two within a month. "Yeah," he said, "might as well go for it."

"Bad things happen in threes."

"That's what I was thinking.—You ever hear 'good things happen in threes'?"

"I didn't know good things happened anymore. Do they?"

"I don't know," Kelley said. "I don't know."

He was thinking of the two bad things in a row—the scene with Jenny and the call from Quaid. He hadn't told Frannie and Duke about the call. Why let them worry? (Also, why punch a hole in your cover? If the money comes from Chook, let them think it's from Lester. . . .)

"H'lo there, sir."

He looked up quickly into Heidigger's big brown syrupy eyes. He'd been standing at the empty urinal, aimed. Heidigger was leaning with his back against the wall. Kelley said, "Hi."

Heidigger waited, jingling his change.

"Are you here on business," Kelley said, "or just browsing?"

Heidigger switched his attention to the wall. "Can I see you for a second, sir?"

"You're seeing me now."

"In private, sir."

"This is as private as it gets." Kelley zipped his fly up and headed for the sink.

Heidigger appeared to be casing the obviously empty room and deciding it was empty. "Well, sir, it's about the sabotage, sir."

"It begin again?" Kelley looked up in the mirror.

"No sir. It's just that I know where it's from."

"Quaid?"

"No sir. Uh-uh. It's Federal, sir. I traced it. You want

237

to know how, sir?" Heidigger, eager as a puppy. Kelley, not giving a damn about the how, just the who: Chambers.

"Yeah," he said, "how?"

"Well you see, sir," Heidigger was leaning on the sink, "I had a long conversation with Federal's computer. It was really quite friendly."

"I see," Kelley said.

"So we just got to talking. You know, about top-secret programs it had? I mean I told it I was interested in one of those programs and it asked me which one and I said I didn't know, which ones've you got, so it gave me the list, sir."

Kelley, engaged now, lit a cigarette. "Go on."

"Well of course it was coded."

"Of course."

"But one of the codewords, sir, was SNAFU. And the word kind of popped. See, one of the things I'm a buff about, sir, is the Second World War and that's a *word* from that war. It means Situation Normal All Fouled Up."

"Fucked up."

"Really? *Fucked* up, sir?"

"People said 'fuck' even then. Go on."

"Well anyway, sir, it's a word I figured most people wouldn't know. I mean computer people, sir. They're mostly too young. But I figured Mr. Chambers used to fight in that war and I figured it's a program he'd personally—"

"Yeah."

"So I called the computer, sir, and asked for SNAFU and it gave it to me, sir. And that's what it was."

"It *gave* it to you?"

"Yes sir." Heidigger shrugged. "Computers can really be sophisticated, sir, but they can also be suckers."

"Yeah." Kelley looked at his face in the mirror. "Yeah. Can't we all."

The kinder cut in the afternoon paper, which Kelley read in the Sky Captain's Lounge, was a page-three item, THE HIGH AND THE MIGHTY—a short history of Famous People Who Were Busted for Pot. From Robert Mitchum and Lila Leeds in the 1940's, through several Beatles, through Kelley and Claire. The article took no sides in the matter but at least put Kelley in respectable company. He wondered if the papers in Kansas did the same.

He looked up from the table at Frannie and Duke coming towards him up the aisle.

"Wow, a lunch with the boss," Duke said.

"Relax," Kelley told him. "It's instead of a raise. But eat anything you like. Feel free."

"Have cheese with your burger," Frannie said.

When the waitress had left, Duke said, "I want to tell you something weird. This morning the calls for reservations have tripled. I don't know what it is. I don't know if it's the ads or you're pulling in every weedhead in town."

"Maybe they think we sell reefers on board."

"I don't know," Duke said. "Beats hell out of *me*. McDermott said we even had a day in the black."

"Oh yeah?"

"We made a profit of ten thousand dollars."

"Ten thousand *dollars?*" Kelley started laughing. "Jesus. Tell the waitress forget about the cheese."

"It's a start," Frannie said. "Oriental wisdom: the longest journey begins with a step in the right direction."

"Or the wrong direction," Kelley said flatly.

The waitress came back with the burgers and beer. When she'd gone, Kelley brought up the subject on his mind. "Speaking of steps in the wrong direction, I think that leak in the auditor's report is what threw me to the wolves."

"By wolves," Duke said, "I assume you mean Quaid."

"Or at least it narrowed my options," Kelley said. "So I'm curious about it." He repeated the story that McDermott had told. About the auditor's report being locked in his safe until he handed it to Frannie. "If I buy that," Kelley said, "what happened from there?"

"From there?" Frannie shrugged. "I brought it to you. And then you gave it back to me just as you were leaving to be dumped by Rosetti."

"Uh uh," Kelley said. "I didn't. I told you it was sitting on my desk."

Frannie thought it over and nodded. "You're right. So it might have been in there for forty-five minutes."

"And you weren't away from your desk in that time?"

"Oh Jesus, I don't remember," she said.

"So try to, huh? I don't mean this second, but think about it, huh?"

"It's McDermott," Duke said. "It's gotta be, doesn't it? The whole situation you said the other day. Gene-vieve Hollis's selling to Quaid. Then you've got the Hollis-McDermott connection. So if Jenny's in control, then George is taking orders from *her*. Am I right?"

"And *she*," Frannie said, "wants Quaid to win out. And George would get—what? He'd be keeping his job with a million-dollar raise or a million-dollar bonus."

"Could be," Kelley nodded. "It probably is. But just think about it, huh? Go into a corner and meditate a little."

In the late afternoon, after Frannie was gone, Kelley phoned Kindler at the V.A. hospital, shot a little breeze, and then got to the point: the combination to

McDermott's safe. It turned out to be 7-12-42, which was very possibly McDermott's birthday.

Kelley made a few other telephone calls, had a few more Scotches and a dozen cigarettes, and then he was walking deserted corridors, entering McDermott's office like a thief, opening the safe and removing the leather-bound corporate checkbook.

The corporate balance was thirty-eight million and a couple of grand. Take half-a-million out for the payroll on Friday—three days from now. And on Monday, take the usual monthly expenses of thirty-one million, and take the extra six-point-six for the fuel, and the ballgame was over.

He closed the book and put it back on the shelf. All right, he told himself, now is the time. He took the employee pension fund book, a checkbook which no one would probably look at for a couple of months. He tore out a check. Sitting at George's orderly desk, he wrote on the stub: *Jan. 28, to B. Kelley, 60 day loan at 12% interest, $2 million.*

He folded the check, leaving it blank, put it in his wallet, replaced the checkbook and locked up the safe.

"Attitude." Chook was sipping his beer. "We're back to your very bad attitude again." He sat in the Route 35 motel room, a Man of Distinction, pulling at his Piel's, his Gucci loafers resting on the wood-grained plastic table. Today he was wearing a cashmere sweater and a good pair of cords. On his wrist was the two-toned Cartier watch. Chook D'Aquino, dressed for success. "You got an attitude that goes, this man's gonna fuck me. Now why would I fuck you?"

"I can think of maybe two million reasons," Kelley said.

"Bullshit. The two million reasons is nothing. I also got a good reputation, you know? You know how it goes? I get a shipment, I gotta be quick, move it fast. I gotta pay my expenses. I got guys on my neck. These are heavy leaners. So now you start telling your buddies I fuck you, so where does that leave me? You see how it goes? They don't trust me no more."

"You mean Zeedee."

"That's one. I gotta have buyers," Chook said. "Like a store. It's a business. I gotta have buyers, I gotta have product. So you give me your money by Friday, okay?"

"And when do I see it?"

"Next morning, next night. Like that."

"Like that."

Chook waited a beat, staring at Kelley with a serious face. "Like I said, you got problems with your attitude, man."

"And that's only half of the problem," Kelley said. "I can't get you that much money that fast."

"Then it's off," Chook said.

"Not in cash," Kelley told him.

"In what then—a check? American Express?"

"Diamonds."

"Diamonds." Chook grinned. "Or how about glass?"

"I don't think so," Kelley said. "I don't think that would be in my enlightened self-interest."

"I don't know how you talk, man."

"I'm talking you'd kill me."

Chook thought it over and nodded. "You're right. Except for the guys who could dust me off first."

"Alvy," Kelley said.

"You know Alvarado?"

"You provided him with background about me, am I right? You told him I used to fly cargo with a friend."

"It's a business," Chook said, "like I told you. We gotta be sure who we know."

"Right. Okay. So you told Alvy what?"

"Like you said. Like he must've told you I said."

"Okay, so where'd you get a story like that?"

"From Zeedee, man. Shit. Where else would I get it?"

Kelley lit a cigarette, looking at Chook D'Aquino through smoke.

"No, man. I tell you. I remember it better. Where I got it, I got it from the candy-man."

"Oh?" Kelley looked up. "You mean Candy's old man? Marcus Imry?"

"Yeah."

"He's a customer?"

"Sure. Like you know. Like I say, man, we gotta know who we cut in."

"Fine. So you know. And Alvy can move the diamonds pretty fast."

"I don't know," Chook said. "It's different. It's cute."

"So where does that leave us?"

"I'll ask. Can I call this a definite offer?"

"No." Kelley put out his cigarette and stood. "I think what you'd call it is a possible question."

23

AGAIN, AS ALWAYS, the need for air. He drove back to Newark and picked up the Beagle.

Superman again. Able to leap tall buildings in a single bound. The sky around him was empty and clear. He remembered skies that were red, and crowded with incoming death. But no bolts would come out of this particular blue. No lightning would strike. He was, at this moment, free as that mindless proverbial bird, except, like the bird, propelled by his instinct, motored by the limiting nature of his breed: an edge-player moving towards the ultimate edge.

There was no choice. It was back once again to the posse or the cliff. But the posse was closer, the cliff was steeper and the waters more troubled. If he looked too closely he could shy from the leap and the time to make it would have come and gone. And then he could sit in the morning-after rubble of his only dream and kick himself for being such a chickenshit coward.

He had never, he thought, been a coward before. On the other hand, he'd never been a felon before. He had, in the course of his checkered career, crossed a few lines, skipped a few steps, flown, as it were, in the face of convention. But up to this point he'd committed no crimes. Even the caper of the weekend, he felt, didn't count as a crime. It was merely an exercise in terrible luck. Or pot-luck, call it, at the trough of life. And sure, it was a case of stupidity too. But without feeling guilty of rationalization, he could still in good conscience blame it on luck. He'd been *stupider,* for Christ's sake, to bring it from Paris.

So it came back to luck.

For the crapshoot itself, he could picture the moves. Tomorrow he'd deposit the check in his account. He could buy the diamonds from Morty Savage. Call him tomorrow at the Diamond Exchange, tell him to line up the best he could find, only keep it confidential. Morty would do it, and on Friday morning he'd accept Kelley's check. Up to that point, it was all within the realm of a legal transaction, fuzzy at the edges, but relatively safe. Including the questionable "loan" from the office. By the time the stub of that check was discovered, he'd either have paid back the interest and the loan, or be under indictment. In which case he still had the salable assets—the houses and the cars—to cover the payback and cover his bail.

Bail. He was skyhawking, thinking of bail.

Its corollary, jail. The ultimate bad luck. It came back to luck. Anything's possible, Ryan had said, and endless possibility cuts both ways. The only limits are the ones you personally decide to draw. The universe itself is completely indifferent. Punishment doesn't have to follow from crime. Villains get rewarded, angels get trashed, and once in a while it's the other way around. The only laws are the laws of chance.

The only limits are the ones you personally decide to draw.

And it cuts both ways.

Because the point of Blue Sky was to exceed limitation. "Let your reach exceed your grasp or what's a heaven for?" Possibly the only lines of poetry he knew; committed to memory in Elgar, Kentucky, when his grasp could only take him from the cottage to the mine. And later, he'd reached—first up, and then down—

wanting to grab all the grounded people and physically yank them up into air—take shopgirls to Paris, and bellhops to the sea, and miners to the top of the fucking Himalayas. Give the working-guy a chance to look around at the world. Or what's an airline for?

Weather forced him to land in Montreal.

He checked into the Bonaventure Hotel and ordered a room-service sandwich and a bottle.

Sitting on the bed with the television burbling and a glass in his hand, he beeped to his answering machine in New York.

And there was the message.

"Alvy say fine. Go ahead with the stones."

Then Claire's voice. "Burke? I just, uh, wanted to talk to you, I guess. Do you have the number here?" And then the number.

"Listen—call me." It was Frannie's voice now. "Before midnight. Oh well. Let me tell you right now, because I might fall asleep. About the auditor's report? Okay, so you left it sitting on your desk and I went to the ladies' room. And then I came back and I remember Ashe Warner coming out of your office. He said he'd put a couple of proofs on your desk. And he had. The stuff about Blue Sky's Smilin'. I don't know if that helps. But he could have been in there for fifteen minutes. But I don't suspect Ashe. My goodness, do you? I'll see you tomorrow."

"Oh Christ, the machine." Miranda, shouting through Brazilian static. "Kelley, we ran into Lester last night. Can you hear me through this? He told us it was off. Paul said, remind you to call his friend Roque. Some film producer with a whole lot of money who might—" A long burst of static cut in.

Click. Buzz. Silence. He hung up and looked at his watch. It was after eleven.

He wondered idly if he'd wake up entire neighborhoods in Kansas with the ringing of the phone. He wondered what he'd say to Claire on this night, or on any other night. Because the truth would be poison. She came from a family of straight shooters. She believed devoutly in How You Play the Game. She believed, or hoped, he would play by the rules; the rules of conscience if not of the law. And his conscience, this time around, wasn't clear. He thought about the Barb for the first time in years; he could picture her walking away down the beach. As Claire would walk away. He'd be no good to her if he did this; and no damn good to himself if he didn't. And the single point of honor would be not to lie.

She answered on the edge of the second ring as though she'd been sitting there, waiting by the phone.

"Are you all right?" she said.

"No. Are you?"

"No." She laughed. "Well . . . as good as expected. Mark's okay."

"He'd have to be."

"Why?"

"He's got you for a mother."

"And the world for a world. I actually did get a phone call this morning. An irate mommy. 'I don't want my Billy to play with your son.' "

"I'm sorry."

"I think we can live without Billy." She paused. "I don't think we can live without you."

Kelley said nothing. Lying on another strange empty bed in another hotel room, thinking it would always be strange empty beds, or beds filled with strangers. Wanting, more than anything else in the world, just to hold her right now.

"Hey, listen. I don't want to lose you," he said.

"You won't. Why would you?"

"I might have to," he said. "It could happen like that."

She was silent for a time. "Is this about the loan?"

"It's off. Canceled. Forget it. All I've got is a couple of days."

"And you think you'd lose me if you lost the airline?"

"No. I'd lose myself. And the rest of it would follow."

"You said you'd start again."

"In a three-room apartment. Doing four flights a day up to Albany and Utica. That's how I started."

"You could do that again."

"I'm forty years old."

"Ancient."

"Tired."

"Bullshit. I'll do your advertising for you."

"On spec. I'd clear about twelve grand a year."

"Burke?"

"That's the first time you've called me Burke. Does that mean something?"

"Yes. No. I don't know. It means that I love you."

"Jesus. You've never said *that* before either."

"I said I'd marry you."

"True," he said slowly. Seeing it. Claire in his bed every night. Saying I love you. Claire and the kid. Flying some bright little boy in the cockpit and watching him love it. Everything love. It was pretty to think so.

"How long will you be staying in Kansas?" he said.

"Till Saturday."

"Good."

"You don't miss me," she said.

"I miss you intensely. I miss you now, and I miss you retrospectively and also foreseeably. Is that good enough?"

"Will I see you on Saturday?"

He said, "There's a chance."

"I don't want to say good-bye."

"Then don't. Hang up. I'll wait till you're gone." He waited till he heard the click and the droning buzz on the line. The television set still burbled, an old-time American western. He stared at it blindly; he pulled at his Scotch.

The old gunfighter. Going soft. Getting over the hill. If he thought about Claire too long and too hard, he'd consider the dangers, think about the homestead and hang up his guns.

And the bastards and the backshooters ride away grinning with the town in their hands.

And certainly that was the new, promotable Hollywood ending. The *Dallas* ending. The neo-morality of killer-take-all. They could re-release *Jaws* and the shark would be applauded. So why was he beating his brains out at all? Not to be a hero. Surely not that. No, it came down to just being himself.

He thought about Frannie's message on the phone: "You don't suspect Ashe?"

And he hadn't. Till now.

But now it was definitely Ashe he suspected.

Ashe, who'd been hired on the word of Rosetti. Rosetti, who was suddenly Federal's man. Or not so suddenly. Think about that. Ashe would be offered a position at Federal. Maybe he'd already met with Chambers and fixed it all up. He'd be Head of Marketing for Federal Airlines, one of the biggest airlines in the world. The job could pay a quarter of a million a year. Plus Federal stock. And a contract with a Golden Parachute clause so that even if they canned him, he still couldn't lose, he'd go on collecting.

Executive Position. Establishment Strokes. Oh yeah, Kelley thought. Warner was the man.

Thinking, he must have drifted into dreams, dreaming of the high-noon showdown again, walking alone along the edge of the street, Chambers coming towards him. Rosetti on the roof. Ashe in the courtyard. He knew where they were. A three-cornered ambush waiting ahead of him, lurking in the sun.

The bullet was sudden and took him by surprise. He stumbled, back-shot, the impact spinning him around in the dust and he squinted, narrowly, to look for the gun. But the sun was too glaring and the shadows too dense. And besides, he was dying.

He woke about a second before he was dead.

24

THE DIAMOND CENTER, where some of the finest diamonds in the world were cut and sold, was one of the grubbier streets in Manhattan. Savage's office, where on any given day there was ten or twelve million dollars' worth of stones, looked like a down-at-the-heels emporium which might or might not be a front for a bookie. In fact, Morty Savage had an unfailing eye for the quality, artistry and worth of a stone.

Kelley sat across from him now at the scarred mahogany desk with the gray winter light coming in through the large rain-streaked windows. Across the street, in a similar office on West Forty-seventh, a middle-aged woman leaned on a windowsill and stared at the street.

Morty said, "I got. You don't like what you see here, I get something else but I tell you I got. You don't like it, you're nuts."

Morty was sixty, with a grizzled beard and a birdlike eye and one of those accents you walk away humming. On his desk was a foot-long blue velvet mat over which presided a gooseneck lamp like a hunched old lady snooping at the wares. He turned on the lamp, went over to a vault and came back with some stones, placing them, singly and slowly, on the mat. Then he stood over them and folded his arms.

Kelley started reaching for one of the diamonds, and Morty said, "Nah.—Not *bad*," he amended.

"Okay, but not good."

"But not great," Morty said. "Let me hit you with a great. Here—" He handed him a jeweler's eyeglass and picked up a stone. "This is fourteen carats. Fifty-six facets. Look. Like the perfect light of an angel's halo, no? Like the secret heart of a flame."

"How much?" Kelley said.

"For you? For you with no poems in your soul? Say half a million dollars."

"And what if I recited you Roses are red—"

"Five hundred thousand."

Kelley looked up; Morty was grinning. "What else have you got?"

"You don't like what you see?"

"I like," Kelley said. "I'd like to see something else."

"Too?" Morty laughed. "Take two, they're small. Why not? You're a wealthy young fella these days. You mind if I ask what you're buying this for?"

"Investment."

"Ah, investment. Not love."

"Does it make any difference?"

"To you, not to me. So *here*—" Morty said, "I got the jewel of jewels. Here I got a thing to make billionaires plotz. Here I got a million and a half worth of jewel, wouldn't change you recite me how Mary had a lamb or the Portuguese sonnets. Here—take a look. Like Richard gave Elizabeth. Forty-two carats. A Nassak. A star in the diadem of night. Investments," Morty ranted as Kelley picked it up. "Everything you do for investments today. No love, just money. Listen—like putting a rainbow in a vault."

Kelley held the stone and instead of the fire what he felt was the ice. The chill went through him with the same cold certainty he'd felt once before holding dice in Las Vegas. He put it on the velvet and stared at it.

252

"So?" Morty said. "What's the news?"

Kelley said nothing; again, he picked up the first of the stones and again felt the same incredible zap, the tingle of omen. "Conscience," he said, "makes cowards of us all."

"I told you," Morty said. "Shakespeare, Mother Goose, it wouldn't do you any good. I'm giving you, you'll pardon me, rock-bottom price. The two of them I'm giving you for two million flat, Mr. Millionaire Investor."

"Swell," Kelley told him. "I'll let you know Friday."

"Friday." Morty nodded. "A bargain like these, it's gonna lay here till Friday? People gonna hear I got bargains like these, they're gonna come from all over. Staten Island. The Bronx. Friday," Morty said. "Before sundown, all right?"

When it opened a year ago, the Palmer Palace, as Kelley remembered, had been greeted by the architectural critics with opinions ranging from high praise to low slurs. Fans had called it "the most exciting hotel in the world." Others had called it the "Pity Palace," and Peter Repozo of the New York *Times* had called it simply "The Red Menace." The lobby, with its huge landscaped atrium, was done completely in sienna marble, walls and floor, all of it imported slab by slab under the direction of Rebecca Palmer, whom Kelley'd come to think of as the Red Queen.

The elevators had brass doors and mirrored interiors and the piped-in music was a Haydn quartet, a little something for everyone.

Kelley got out at the forty-eighth floor, at the overly advertised Ivory Tower, "your customized penthouse aerie in the sky," a statement that was no more redundant than the decor. Palmer was nothing if not literal. The walls, furniture and carpeting along the hallways were ivory, and one story had it that Rebecca had taken the swatches to the Congo and there held them up against an elephant's tusk.

Jean Roque was staying in Suite 21. Kelley remembered he'd met the man once, at a party last summer, when Paul had brought him to the house on the bay. He remembered that Roque had a curious, dry, academic refinement, a title on the order of Baron or Duke, and a barrel of money both new and old. He was owner of a chain of European hotels, a Burgundy vineyard, and a yacht that was big enough to serve as an ark.

Clearly, the fellow had money to burn. A penthouse suite would be immolating eight hundred dollars a night, and as Kelley stood at the ivory door, he wondered again about what kind of stone he was about to upturn. Paul had said, "if your back's against the wall," the implication being that the deal to be offered would be less than ideal. He could only imagine, since Roque was French, it had something to do with the service to Paris. Possibly a tie-in with Roque's hotels. Or possibly Roque had an eye for the route. And that, Kelley thought, had a certain solid and reasonable logic. And yes, he would certainly offer that chip in exchange for a timely infusion of cash. As he knocked on the door, he felt suddenly heartened.

Roque said, "Ah, but how nice of you to come." Roque, in a dressing gown, looked almost royal. At the age of sixty, he was dark-haired and ruddy with a nose like a falcon and eyes that were surprisingly warm and serene. He led Kelley into a Frenchified living room, damask and gilt. A sulky young blondie looked up from the sofa. A hooker, he imagined; a hundred a night. She had one of those elaborate worked-on hairdos, piled on her head and working its way into cascading curls, copied, no doubt, from a sketch of a goddess. That, Kelley thought, or a fast-food waitress on Interstate 5.

"Allow me to present Suzanne," Roque said. "Suzanne La Salle." He said it like you might say the Duchess of Windsor.

Kelley said, "Hi." The girl, mid-twenties, had a sex-kitty face, big tits, small frame.

Roque said, "I promise you will hear of this name."

The girl followed Kelley with her kitty-cat eyes while Roque crossed over to the bar in the corner and Kelley took a chair.

"Bloody Mary?" Roque said.

"Be fine."

Roque poured from a pitcher on the bar, and came back to the sofa, where he sat beside the girl, taking hold of her small, and undoubtedly very skillful, little hand. "This one," he said, "has an incandescence that will light up the screen."

The girl bit a cuticle.

Kelley said, "Yes."

"You can see it, can you not?"

"Absolutely," Kelley said. "She's kind of a Pia Zadora east."

"Comment?"

"Another actress with incandescence."

"Ah, but there's no other like her in the world."

Try the corner of Forty-second, Kelley thought.

The girl said, "I've gotta have a manicure, Jean."

But Roque wasn't ready to relinquish the hand. "The camera, it utterly adores her," he said. "It makes love to her features, finds the soul in her eyes."

The girl said, "I've gotta have a pedicure, too, and I told you, I've got an appointment at two."

"Ah yes," Roque beamed. "We have to take care of those precious little toes."

"Make 'em nice so you can kiss 'em," the girl said with ease. She extracted her hand and stood. "You're gonna meet me at a quarter of four?"

"I will be there," Roque said.

She moved to the foyer and was next seen modeling a

floor-length sable. "Don't be late now," she chided. "I miss you already."

"Ah, sweet." It was Roque who was glowing right now, watching as she clicked her heels across the floor, waiting, suspended, till she'd gone through the door and then staring at the doorway. He finally sighed and then, turning to Kelley, he said, "And of course you must think I'm a fool."

"Not at all. She's attractive."

"And still—I could be her grandfather, no?"

Kelley said nothing.

"May and December. Ah well," Roque said, "we'll be married in the spring, and then of course we start production in the summer. It's a wonderful film and Paul DuLac, as you know, will direct. He believes as I do, that Sooz is a brilliant and natural star."

"Paul knows a good thing when he sees it."

"I told him to go all-out with production. I told him, for Sooz, we have nothing but the best. It's important I give her a magnificent setting. You can see what I mean."

"Like a jewel."

"But exactly. But exactly," Roque said. "I am also on the lookout for a suitable home. I have searched all over. It's important, I believe, for Sooz's career that we live in the States. Or at least for a while. But I tell you, for two and three million these days, what you get is a box, what you get is a house without character or style. An acre of land in some dreary little woods. No, I am looking for a lovely estate. I was saying to Paul, like the one of your friend. You have wonderful space and then you have the ocean like a carpet at your door." Roque sipped his drink. "I suppose you wouldn't know of any places like yours—I mean, up for sale?"

And Kelley almost laughed. Because Roque wasn't after the air route to Paris, he was after the house. And what could he offer? A few million bucks? And by the time all the dealings on a house had been settled, with inspectors and lawyers and everybody else, about five or six dragged-out months would have passed.

"Sorry," Kelley said. "I'm completely unfamiliar with the real estate market."

"I'd be willing to pay," Roque said, "up to, let's say, five million dollars?" He paused. "For a place on the order of yours."

"Well, see, the thing about mine," Kelley said, "is it's already sold. In fact, we're about to do the closing tomorrow. And the price, by the way, for five-some acres of beachfront land, came to six-point-six."

"Oo-la," Roque said. "Oo-la, *c'est merdique!* I was thinking to call you, you know? I was thinking that you might want to sell."

Kelley just shrugged. *"Je suis desolé."*

"I have looked all over," Roque said with dismay. "There is nothing its equal." He stared at his glass.

And come on, Kelley thought, start to make the connection.

And apparently the thought-wave zoomed through the air because Roque looked up at him, bright as a bird. "But you say, I think, you haven't yet totally finished the deal."

"Oh well," Kelley shrugged. "Tomorrow at noon. So it's pretty much finished."

"Except if I offer you . . . half-million more?"

Kelley shook his head. "Listen, it's not just the money," he said. "It's the time. You can figure I'm hard-put for cash and tomorrow what I'm getting is a letter of credit. So we're talking now six-point-six in my hand against birds in some Maytime mulberry bush. No. I'm sorry. I repeat. *Desolé.*"

"But I, too, could provide you with a letter of credit."

"By noon?"

"The impossible can always be done."

Kelley appeared to give it serious thought.

"On condition," Roque said, and when Kelley looked up, he added, "the condition that Sooz likes it too."

"Sooz. Uh huh." Kelley looked at his watch. He hadn't yet deposited his check in the bank. He'd be cutting it close. A gamble on an alley-cat liking his house. "If you want to meet me at the heliport—"

"No. My little lovebird does not like to fly. However, perhaps if you'd join us in a car . . . ?"

"Why don't I meet you at the house, say, at seven."

"Call it done." Roque stood. "And I do hope she likes it."

Kelley just shrugged. "It's no sweat either way."

25

FLYING ALONE ALONG the edge of Long Island, he refused to be distracted by dim hallucinations of eleventh-hour rescue. Even if he did get the money tomorrow it would only, after all, be enough to let him squeak through the first of the month. The same set of problems would be looming once again in the next thirty days. And thirty after that. The problems would remain but the answers would have dwindled their way down to zip. If he fucked up with Chook now, even the doorway to Attica was closed.

So he'd meant it when he'd said no sweat either way. And still he couldn't shake that feeling of omen when he'd sat there this morning in Savage's office with the stones in his hand.

Omen. The word itself made him laugh. He had not been joking when he'd muttered the line about cowards and conscience. For surely the "omen" had been nothing but the chirpings of a Jiminy Cricket. Or possibly call it the bleat of his will. He did not want to do this. If Roque's seven million could get him through the week, then . . . Cool it, he told himself. See how it goes.

The water below him looked gloomy and choppy in the winter afternoon. Sooz, he decided, could go either way—love it or hate it or lift her little shoulder and chew her little nail. Still, he thought it wiser to arrive a little early, to make an inspection and alert the old caretaker living on the grounds that some company was coming, prospective employers.

The house was in sight now, just beyond the private dock on the bay, the back of it facing on a quadrant of beach from the vantage of a small hillside of rock, a redwood stairway leading to the sand. Hard as he looked, he could see no flash of romantic image. He could see no laughter and splashing on the beach, no love on the hillside. There was nothing but the empty image of himself, standing alone along the edges of the hill, getting away from assorted babbling strangers in the house, occasionally taking the boat out alone, and once, at a time when Karen was away, he'd been here with Miranda. End of report.

As he circled the land now it occurred to him it could have been a wonderful house, a pleasure palace when they'd built it in the twenties. A twenty-room mansion with a limestone facade. He'd imagined a bootlegger living on the land, living on the fat of it, moonlight swimming, parties on the lawn, and yet the reality, including the parties, hadn't touched him at all. He'd walked through extravagant scenes like an extra. The fault, he decided, was undoubtedly his.

He landed in a clearing at the edge of the lawn. There were cars on the circular path of the driveway—a beat-up Beetle and a dusty Ford. As he passed them, he paused and peered through the windows. There were keys in the ignitions; some Harvard textbooks on the back seat of one. Not likely to belong to the typical cronies of Albert McKendrick, the taciturn Yankee who minded the grounds. So Kelley felt a certain tinge of apprehension as he got out his door keys and let himself in.

The first thing he saw was the clutter of baggage and coats in the hall. Karen's suitcase, opened and raided, another beside it, a couple of dark mink coats on the floor, a man's leather jacket lying on the chair, its arms hanging loosely and trailing on the floor, as though it had collapsed there in total exhaustion.

There was hard-edge music coming from the den, a masculine voice saying, "Yeah, oh yeah," though whether from the record or coming to him live, he was still uncertain. He crossed the hallway; a number of images crossed through his mind but none of them prepared him for the one that was waiting when he opened the door.

Karen and Candy were fucking, or whatever you'd call it, on the rug. The stereo was playing, a fire was burning, the boys, both naked, were watching it with adolescent spittle on their chins and one of them was grinding out an X-rated movie with the video camera unsteady in his hand.

Kelley's first move was to sock the kid backhand and go for the camera. His next move was almost to hurl it at the wall but a cannier and much more furious instinct compelled him to aim it directly at the boys, preserving their fuddled and fried-out expressions, their strung-out bodies, their withering dicks. He panned back to Karen and Candy on the floor, the two of them rising, languidly almost, blinking like mermaids coming to the surface of a tropical sea.

There were ludes and a bottle of liquor on the floor.

He clicked off the camera and put it on the table.

Candy giggled.

Karen said, "When Johnny comes marching home," and, rubbing at her breast, said, "Tra-la, tra-la."

He turned off the stereo and opened the large French window to the porch. The air was icy. The college boys, lying there heedless and fuzzy, both, Kelley thought, too young to be quite so calmly corrupt, stared at him blankly as though he were some kind of creature in a dream. His instinct to slam them was muted by the fact of their apparent confusion. The ludes and the liquor, the sex and the sleaze; they were clearly on their way into overload now, but they caught his intention. One of them shakily scrambled to his feet, muttering, "S'cool, man. S'cool. Gonna go."

"True," Kelley said, and pointed at the open window to the garden. "Right this minute and right as you are."

"S'cool."

"More than that," Kelley told him, "it's freezing. So pick up your clothes and you'll find some motivation to put the things on. Move. Now."

The kid made a stumbling dive for his clothes. The other kid apparently found it amusing. He lay there laughing. Kelley found a belt in some jeans on the floor, pulled it out of the belt loops and moved on the kid.

Karen said, "Oh! a little whip-action. Good."

Kelley just glared at her and bent to the floor, encircled the belt around the giggling body, hooked it up neatly, and used it as a handle to drag the kid's gangling frame across the carpet and out through the door. The other kid had gotten the message and fled; out on the lawn, he was coping with the tangled confusion of his pants. Kelley picked the rest of the clothes off the floor, tossed them to the garden, and locked up the door.

"Now," he turned to Candy. "You want the same treatment or you want to get dressed?"

"*Me?*" Candy said. Incredulous. Hurt.

Kelley said, "I'll give you to the count of eleven."

He picked up the camera, brought it to the hall, locked it in the closet, and grabbed the fur coats.

Back in the living room, he tossed them at the women. "Three," he said. "Four." He looked down at Karen, whose flesh had turned bumpy and blue from the cold. "If I were you, kiddo, I'd get into that coat. And if not for your health, then for basic aesthetics. You're just about as lovely to look at as a corpse."

262

He crossed to the telephone. Candy hadn't moved except to put on the coat. She was skinnier than Karen, her blond hair tangled and matted with sweat. He said, "You've got a choice. I'm either gonna call your husband or the cops. On the other hand, you want to get dressed and get out, I'll have the caretaker drive you and drop you at your door. The count is now seven." He picked up the phone. "Eight." He was dialing.

Karen said, "Christ. What a humorless prick."

"Nine."

Candy stood. "Oh Jesus. All right."

Karen, still naked, watched him from the floor. "Upright," she said. "The *up*right prick."

"Wanna bet?" Kelley said. "You could wither Colossus."

He dialed McKendrick in the caretaker's cottage, explained the situation as "a couple of people had too much to drink," and offered "a truly fantastic bonus if you'll drive them into town."

The bonus shorted the expected objections and five minutes later, Kelley heard the sound of the truck pulling up. He helped McKendrick round up the boys, and tossed them in the truck bed along with their bags.

Candy, in the front, was beginning to weep.

McKendrick said, "Gonna be a hard-earned bonus."

Kelley simply wished him a bon voyage.

He stood in front of his moonlit house, in the silent wake of the departing truck, attempting to determine exactly what he felt.

He felt as indifferent and empty as a yawn.

Karen was still as he'd left her, on the floor in front of the fireplace, sprawled on the thickness of the white fur rug, wrapped in the coat now, smoking a cigarette and drinking a bourbon.

He picked up the scattered Quaaludes from the floor and tossed them in the fire. Christ, she was now doing bourbon and ludes. Aloud he said flatly, "Kentucky-fried cunt."

Karen said nothing, constructing an amused and superior grin. He looked at her, skin and bones under fur, untouchable eyes under smeared mascara. She looked like the aftermath of Dracula's kiss. "Look at you," he said. "My God, the Geneva Convention was created so that prisoners of *war* look better than—"

"Stop it."

"I think it's up to *you* to stop it, don't you? What the hell have you been doing to yourself?"

"You know damn well what I've been doing," she said.

"Do I? I didn't even know you were a dyke. I didn't even know you gave moonlight biology lessons to sophomores. Is that what you've been doing?"

Karen said nothing, just sipped at her drink.

"How long have you and Candy been—whatever that is."

"Oh Jesus, you're a cretin."

"Undoubtedly."

"Years."

"And doing it for show?"

"A cretin with no imagination," she said. "We did it with the boys and the boys did each other."

"I see. And a good time was had by all." He picked up the bottle and took himself a swig. "And years ago, I guess, you told Candy that I used to fly cargo with Ryan. Just a little morsel of pillow-talk, eh?"

"You raped me that night."

"Uh huh. Well, that was certainly fine retaliation."

"But then, as it happens, it happens to be true."

"As it happens, it's not. But that's irrelevant, Karen. Tell stories like that and your sweet friend Candy tells them all over town. Like she babbled to Miranda how you had yourself spayed. I hope her mouth has some compensating virtues."

Karen said nothing, just pulled at her bourbon and stared at the crackling logs on the fire.

Kelley stood wearily and paced to the window. "I'm expecting some people in a couple of minutes. I want you to go upstairs and lie down."

"You do?" Now she laughed. "Well now, isn't it tough, in this hard-luck world, how you can't, as Mick said, always get what you want."

He turned from the window. "And what is it you want? Seriously, Karen. What the hell do you want? In this hard-luck world. What makes you happy?"

"Happy?" she said. *"Happy?* Oh yes. That's the seventh dwarf, isn't it? Happy. Mmm-hmm. How *is* the little fellow? Haven't seen him around. It seems to me I read someplace that he died."

"No," Kelley said, "that was Snow White that died. She fucked herself to death."

"Ah, then she must've died Happy," Karen said. "Maybe that's what I read."

"For a stoned conversation, you're doin' pretty good."

"Mmm. For a good conversation with a stone. That's what you are, you know. Rolling and rolling and gathering nothing."

"And what have *you* gathered?"

"My rosebuds," she said, and giggled. "My bed of roses. Oh boy. They promise you a garden and all they ever give you is a lousy little bed.—So how about you, Kelley? Got what you want? Or still just beavering to get what you need?"

He looked at her flatly. "What I want is a divorce."

"Oh no," she said, "no. Over my—uh-uh—over *your* dead body."

He nodded. "Gonna make a little trouble?"

"You bet. And a whole lotta money. And a whole lotta stink. Those pictures of you and Miss Cutie upstate? I looked at those pictures and I thought, I wonder if he'll try something now. And I thought I could make Miss Cutie look just about as cute as a bug. For openers," she said.

Nodding again, he took another long slow pull from the bottle. "Thing is," he said levelly, "I've got that tape. Are you listening, Karen?" He had her attention; a sudden clearing in the fog around her eyes. "If you want to make trouble, I can make a lot more. I can show it in the courtroom. I can send it to *Hustler.*"

She stared. "You wouldn't."

"Try me," he said. "Now listen—you want to go get yourself straight, I'll do anything I can. I'll pay for any doctor or farm of your choice, but that's it and that's all."

The doorbell was ringing.

Karen just sat there with rage-lights emanating out of her eyes. "You can't do that," she said.

"I can and I will. If I have to. Now I think you better go to your room."

The bell rang again.

"Why?"

"Take a look in a mirror, you'll see."

That did it. She suddenly bolted from the chair, her eyes getting wilder and brighter with rage. "I'll find it," she hollered. "I'll find it and burn it."

She was halfway through the hall when the door just opened. And there was Roque and his furry little friend, all sable and pout.

Roque said, looking from Karen to Kelley, "I'm sorry. It was partly open and—"

"Fine," Kelley told him. "I was coming to answer it. Karen, I imagine you remember Jean Roque. The movie producer. And this is Suzanne, uh—"

"La Salle." Roque was in there promoting the name.

"La Salle?" Karen smiled. "As in French for 'the room'?"

"That's right."

"And we all know *which* room, don't we."

"Come in," Kelley covered. "Let me offer you a drink."

But Suzanne turned to Roque. "What the hell did she mean?"

"I don't know." Roque looked as though he probably didn't.

"Let's see," Karen said. "Now what could she have meant? The scullery? The basement?"

Kelley said quickly, "I think you ought to go upstairs now and rest."

"The *rest* room," Karen said. "Maybe that's what she meant."

"You'll have to excuse my wife," Kelley said. "As you can see, she's been ill."

"The darkroom," Karen said. "Am I getting any warmer?"

"It's a serious mental illness," Kelley said. "She's just coming back on a leave from the asylum. You can see her suitcase."

But Karen wouldn't quit. "A pay-by-the-hour hotel room?" she tried.

Kelley said nothing. He gestured quickly at the living room doorway, encouraging Roque and Suzanne to come in while giving them a look that promised explanation and pleaded for calm.

Roque took the cue; he moved through the doorway. "Oh look," he said, "Sooz. It's got leaded windows. And ah what a view!"

Closing the mahogany doors behind him, Kelley said, "I can't apologize enough." He turned to Suzanne. "It's pretty young women who set the thing off. Years ago she used to be as pretty as you.—Almost," he added.

Outside the door there was a crash and a curse.

"Perhaps," Roque said, "we should come another time."

"Not me," the girl snapped. "We got lost and it was creepy on the road, and it was cold."

"She got a chill," Roque said.

"Then some whiskey would help."

"And it's colder in the goddam house," the girl said. She settled on the couch now, burrowed in her coat.

"It's been closed," Kelley told her, "for a couple of months." He was pouring some Cutty from the living room bar. He returned with the glasses. "Drink up. You'll get warm."

The girl took the whiskey and drank it in a gulp. Meanwhile, thundering footsteps in the hall. "What's she *doing* out there?"

"Karen thinks the Russians have been taping her dreams. She also thinks the tapes have been hidden in the house."

"Ah, what a terrible pity," Roque said. "It must—it must cause you a great deal of pain."

"It does," Kelley said. "In more places than one. But don't let it color your impression of the house. Come on, I'll turn the lights on, we'll look at the grounds."

"I don't want to see the grounds," the girl said. "It's too cold."

"Oh my sweet," Roque assured, "it won't be cold in the summer. Imagine! We can swim on our own private beach. We can buy a little boat."

Neither possibility appealed to Suzanne. She was probably thinking how her hair would get wet.

"How about we look at the house," Kelley said.

There was nothing in the house that appealed to her either. Not the master bedroom with its fireplace, patio and view of the ocean, not the marble bathrooms, not the country kitchen, not the landscaped garden or the wood-paneled walls.

"It's okay, I suppose. Old-fashioned."

"Old-fashioned?" Roque had to laugh.

"Then old," she said. "Just plain old, okay?"

"Old?" Once again, Roque couldn't believe. "But, my darling. My house in Burgundy is old. About three hundred years."

"So," she said. "I bet it has roaches and rats."

They were back in the hall. Karen was tugging at the door to the closet. Pulling on the handle, pounding on the frame.

Kelley said nothing and walked right past her to the paneled front door. Roque and the furball followed him out.

"Well," Kelley said, as they stood on the drive. "I guess it doesn't quite measure up for Suzanne."

"I think we need a chance to discuss it," Roque said.

"There isn't much time."

Roque turned to the girl. "Remember how you didn't like the bracelet?" he asked. "Until I told you it was seventeenth century enamel? And you wore it and everybody fell to their knees? I am telling you, my darling, it's the same with this house."

The girl looked up at it. "Well . . ."

Roque watched her. "Well?"

She shivered.

"Ah, she is cold. We will talk in the car now. I'll call you tonight."

"I'll be here at the house."

Karen, from the door, said, "You'll be in your fucking coffin in a minute, you don't stop talking to that fool and that slut and come open this closet."

Her coat had come open. She was naked in the overhead light of the porch.

Roque clucked his tongue. *"La pauvre petite chose."*

The "poor little thing" was pounding on the closet when Kelley walked in.

He went to her slowly, shaking his head. Then he picked her up, threw her over his shoulder and carried her, kicking and screaming, upstairs, dumped her in the shower, turned on the water, and waited till her shrieks had subsided to moans and then ebbed into soft, inconsolable tears.

He toweled her tenderly and got her into bed, then sat there and held her when she asked to be held, and listened while she told him she'd be different and good. He told her to hush now, sleep, go to sleep. And sometime, just around midnight, she did.

And Roque hadn't called. There still remained the chance that he'd call in the morning, one of the three impossible things that could happen before breakfast, but the odds weren't good.

He paced around the silent husk of this chilly bootlegger's house, fixed himself another bourbon and water, and stared through the window at the pale and jagged remnants of the moon.

The particular game he'd been playing was over. The Old Ballgame had a strict set of rules, and the rules were the old Three Strikes and You're Out.

Hollis: one.

Quaid: two.

Roque: three.

In the end, even *he* couldn't say he hadn't tried. To play the game fairly. To win by the rules. Or *almost* by the rules. A little bending and stretching. A dubious exercise in moral isometrics. But now he was entering a difficult and much more dangerous game.

It occurred to him that up to this desperate minute he'd only been going through a series of motions— rehearsing for an action he knew he'd never take. Now he was finally aware that he'd take it. He still felt the chill of those diamonds in his hand; he still had the instinct that somewhere, something was about to go wrong. He understood clearly in the light of this particular cloud-covered moon that he was violating something much deeper than the law, that he was violating his own character.

And still, he would do it.

At six in the morning, with Karen still asleep, he telephoned the Betty Ford Sanitarium in Southern California and made a reservation. For Karen Houghton. Then he called the office and booked two seats on the one-o'clock plane and a single return on the Red Eye tonight.

On the flickering ghost of an outside chance, he telephoned his answering machine in the city. No message from Roque. Only the serious voice of D'Aquino:

"Same motel room. Friday at noon."

26

THERE WERE TWO police cars double-parked in front of the Diamond Exchange, clogging the morning rush-hour traffic. A couple of drivers were sitting on their horns. Things were being yelled out of taxicab windows. Kelley's driver said, "Christ, what a town. Always something, you know?"

There were two more uniformed cops in the lobby, a couple of bluesuits standing like posts.

Kelley had a flashing paranoid thought: the cops saying, "You there. Yeah, you. You with the blank check in your wallet for two million dollars that you're gonna buy dope with—c'mere."

There were two more cops up on Savage's floor, standing in the hallway. Kelley turned the bend. Morty Savage's office was open; a squad was inside, three more uniforms and half a dozen guys who could only be detectives.

"What happened?" Kelley said.

A guy in a black-and-white checkered jacket looked up at him vaguely. "You authorized?" he said.

"To do what?" Kelley asked him.

But the guy turned away and started talking to a red-headed cop with a ripe-looking boil.

"Mr. Savage all right?" Kelley said to another.

"In there." The man thumbed at the closed inner door.

It wasn't, Kelley figured, exactly the moment for a private transaction. "Guess I better come back later," he said, to no one in particular, and headed for the hall.

Morty Savage came out of his office with a circle of cops, saying, "What could I tell you from an inside job? Inside, outside. All I know, they were inside the vault, now they're *out*side the vault. Oy Gott." He looked up. "Kelley. So what could I sell you today? A radiator, maybe? A couple of chairs? Maybe you'd like to invest in a foolproof burglar alarm. I got one of those too."

"You were robbed," Kelley nodded.

"Robbed?" Morty laughed. "I am cleaned out better than my grandmother's kitchen at Passover. Listen— it's a prank of the gods. I told you, like a joke, I told you how they'd hear what I got in this office, they'd come from all over? Mozel. They came. I don't know," Morty said. "I don't know, I don't know. You want to do business, come back in the summer."

"I'm sorry," Kelley said.

"Listen. I'm covered. A bath I won't take. But in pure aggravation, I will age twenty years. You want to do business, come back in a month. If Methuselah comes to the doorbell, it's me."

A cop turned to Morty. "We need some information."

"Information?" Morty said. "So what the hell am I? The Answer Man? What?"

Ten in the morning. And the only thing to do now was start getting drunk. And the only place to do that at ten in the morning was a Blarney Stone bar. The luck of the luckless—a chain open twenty-four hours a day and catering to every kind of bad-luck boozer with a nickel in his pants.

Kelley sat at the bar. He ordered a whiskey and drank to the disappearing trail of his luck. Not only had she shown him her fast-moving back, but she'd *mooned* him. He had to admit it was funny. And the only thing to do now was sit back and laugh. The game, in all its wry variations, was over. There was no way on earth to get two million bucks' worth of quality diamonds in a couple of hours. With a blank check. From the pension account. Of a shaky airline. Monday, he could glue the thing back in the book.

And that would be that.

He telephoned Zeedee from a booth on the corner. Too weary to explain it, he just told him, "Sorry, can't do it, ole buddy."

"Can't," Zeedee said, "or won't?"

"Doesn't make any difference, I think. You better tell Chook."

"He'll love it."

"I'll bet."

"You're a shmuck," Zeedee said. "So what happens from here?"

"Nothing," Kelley said. "We who are about to die salute you."

"You who are about to suicide, you mean.—Thing is, I never did count on you a lot, so we got ourselves a backup. I gotta hang up. I gotta put plan number two on the stove. But never," Zeedee said, "say I didn't try to help you."

"Never," Kelley promised.

"I'll see you."

"I guess.—Good-bye, Zeedee."

"So long, sucker."

* * *

He got to the apartment, a little unsteady, at a little after two. It was so fucking quiet he turned on the radio just to hear noises, to drown out the threatening babble in his head—the ifs and the maybes, the mights and the shoulds, and all the other squeaky conditional tenses that hadn't been silenced in the onslaught of booze.

He poured another drink now and raised it to the Serious Man on his wall. Nowhere to Nowhere. Zero to Zip. The perfectly circular round-trip of life. He thought about Claire and, reaching for the bottle, he thought of a limerick:

Poured out a Cutty, and sat in his study, and frightened Miss Muffett . . .

Well . . . he'd done nothing to frighten her now.

Or to frighten himself.

It was almost, in a weird kind of way, a relief. It was over. The treadmill had finally stopped. He could rest for a while, just sit and relax, yield to what was clearly a conspiracy of fate. He'd done what he'd had to, and luck, or the absence of luck, did the rest. As to what he'd do now . . . he'd do what he had to.

He looked at the Serious Man. What the hell. There were, he decided, no destinations; there was only the whirligig blast of the trip.

So he'd start all over. With three Dakotas. But first, he would get about as drunk as he could. He crossed to the bar again, weaving a little. The voice from the radio warmed up the air. Babble-de-babble. He reached for some ice.

"Millionaires Tom Cubbitt and Zachary David were arrested today . . ."

He turned, let the ice cube slide to the floor.

". . . collared in a Route Thirty-five motel room, and charged with attempting to purchase, import and distribute cocaine. With them in the room was a suitcase with

one-point-eight million dollars, a sample kilo of high-grade coke, and federal informant Chook D'Aquino . . ."

Kelley made an animal sound in his throat.

"Mr. Cubbitt's attorney is claiming it's a clear-cut case of entrapment. D'Aquino, in government employ since the fall, under the direction of federal officer Axton Chambers . . ."

The voice kept blatting, but nothing came through. Only the loud and reverberating thud—the pieces of the puzzle falling into place.

Chambers.

Chambers.

Rip had a brother named Axton Chambers.

Kelley had even met the guy once, at the Wings Club dinner where Rip had been speaking—an aging linebacker running to fat; a crew-cut head and a Dick Tracy jaw. No one had told him, this is Axton, the fed, but then how many guys are named Axton Chambers?

No. So forget about coincidence here. The trap had been baited by Axton Chambers and Kelley had been meant to get caught when it sprang.

He could practically picture the way it came up. Ax saying, "Listen, I caught a real beaut. A guy we're gonna use to make a coupla busts. And the thing of it, Rip—the guy's selling product to a bunch of your friends."

"My friends?" Rip says. "What friends're those?"

And the obvious answer is, Marcus and Candy. And Rip says, Shit. And then he remembers. Maybe not then. Maybe not that minute, but he puts it together in the middle of the night.

He remembers the story that Kelley flew smack. Because that's the kind of story that sticks in your mind. You find a peck of dirt about your hardiest rival, you keep it; you're gonna make him eat it someday.

And Rip would remember where he heard the thing too. From Marcus Imry. At a Palm Beach party. The weekend he was making a play for Miranda and Miranda's husband was in bed with his wife.

And the rest of it would come to him quicker than a fox. How neat it all was. That Candy, Zeedee and Karen were friends was as public as society pages of the *Times*. The ladder was there. And Kelley could be reached—given his currently tight situation (tightened by the leak in the auditor's report) and given his less than respectable past.

So Rip says to Axton, "I got an idea. You want to set someone up . . . ?"

And that's how it happened: Chook as the bowler, Zeedee as the ball, Kelley as the pin.

BAM!

Only Zeedee, who'd sincerely been trying to help, gets caught in the middle. And Cubbitt, coming in as the last-minute sub.

Jesus. Jesus Christ, Kelley thought.

Instincts and omens; symbols and signs. Everything he should have listened to and trusted and hadn't. His luck had worked overtime here.

He was broke but still free; he was down but he hadn't brought the house down with him. He'd been saved, and maybe there was purpose in that. Or maybe it was something like a skywriting stint: the fates in an airplane, spelling out, "Hey, man, it coulda been worse." Cosmic consolation. Jokes from on high.

He paced the apartment, occasionally laughing, though it wasn't very funny that Zeedee got caught.

He thought about Claire.

He thought about the headline BEAU BOPS FOE, and thought, Oh Christ, is she caught there again?

He picked up the telephone and noticed his machine had been working like a dog: sixteen messages.

He let them rewind and then pushed on the button.

"Mr. Kelley? Bill Hagen of the New York *Times*. We'd like your reaction to this morning's ruling by the FAA. Of course we can imagine you're terrifically pleased, but we'd like to get a quote. We'll try you again."

Kelley had no idea what he meant.

"Mr. Kelley, this is Ed DeWitt, A.P. That emergency amendment to part one-twenty of the FAR regulations. I guess that puts you as the man of the hour. We'd like to get a statement. And, hey—congratulations."

Still in the dark.

"Mr. Kelley? Ann Tobin of *Time* magazine? That Kellometer of yours—that wind-shear detector? In light of the government's new regulations, we'd like to do a feature on how the thing works. Can we make an appointment?"

"Mr. Kelley. This is Kelton Crabbe, *Daily News*. We've been trying to figure how rich you're gonna be. At fifty percent of fifty thousand dollars for every single airplane that's flying in America, what does it come to? The way we figure, it's close to a billion. So how does it feel to be a new billionaire? . . ."

He clicked off the tape and then stared at it blindly, trying to figure out what he'd just heard.

FAR regulations.

Part one-twenty.

Emergency amendment.

Wind-shear detector.

Put it together . . . Come on, now, he told himself: put it together.

A couple of disastrous wind-shear crashes in the last few weeks.

The Kellometer works; it's the only cockpit detector in the world.

And the FAA just enacted a fast emergency amendment. That every airplane flying under Federal Air Regulations has ninety-one days to install a Kellometer, Kelley's invention. The thing costs fifty thousand dollars per plane and Kelley, as inventor, gets fifty percent.

Was that what had happened?

No.

Yes.

No.

But then again, why the hell not? Luck was on an all-out rampage today.

He turned up the radio.

And that's what had happened. That's what had happened while Kelley had been taxiing to West Forty-seventh on his way to the gallows. Kelley had been saved, and so had Blue Sky. Because no one was about to foreclose on him now. The banks would be fighting over who'd lend him money.

Burke M. Kelley, the new billionaire.

He looked up quickly at the Serious Man and laughed till the tears came streaming down his face.

Saturday brunch, walking into McMullen's, Claire on his arm, everybody's heads doing three-quarter turns.

And there, at a quiet table in the corner, was the final irresistible present from fate. There, all together, was the whole ball of wax.

Ashe Warner and Frank Rosetti. And the Chambers connection, Axton and Rip. They were sitting and possibly crying over beers, and Kelley turned to Claire and asked her, do you mind if I make another headline? Just one more headline and that'll be it.

The Sunday papers had a blast, page one:

HIGH NOON IN MANHATTAN:
KELLEY SLUGS CHAMBERS
Federal President Sues for Assault

FREE!!
BOOKS BY MAIL
CATALOGUE

BOOKS BY MAIL will share with you our current bestselling books as well as hard to find specialty titles in areas that will match your interests. You will be updated on what's new from Pocket Books at no cost to you. Just fill in the coupon below and discover the convenience of having books delivered to your home. Please add $1.00 to cover the cost of postage and handling.

- -

BOOKS BY MAIL

320 Steelcase Road E.,
Markham, Ontario L3R 2M1

Please send Books By Mail catalogue to:

Name_____
(please print)

Address_____

City_____

Prov._____ Postal Code _____

(BBM2)